芭拉蒂·穆克吉小说中的移民书写研究

A Study on the Immigrant Writings in Bharati Mukherjee's Novels

苗颖 ◉ 著

苏州大学出版社
Soochow University Press

图书在版编目(CIP)数据

芭拉蒂·穆克吉小说中的移民书写研究 = A Study on the Immigrant Writings in Bharati Mukherjee's Novels / 苗颖著. -- 苏州：苏州大学出版社，2024. 7. -- ISBN 978-7-5672-4899-1

Ⅰ.I712.074

中国国家版本馆 CIP 数据核字第 20243P4W89 号

Bharati Mukherjee Xiaoshuo Zhong De Yimin Shuxie Yanjiu
芭 拉 蒂 · 穆 克 吉 小 说 中 的 移 民 书 写 研 究
A Study on the Immigrant Writings in Bharati Mukherjee's Novels

著　　者：苗　颖
责任编辑：金莉莉
封面设计：刘　俊

出版发行：苏州大学出版社（Soochow University Press）
社　　址：苏州市十梓街1号　邮编：215006
印　　刷：镇江文苑制版印刷有限责任公司
网　　址：www.sudapress.com
邮　　箱：sdcbs@suda.edu.cn
邮购热线：0512-67480030
销售热线：0512-67481020

开　　本：700 mm×1 000 mm　1/16
印　　张：10
字　　数：210千
版　　次：2024年7月第1版
印　　次：2024年7月第1次印刷
书　　号：978-7-5672-4899-1
定　　价：49.00元

若发现印装错误，请与本社联系调换。服务热线：0512-67481020

序 言

芭拉蒂·穆克吉（Bharati Mukherjee）是最早一批既获学术界的认可，又受广大读者喜爱的印度裔美国作家之一。穆克吉创作迄今为止，已逾四十载，其作品精湛地再现了移民生活离开与融入的张力。

学术界对穆克吉作品的研究始于20世纪70年代。其中，在流亡书写阶段与移民书写阶段，穆克吉作品主题与风格的截然转变引起了广泛的探讨。但截至目前，穆克吉在移民书写阶段写作重心的逐步微妙的转变，尚未得到系统的研究。

本书对穆克吉移民书写阶段主要作品中移民的身份建构进行了研究。这既是对现有穆克吉前期研究的延续，又是在论述主题上的创新。穆克吉的移民书写，截然不同于印度裔作家R.K.纳拉扬的"扎根"书写及V.S.奈保尔的"无根"流亡书写，在后殖民书写中独树一帜。穆克吉颂扬移民在文化碰撞中拥抱混杂性与流动的身份，同时又对全盘融入的思想进行了强烈的批判。

本书主要应用后殖民主义理论对穆克吉的四部小说《詹思敏》《世界的拥有者》《理想的女儿》《树新娘》的移民书写进行了探讨。不同移民的身份建构、变形中的自我肯定、越界中的反叛与回望故国、对不同文化的反思，为追溯与梳理穆克吉融合美学的本质与发展提供了参照。

本书简要介绍了穆克吉的文学成就、个人移民经历及其在移民书写中独特的地位，同时也对穆克吉研究的国内外现状进行了梳理和评析，并简要介绍了本研究的理论框架与结构。

在《詹思敏》中，詹思敏变形中的自我肯定存在双面性。一方面，詹思敏发挥与混杂性密切联系的主体能动性，主动转变，在移居国努力生存；另一方面，詹思敏在自我肯定中又不断自我东方化，该自我东方化局限了其能动性。变形中的自我肯定，拥抱混杂性，解构僵化的身份认同；但对去语境化的混杂性的肯定，又反映了穆克吉小说写作中隐含的东方主义立场。

在《世界的拥有者》中，移民人物在越界中进行反叛。汉娜表现出反叛精神，跨越性别与种族边界，并以其他形式，解放了自身的女性特质。《世界的拥有者》在对美国文学经典《红字》进行后殖民主义重写的过程中，颠覆了男/女、白人/黑人的二元对立，解构了白人、男性的美国国家起源神话。越界中的反叛意识，反映了穆克吉移民书写中的解构主义倾向及对印度文化的初步再认可。

《理想的女儿》《树新娘》进一步刻画了移民的身份建构及对不同文化的反思。两部小说中的塔拉对两个姐姐与自己所代表的三种迥异的文化认同，即隔都化、狭隘民族主义与盲目全盘融入，进行了反思。在反思与寻根之旅中，塔拉再次肯定了印度文化的优势，并逐步意识到对文化差异的开放态度对打破僵化的身份建构及对立的二元建构极具重要性。在移民书写中，对不同文化身份的反思，反映了穆克吉的世界主义思想倾向。穆克吉在移民书写中所进行的身份建构与文化反思，反映了穆克吉思想的逐步发展与成熟。

因笔者的水平有限，书中的疏漏与不足之处在所难免，恳请读者批评指正。

苗 颖

2024 年 1 月于上海

Contents

Introduction ·········· 001

Chapter 1 *Jasmine*: **Self-assertion in Metamorphoses** ·········· 022
   1.1 Hybrid Identity as Agency ·········· 023
   1.2 Self-orientalization as Tools ·········· 035
   1.3 Mukherjee's Celebration of Fluid Identities ·········· 046

Chapter 2 *The Holder of the World*: **Rebelliousness in Transgression**
·········· 059
   2.1 Transgression of Gender and Racial Boundaries ·········· 062
   2.2 Liberation of Female Sensuality ·········· 075
   2.3 Mukherjee's Deconstruction of American National Myth of Origin ·········· 084

Chapter 3 *Desirable Daughters* **and** *The Tree Bride*: **Self-reflection in Immigration** ·········· 097
   3.1 *Desirable Daughters*: Reflection upon Different Cultural Affiliations ·········· 098
   3.2 *The Tree Bride*: Criticism of Colonial History and Re-evaluation of Homeland Culture ·········· 113
   3.3 A New Turn in Mukherjee's Writing of Immigration ·········· 125

Conclusion ·········· 141

Works Cited ·········· 146

Introduction

Bharati Mukherjee, a National Book Critics' Circle Award winner, is one of the most world-known American writers of Bengali origin. Her writings, mostly exploring the migrant experiences, are usually included in the growing category of American immigrant literature.

Mukherjee often writes about the new Indians who migrate to metropolitan centers of the America or other white settler countries as part of a post-1960s pattern of global migration. She distinguishes herself by the virtue of successfully representing migrant issues and her novels wonderfully capture the tension of departure and assimilation in migrancy. Mukherjee's literary achievements are highly valued in the academic circle. Her novels and short stories are often studied in university literary courses and are included in most anthologies of multi-cultural writings and minority literature in America. As a writer, she is considered "in the company of writers such as Salman Rushdie, Rhonton Mistry, and Vikram Seth"[1] and in successfully representing the experiences of recent Asian immigrants, she also "joins the likes of Maxine Hong Kingston and Diana Chang"[2].

Mukherjee is very versatile in her writings and her literary creation spans about four decades. From 1971 to 2011, Mukherjee has published eight novels [*The Tiger's Daughter*(1971), *Wife*(1975), *Jasmine*(1989), *The Holder of the World*(1993), *Leave It to Me*(1997), *Desirable Daughters*(2002), *The Tree Bride* (2004), *Miss New India* (2011)], two short story collections [*Darkness*(1985), *The Middleman and Other Stories*(1988)], one memoir [*Days and Nights in Calcutta*(1977)] (with Clark Blaise), some essays and four non-fictions (one of them also with Clark Blaise).

---

[1] Frank Day. *Bharati Mukherjee*[M]. New York: Twayne Publishers, 1996: ix.
[2] Frank Day. *Bharati Mukherjee*[M]. New York: Twayne Publishers, 1996: ix.

Many awards and honors bestowed upon her gradually established Mukherjee's status as a major writer. Mukherjee's second novel *Wife* was selected into the finalist for the Governor General's Award of Canada in 1975. Her short story "The World According to Hsu"[1] was granted the Canadian Journalism award in 1980. Her essay "An Invisible Woman" was awarded the Canadian National Magazine Award's second prize in 1981. Her short story collection *The Middleman and Other Stories* was granted the National Book Critics Circle Award in 1988, which made her the first naturalized American to have ever won the award. *The New York Times Book Review* also included her novel *Jasmine*, which is a much acclaimed success, in the list of the best books of 1989. Besides, Mukherjee has gained fellowships from both the Guggenheim Foundation and the National Endowment for the Arts, and membership in the American Academy of Arts and Sciences. In 2006, she was invited to chair the committee of the National Book Award for Fiction.

Mukherjee's writings are marked by her diasporic location and cultural background. On 27 July, 1940, Mukherjee was born into one of the highest caste Bengali Hindus, Brahmins family, in Calcutta India. Since 1947, Mukherjee travelled with her family to Europe and subsequently lived in London and other European cities. This period of education in Europe improved Mukherjee's mastery of Western knowledge and her use of English language. After returning to Calcutta in 1951, Mukherjee attended the Loreto Convent School. In 1959, Mukherjee got a BA with honors in English from the University of Calcutta. In 1961 she received a MA in English and Ancient Indian Culture from the University of Baroda. After graduation, Mukherjee travelled to the United States to further her study of creative writing in the University of Iowa. In 1963, she received a MFA from the Iowa Writers' Workshop and in 1969, she earned a PhD in English and comparative literature from the Department of Comparative Literature. After marriage, Mukherjee moved with her husband, Clark Blaise, to his home country, Canada, and began to teach at McGill. However, Mukherjee found life in Canada depressing. The multiculturalism promoted by the Canadian government was racialist. In 1980,

---

[1] Liew-Geok Leong. Bharati Mukherjee [G] // *International Literature in English: Essays on the Major Writers*. Ed. Robert L. Ross. New York: Garland, 1991: 489.

Mukherjee moved back to America. In America, Mukherjee became more mature in her writings and gained wider recognition in the academic circle. Mukherjee's personal cultural background, expatriate and immigrant experiences strongly influenced her writing career. Her writings, containing so many autobiographical elements, are the full expression of her perception of migration.

Mukherjee's writings bear distinctive features and academic significance. Firstly, in her writings spanning more than four decades, Mukherjee gradually changes her literary affiliations and matures in both aesthetics and style. In her early phase of writing, with the publication of *Darkness* as the dividing line, which is referred to by her as the "expatriate" or "exile" phase, Mukherjee writes in a vein similar to those alienated exilic writers such as Joseph Conrad, E. M. Forster, Vladimir Nabokov and V. S. Naipaul. In this phase, Mukherjee identifies herself as "an extravagant admirer" of V.S. Naipaul who has "written most movingly about the pain and absurdity of art and exile, of 'third world art' and exile among the former colonizers; the tolerant incomprehension of hosts, the absolute impossibility of ever having a home"[1]. She admires him for "articulating a postcolonial consciousness without making it appear exotic"[2]. She admits that "in myself I detect a pale and immature reflection of Naipaul" [3]. Also, Mukherjee's writing style and narrative technique in her early works are strongly influenced by British literary models.

With the publication of the short story collection *Darkness*, Mukherjee begins her immigrant phase of writing. Mukherjee explains this shift as a movement away from expatriation to immigration. In this phase of writing, Mukherjee seeks to place herself among the writers who write in the immigrant tradition. Distancing herself from alienated exilic writers, such as Naipaul, she finds herself a new literary model, Jewish immigrant writer Bernard Malamud. She says that "[l]ike Malamud, I write about a minority community which escapes the ghetto ... Like Malamud's, my work seems to find quite naturally a

---

[1] Frank Day. *Bharati Mukherjee*[M]. New York: Twayne Publishers, 1996: 287.
[2] Bradley C. Edwards. *Conversations with Bharati Mukherjee*[M]. Oxford: Mississippi UP, 2009: 17.
[3] R. K. Dhawan. *The Fiction of Bharati Mukherjee: A Critical Symposium*[M]. New Delhi: Prestige Books, 1996: 27.

moral center"[1]. There is a long tradition of immigrant writing tradition in Jewish American literature. Some scholars have pointed out that Jewish immigrant writings have been shaped by the model minority discourse, which emphasizes assimilating into mainstream American culture while detaching from original ones. Besides Malamud's works, many other Jewish American writers' writings are also about assimilation in explicit or obscure ways. For instance, Mary Antin's *The Promised Land*, Anzia Yezierska's *Red Ribbon*, Henry Roth's *David Schearle*, Saul Bellow's *Herzog*, and Philip Roth's *Alexander Portnoy* are all writings in this vein. In the immigrant phase of writing, Mukherjee's writing style and narrative technique have also changed to be more Americanized. Works in this period are often narrated from an intimated first person point of view. Mukherjee explains, "[b]y the time I wrote *Darkness* I had adopted American English as my language. I moved away from using irony and was no longer comfortable using an authoritative point of view"[2].

Mukherjee makes strict distinction between expatriation and immigration in her writing theory. According to her understanding, expatriation and immigration have different focuses, with the first one on the native land that has been left behind and the second one on the newly arrived land that one enters as an immigrant. Therefore, in Mukherjee's perception, expatriation is backward-looking, while immigration is forward-looking. Expatriate writing dwells mainly on reflecting levels of alienation like existential suffering and self-estrangement, while immigrant writing is about lives in the new country. The expatriates in Mukherjee's definition are quite similar to diaspora in Clifford's term. Clifford claims that immigrants, despite their loss and suffering, can be assimilated into the host country while diaspora cannot merge into the host country for they are "peoples whose sense of identity is centrally defined by collective histories of displacement and violent loss"[3]. Mukherjee's change from the expatriate phase of writing to the immigrant phase of writing echoes with the change of trend in postcolonial writings. In the first part of the twentieth century, many

---

[1] Bradley C. Edwards. *Conversations with Bharati Mukherjee*[M]. Oxford: Mississippi UP, 2009: 27.
[2] Bradley C. Edwards. *Conversations with Bharati Mukherjee*[M]. Oxford: Mississippi UP, 2009: 27.
[3] James Clifford. *Routes: Travel and Translation in the Late Twentieth Century*[M]. Cambridge: Harvard UP, 1997: 250-251.

postcolonial writings focus on the limbo existence of displaced migrants. Drawing to the end of the century, many switch to the depiction of migrants in the metropolitan center.

After grounding herself in the great tradition of immigrant writing, Mukherjee is determined to add more dimension to it. In her immigrant phase of writing, Mukherjee begins to write about immigrants struggling to survive in the new lands, which represents another strand of postcolonial writings different from expatriate writers' writing of rootlessness and nationalist writers' writing of rootedness. She tells her interviewer Alison B. Carb:

> Unlike writers such as Anita Desai and R. K. Narayan, I do not write in Indian English about Indians living in India. My role models, view of the world, and experiences are unlike theirs. These writers live in a world in which there are still certainties and rules. They are part of their society's mainstream ... On the other hand, I don't write from the vantage point of an Indian expatriate like V. S. Naipaul ... He writes about living in perpetual exile and about the impossibility of ever having a home ... I view myself as an American author in the tradition of other American authors whose ancestors arrived at Ellis Island. [1]

Mukherjee views her works as attempts to obliterating that particular kind of discourse between the Third World and the First World, margin and center, minority and mainstream. In her attempts, she is going to replace binary polarities with hybridity. Also, Mukherjee tries to distinguish herself from those second-generation Asian American writers, for example, Maxine Hong Kingston and Amy Tan. She points out that the abundance of mythological factors in their works are a kind of roots retrieval, while herself "being fresh off the jet, want to get away from a lot of the mythologies that were so genderist, that were created to reinforce patriarchy or the class system—not just caste system, but class system" [2].

Critics are keen to study the differences between Mukherjee's writings in the expatriate phase and those in the immigrant phase. However, there is no

---

[1] Bradley C. Edwards. *Conversations with Bharati Mukherjee*[M]. Oxford: Mississippi UP, 2009: 27.
[2] Bradley C. Edwards. *Conversations with Bharati Mukherjee*[M]. Oxford: Mississippi UP, 2009: 106.

systematic study on Mukherjee's more recent writings in her immigrant phase of writing. Critics commonly hold the opinion that in her writings published after *Darkness*, Mukherjee consciously severs her Indian ties in an effort to be accepted as a writer writing in American tradition through depicting immigrants' arduous struggle to survive in new lands. However, close scrutiny will show that in her immigrant phase of writing, Mukherjee's focus, perception, style and aesthetics of fusion go through gradual changes. Especially, in her more recent novels, there appear the recurring leitmotifs of roots search, which may be viewed as a new turn in Mukherjee's writings. Mukherjee continues her writing into the twenty-first century. In the new cultural context with escalating global migrancy, her writings of immigration assume greater cultural significance. A more systematic and structured study of cultural conflicts and immigrants' identity construction in Mukherjee's major novels written in her immigrant phase of writing would be academically intriguing and rewarding.

Despite her popularity in the academic circle and among common readers, it is always not simple to define Mukherjee's works, partly because of the occasional conflicts between her writing theory and writing practice, partly because of her constant shifting values and identifications in her long span of literary writings.

Generally speaking, Mukherjee studies differ sharply abroad and in China. Since Mukherjee's popularity shots up with the publication of *Middleman and Other Stories*, critics abroad have undertaken various thematic studies on her works. Her narrative of migrants' alienation and limbo existence is widely discussed among these critics. With the boom of new migration and deepening of globalization, Mukherjee's migrant narrative gains ever increasing significance and academic attention. On the other hand, the majority of Mukherjee's works, except *Jasmine*, has been largely ignored by Chinese scholars. Till today, there are no systematic studies on her works in China with her more recent works rarely commented upon.

Studies on Bharati Mukherjee abroad boom after the publications of the short story collections *The Middleman and Other Stories* and *Jasmine*. In fact, it is quite true to say that Mukherjee has built her early fame as a great writer upon the two works. Critics have studied Mukherjee's individual works from the perspective of migration, nationhood, postcolonialism, feminism, and identity construction, etc. However, the aesthetic nature of her works, her writing styles, and narrative technique are rarely explored.

Studies on Mukherjee's works abroad can be roughly classified into four groups, monographs of her works, monographs and PhD dissertations that compare Mukherjee's works with those of other writers, collections of criticism of her individual works from different perspectives and articles and reviews published in academic journals. Besides, there is also a collection of interviews with Mukherjee.

In the first group, the monograph *Bharati Mukherjee* edited by Frank Day (published in 1996) is the most influential one. It offers a comprehensive and systematic study of the writing career of Mukherjee from the publication of her first novel, *The Tiger's Daughter* (1971) till that of *The Holder of the World* (1993). Day divides Mukherjee's writing career into four phases. In works of the first phase, including *The Tiger's Daughter* and *Days and Nights in Calcutta*, Mukherjee looks at India from an exile's perspective. Those works depict sufferings of exiles and their constant longings for "home". The second phase, expatriation phase, starts with Mukherjee's moving to Canada. In this phase, she published *Wife*, *Darkness*, and *The Sorrow and the Terror*. All these works reflect directly or indirectly Mukherjee's personal experiences in Canada, which are characterized by her constant feeling of frustration and exasperation with Canada's policy of multiculturalism. Mukherjee takes an aloof attitude in her writing in this phase and her works resemble to a large degree those of V. S. Naipaul's. The third phase starts with Mukherjee's immigration back to the United States. The publications of *The Middleman and Other Stories* and *Jasmine* bring her both fame and critical attention. Day also designates a new phase of Mukherjee's writing with the publication of *The Holder of the World* (1993), which is characterized by Mukherjee's attempts to place herself in the American tradition of prose narrative. The author's designation of Mukherjee's writings into four different phases is very insightful in the time of the monograph's publication. However, this designation needs further revision with the passage of time and more recent changes in Mukherjee's concerns and perceptions.

Sushma Tandon's monograph *Bharati Mukherjee's Fiction: A Perspective* (published in 2004) analyzes Mukherjee's works from *The Tiger's Daughter* to *Jasmine*, tracing the turn of Mukherjee's writing from the expatriate to the immigrant phase. The author maintains that early works of Mukherjee, including *The Tiger's Daughter*, *Wife* and *Darkness*, shows Mukherjee's expatriate sensibility, which is characterized by a strong feeling of alienation and being caught between two cultures. However, Mukherjee's detached and ironic style is sometimes subject to strong criticism. After feeling expatriate for fifteen years in Canada, Mukherjee moved back to America and began her writing as an immigrant. The author tries to examine the American society and its psyche in which Mukherjee's protagonists try to assimilate in *The Middleman and Other Stories* and *Jasmine*. After a close survey, the author reaches the conclusion that the landscapes of America changes as immigrants change themselves, "the peopling of America is an ongoing sage"[1]. However, the shortcoming of the monograph is that due to the wide coverage of the study, there is no in-depth analysis of Mukherjee's any specific novel.

Verena Esterbauer's monograph *The Immigrant's Search for Identity in Bharati Mukherjee's Jasmine and Desirable Daughters* (published in 2008) studies two of Mukherjee's important novels from the perspective of cross-cultural identity formation. The author points out that there is a wide gap between the concepts of identity in the Eastern and the Western cultures. Exploring the Western image of "Asian", the author points out that cultural factors influence the formation of stereotyped immigrants. The monograph moves on to study the various ways of belongings in Asia and the United States, clashes of traditions and differences in interpersonal relationships in India and America, all of which contribute to the identity formation and transformation of the female protagonists in *Jasmine* and *Desirable Daughters*. This is a comprehensive intercultural study taking various cultural factors affecting identity formation into consideration. However, lacking in theoretical framework renders the monograph a rather superficial listing of intercultural communication conflicts and phenomena.

---

[1] Sushma Tandon. *Bharati Mukherjee's Fiction: A Perspective* [M]. New Delhi: Sarup & Sons, 2004: i.

Atia Anwer Zoon's monograph *Bharati Mukherjee's Female Protagonists: A Search for Female Identity* (published in 2012) runs in the similar vein. The monograph mainly deals with the diasporic journey of women and the efforts of female protagonists to adapt to hyphenated identities. According to the author, the South Asian diasporic experience is best characterized by a state of liminality. The various woman protagonists of Mukherjee's novels are caught between the traditional customs of south Asia and present experience of the Westernized culture of the United States. It is a fairly comprehensive immigrant identity study rendered through analysis of common features of immigrant experiences. However, the main weakness of the monograph is that the author seems to have neglected the specific and individually different features of female protagonists in Mukherjee's novels. The author studies all the female protagonists in a similar and general way, which renders them not significant one from the other, or different from those in novels of other diasporic writers.

The second group of studies includes monographs and PhD dissertations that compare Mukherjee's writings with those of other immigrant or diasporic writers. Cristina Emanuela Dascalu's monograph *Imaginary Homelands of Writers in Exile: Salman Rushdie, Bharati Mukherjee, and V. S. Naipaul* (published in 2007) compares Mukherjee's works with those of other writers. Jenkins praises the significance of the study concerning post-colonial and de-colonial displacement and classifies the monograph as the most concise and outstanding examinations of exile[1].

The monograph explores the theoretical and practical implications of exile across national, generic and ethnic boundaries. The author asserts that given their similarity, these three novelists should be called the most important artists of a new genre: a literature of exile. For they all travelled across the seas, all come to a foreign land, and in their works exile is a constant theme. The author moves on to compare the different features of the three writers' exile writings. Rushdie, with magical realism, in portraying the "imagery home" deconstructs the fundamentalism of both the Western and Islam thoughts. His exile writing emphasizes the changeability and shifting nature of the world. Naipaul, often

---

[1] Critina Emanuela Dascalu. *Imaginary Homelands of Writers in Exile: Salman Rushdie, Bharati Mukherjee, and V. S. Naipaul*[M]. New York: Cambria Press, 2007: x.

using the biographical form in his writings of displacement, has a more negative view of the state of exile. On the contrary, Mukherjee, writing immigration as a quest of negotiating the gender and ethical implications of subjectivity, has a brighter view of the state of exile. Mukherjee presents in her novels the exiles' ability to take action and assert agency.

Markose Abraham's monograph *American Immigration Aesthetics: Bernard Malamud & Bharati Mukherjee as Immigrants* (published in 2011) does a comparative study of works by the Jewish immigrant writer Malamud and the Indian immigrant writer Mukherjee. It is an intriguing comparative study since besides many similarities the two writers share, Malamud is also an acknowledged literary model of Mukherjee. Markose points out that both immigrant writers write with a tone of affirmation about immigrant experience and their immigrant visions can be characterized by a strong moral center. Immigrant protagonists in the novels of the two writers resist the domination of the majority community in America and grind their ways into America firmly. Markose moves on to compare the two writers' different perceptions of transgressions, sufferings, and their use of myth and tradition. Malamud, a second-generation Jewish immigrant and Mukherjee, a first-generation Indian immigrant, both are actually quite deeply influenced by their own cultural heritage and show different focuses in cultural assimilation. Markose believes that Malamud writes about some essential aspect of the Jewish experiences, the biblical past, the rise of Hitler, the Holocaust, the new state of Israel in the quest for Jewish moral salvation and self-realization. Markose shows that Mukherjee's female protagonists, molded by the long tradition and history of spirituality and adaptability in Hinduism, transform themselves by fighting adversity in their process of immigrancy. In this monograph, Markose praises the unyielding spirits of Mukherjee's protagonists in their identity formation and reformation.

There are also several PhD dissertations that compare Mukherjee's writings with those of others. Sunanda Chaudhury Vaidya's *Myths of Interaction: Reading between the Politics and Ethics in the Works of E. M. Forster, Salman Rushdie, Bharati Mukherjee and Mahasweta Devi* compares the political use of myth in the four authors' writings. Krystyna Zamorska's *Ethnic Fictions:*

Cultural Mediations in Contemporary American Writing selects Mukherjee as a representative of authors with South Asian ancestry. The dissertation compares the ways in which Mukherjee's *Jasmine* and other works of native American, African American, Polish American, and the Caribbean authors redefine American narrative. Anupama Jain's *Hybrid Bildungs in South Asian Women's Writing: Meena Alexander, Bharati Mukherjee, and Bapsi Sidhwa Re-Imagine America* reads Mukherjee's writing together with those of other South Asian writers such as Meena Alexander and Bapsi Sidhwa as bildungsroman and compares their subtle differences in writings. Shazia Rahman's *Resisting Women: Orientalism, Diaspora, and Gender* compares Mukherjee's works with those of Anita Rau Badami, Rachna Mara, Kirin Narayan and Sara Suleri to show how their writings contest Orientalist stereotypes of South Asian women. Yan Jiang's *Homemaking in Asian American Women's Writing: Chuang Hua, Bharati Mukherjee and Meena Alexander Performing the Diasporic Home* compares identity transformation in Mukherjee's *Jasmine* with those in Chuang Hua's *Crossings* and Meena Alexander's *The Fault Lines* and suggests that Asian immigrants' homemaking is performative. Basically speaking, the comparative studies usually compare Mukherjee's writing with those of other migrant or disporic writers, especially those with Asian ancestry. There are still many other PhD dissertations written in the similar way which are omitted here.

Besides monographs and comparative studies there are also several book length collections of critical essays, among which, *Bharati Mukherjee: Critical Perspectives* edited by Emmanuel S. Nelson (published in 1993) is one of the most influential works in Mukherjee studies. The collection includes eleven thematic, stylistic and aesthetic studies of Mukherjee's novels. Maya Manju Sharma analyzes Mukherjee's expatriate sensibility reflected in *Wife* and *The Tiger's Daughter*. Sharma makes a biographical study of Mukherjee, pointing out that Mukherjee is bicultural from very young age in life, the experience of which greatly influenced her creative writing. Sharma's claim that Flannery O'Connor is a clear influence on Mukherjee is very innovative and insightful. Approaching Mukherjee's novels from a new angle, Pramila Wenkateswaran studies the Indian mythical factors in the texts. She believes that the reincarnation in Indian myth clearly influences Mukherjee's construction of fluid, changing identities of her protagonists. Brinda Bose in her article exams the ethnicity, gender, and migrancy in *The Tiger's Daughter*, *Wife* and *Jasmine*. Bose also touches upon a leitmotif, violence, in Mukherjee's novels pointing out that Mukherjee's protagonists translate their identities in traumatic changes. Samir Dayal further explores the pervasiveness of violence in *Jasmine*. Employing postcolonial theories in his study, Dayal contends that the leitmotif of violence reveals the contradictions in postcolonial subject formation. Janet M. Powers employs Roland Barthes's theory of narrative codes to study the sociopolitical factors as indices and narrative codes in Mukherjee's *Wife* and *Jasmine*. Pushpa N. Parekh studies the narrative voice and gender roles in *Jasmine*. Parekh asserts that Mukherjee unravels the triple voice-strands in her depiction of Jasmine's moving from the position of being told to that of telling.

Bharati Mukherjee: Critical Perspectives edited by Somdatta Mandal (published in 2010) is also a collection of criticism from different perspectives. The authors approach Mukherjee's individual works from different theoretical frameworks, ranging from postcolonial, feminist, psychological, to cultural studies. Besides, different aspects of Mukherjee's oeuvre are explored, ranging from her position as an Asian American writer, her stance on multiculturalism, her perception of expatriation and immigration, to Bengaliness in her works. The collection is quite thought-provoking because several contributors from India offer utterly different ways of reading Mukherjee's works.

There are also many journal articles and reviews concerning Mukherjee's works, which show an increasing interest of both the academic and common readers in the writings of Mukherjee. In view of the large number of articles and reviews published, only a few most representative and relevant ones will be briefly introduced here.

Articles published on *Jasmine* mainly study subjectivity formation, or compare *Jasmine* with works of other writers. Kristin Carter-Sanborn's "'We Murder Who We Were': *Jasmine* and the Violence of Identity" published in *American Literature* studies the use of violence as catalyst in subject formation reflected in *Jasmine* and moves on to provide an overall examination of the dynamics of migrants' subjectivity. Mukherjee's use of violence has become the subject of study in many articles, among which this article by Kristin is probably the most representative one. Robyn Warhol-Down's "*Jasmine* Reconsidered: Narrative Discourse and Multicultural Subjectivity" published in *Contemporary Women's Writing* reads *Jasmine* as a poststructuralist critique of the Bildungsroman tradition and an experiment in the form of feminocentric fiction. Ahmed Gamal's "Postcolonial Recycling of the Oriental Vampire in Emile Habiby's *Saraya*, *The Ghoul's Daughter* and Bharati Mukherjee's *Jasmine*" included in *Pluto Journals* compares the two postcolonial novels. The author points out that both authors use the classical vampiric topoi of otherness and border existences to deconstruct the demonic and ghostly constructions of the Arabs and Indians in colonial and postcolonial contexts. Ashy Sen's "From National to Transnational: Three Generations of South Asian American Women Writers" published in *Asiatic* examines a representative pool of canonical Asian American texts, including Bharati Mukherjee's *Jasmine*, selections from Chitra Divakaruni's short story collection *Arranged Marriage*, and Jhumpa Lahiri's two short stories "When Mr. Pirzada Came to Dine" and "Mrs. Shen's". The author argues that all the narratives can be read as counter hegemony. Rosanne Kanhai's "'Sensing Designs in History's Muddles': Global Feminism and the Postcolonial Novel" published in *Modern Language Studies* explores the relationship between global feminism and transnational cultural patterns that affect women of color using Mukherjee's *Jasmine* and Jamaica Kincaid's *Lucy* as exemplary texts.

The numbers of articles published on *The Holder of the World*, *Desirable Daughters* and *The Tree Bride* are relatively small compared to that on *Jasmine*. Yet some of the articles offer very refreshing and illuminating readings. Jennifer Drake's "Looting American Culture: Bharati Mukherjee's Immigrant Narratives" published in *Contemporary Literature* studies the myth and history writing in *The Holder of the World*, which provides an alternative version of myth and history for America. Shao-Pin Luo's "Rewriting Travel: Ahdaf Soueif's *The Map of Love* and Bharati Mukherjee's *The Holder of the World*" published in *The Journal of Commonwealth Literature* compares the two novels from the point of view of travel writings. The author points out that the travels of the protagonists show the interconnectedness of cultures. Krishna Sen's "The Bengal Connection: Transnationalising America in *The Namesake* and *The Tree*

Bride" published in *Comparative American Studies* shows that by inscribing ethnicity and history of Bengal to American culture, the two novels transnationalize the host culture.

Besides, as a professor teaching literary creation, Mukherjee is also very voluble about her own writing theory and practice. *Conversations with Bharati Mukherjee*, edited by Bradley C. Edwards (published in 2009), is a collection of thirteen interviews conducted with Mukherjee from 1973 to 2007. In these interviews, Mukherjee answers a wide range of questions concerning her writing technique, aesthetics of fusion, the depiction of violence and terrorism in her works, her own perception of postcolonial and feminist theories, etc. Mukherjee seems to enjoy sharing her opinions with others. However, if the interviews are traced closely, contradictions of opinions are abundant, which may be due to her constant revisions of her own ideas and maturity of thoughts. The collection provides insights into understanding Mukherjee's works as it includes a lot of comments on works by Mukherjee herself.

To sum up, although Mukherjee studies abroad starts in the 1970s, it booms only after the publications of *The Middleman and Other Stories* and *Jasmine* in the 1980s and the 1990s. Till today, relatively comprehensive studies usually concentrate on analyzing Mukherjee's changes in style and theme between her expatriate phase of writing and immigrant phase of writing. In comparative studies of her works with those of other migrant or diasporic writers, scholars usually endeavor to highlight Mukherjee's specific features in writing. Critics' attempts to compare her writings with those of V. S. Naipaul, Salman Rushdie and Bernard Malamud surely in a way vouch for Mukherjee's literary status and achievements.

However, there are some failings in Mukherjee studies abroad: (1) Critics seem to attach too much importance to Mukherjee's early works, especially *Jasmine*. There are not so many in-depth studies on her most recent works although some of them are highly reviewed. (2) There are many studies devoted to analyze the differences in Mukherjee's writings between the expatriate phase of writing and the immigrant phase of writing. However, there is no systematic study to trace the changes in Mukherjee's writing in the immigrant phase, which also lasts for more than three decades. Therefore, it would be academically rewarding to make a comprehensive study of major novels written in Mukherjee's immigrant phase of writing.

Compared with the flourishing interests in Mukherjee writings abroad, academic studies on Mukherjee's works seem to be relatively insufficient in China. Besides general reviews, there are totally less than twenty academic articles published, most of which are devoted to analyze Mukherjee's most famous novel *Jasmine*. The most important articles of Mukherjee studies in China are as follows.

Huang Zhi's "A Transforming Kali: A Critical Reading of Bharati Mukherjee's *Jasmine*" published in *Journal of PLA University of Foreign Languages* in 2007 applying James Clifford's diasporic theory which shifts the focus of diasporic study from "roots" to "routes", analyzes the transforming identities of Jasmine. Jasmine, through constant transformation of identities, deconstructs her original identity as a subaltern woman. Her shifting identities challenge colonial and patriarchic hierarchy, thus in a way, subvert binary construction of the opposites. The author reaches the conclusion that Jasmine's transformations "provide feasible path for other woman diaspora"[1].

Yin Xinan's "Bharati Mukherjee's Trans-cultural Writings and Her Imitation and Transcendence of V. S. Naipaul" published in *Foreign Literature*, in 2010 is a comparative study of the migrant writings of Mukherjee and those of Naipaul. The author divides Mukherjee's writings into three stages. These three stages are associated with the sense of exile of emigrants from the third world, the sense of inhabitants and the sense of settlement. The author asserts that Mukherjee's writings on the first stage, which concentrate on the portrayal of alienation and homelessness of expatriates, resemble and in a sense strongly mimic those of Naipaul's. However, in the third stage, Mukherjee's writing of assimilation, cultural translation and positive subsequences of migration shows her transcendence of Naipaul's thoughts. The author claims that Mukherjee's imitation and transcendence "reflect the trajectory of postcolonial writers'

---

[1] 黄芝. 变幻莫测的"卡莉女神":解读芭拉蒂·穆克尔吉的《詹丝敏》[J].解放军外国语学院学报,2007(3):94-98.(translated by the author of this book)

thinking about the relationship between the West and the East, and intercultural communications"[1].

Xu Zhenyan and Zhang Li's "Female Subjectivity Construction in Diaspora—A Reading of *Jasmine*" published in *College English* in 2012 studies Jasmine's identity construction in diaspora. The study mainly employs the theory of postcolonialism. Authors claim that "with the awakening of female consciousness and economic independence, Jasmine forms hybrid identities. With spatial mobility, Jasmine completes her subjectivity construction"[2].

Shi Haijun's "Regional Culture and Imaginary Homeland" published in *Foreign Literature Review* in 2001 includes a section that is devoted to the discussion of Mukherjee's writing. In the author's opinion, Mukherjee's writing of assimilation "does not mean losing of Indian culture to American one. Instead, it means that the writer, dwelling on the margins of two cultures, functions as a negotiator in the communication of the two cultures"[3]. The author certainly treats Mukherjee as a representative who stands for a totally distinctive stand of migrant writing.

Yang Xiaoxia "Diaspora Puranas: The Past and Future of the Indian Diaspora and Diaspora Fiction" published in *Journal of Shenzhen University (Humanities & Social Sciences)* in 2012 begins with a survey of India's four major waves of migration and then moves on to study Indian diaspora fictions. The author claims that these fictions reflect the historical changes and the living conditions of Indian migrants. Mukherjee's writing, together with those of others, is considered by the author "to have made great contributions to diaspora fictions"[4]. But still the author questions some of Mukherjee's depiction of immigrants' experiences in her fictions and considers that it ignores more realistic factors.

---

[1] 尹锡南.芭拉蒂·穆克吉的跨文化书写及其对奈保尔的模仿超越[J].国外文学,2010(1):148-153.(translated by the author of this book)

[2] 徐珍岩,张丽.离散中的女性主体性身份建构:解读芭拉蒂·穆克尔吉的《茉莉花》[J].大学英语(学术版),2010(2):114-116.(translated by the author of this book)

[3] 石海峻.地域文化与想像的家园:兼谈印度现当代文学与印度侨民文学[J].外国文学评论,2001(3):24-33.(translated by the author of this book)

[4] 杨晓霞.流散往世书:印度移民的过去与现在:兼论印度流散小说创作[J].深圳大学学报(人文社会科学版),2012(6):10-16.(translated by the author of this book)

Foreign Literature also includes an interview with Mukherjee in 2012 by Liu Jing: "Immigrant Writing and *Miss New India*: An interview with Bharati Mukherjee". In this interview, Mukherjee discusses two topics: immigrant writing and her new novel *Miss New India*, which is published in 2011. Mukherjee discusses the definition, development and significance of immigrant writing in an age of globalization. Mukherjee also tries to differentiate immigrant writings from other postcolonial writings. Besides, Mukherjee thinks her writing is different from those of second-generation immigrant writers, such as Amy Tan and Maxine Hong Kingston, in that they have not experienced the painful processes of unhousement and rehousement. *Miss New India*, which is set completely in India, is the last one of Mukherjee's "New Trilogy", with the other two novels being *Desirable Daughters* and *The Tree Bride*. Besides thematic discussion of the new novel, the interview also includes Mukherjee's discussion of her writing style and changing narrative technique.

Besides journal articles, there are also several M. A. theses on Mukherjee in China, four of which are listed in on-line database. Liu Yuchen's "Reconstruction of Identity: On the Protagonist's Growth of Bharati Mukherjee's Novel *Jasmine*", studies *Jasmine* mainly as a postcolonial Bildungsroman. Wen Yuling's "The Oscillation of Jasmine's identity: A Study of Bharati Mukherjee's *Jasmine* Based on Postcolonial Feminist Theory" studies Jasmine's changing identities. Chang Shufang's "'Third space' and Identity Formation in Bharati Mukherjee's *Jasmine*" introduces the third space in Jasmine's identity construction. From relatively different angles, all the three theses make a text-specific analysis of Mukherjee's masterpiece *Jasmine*. Wan Ling's "A Post-colonial Study of Bharati Mukherjee's Works" studies the protagonists' resistance strategies against the hegemonic discourses in several of Mukherjee's novels. These relatively new studies are also signs of Chinese scholars' increasing interests in Mukherjee's works.

To sum up, there is no comprehensive study of Mukherjee's works in China till today. Most studies in China are devoted to Mukherjee's most-acclaimed novel, *Jasmine*, which shows the limitation of Chinese scholars' interests in Mukherjee studies. However, in the last three years, the increasing number of Mukherjee studies in China may be deemed as a sign of increased interests in the academic circle.

This book studies Mukherjee's writings of immigration in the following four major novels, *Jasmine*, *The Holder of the World*, *Desirable Daughters* and *The Tree Bride*.

Mukherjee's writings of immigration are quite different from those of many postcolonial writers. Many first generations of postcolonial nationalists, for instance, Chinua Achebe, and R. K. Narayan, write about the construction of anti-colonial identities, which give their works a strong sense of rootedness. The works of later postcolonial writers, such as V. S. Naipaul, Salman Rushdie and many others, reflect a strong sense of rootlessness. However, rootlessness may be perceived and represented differently among these writers. Some emphasize the alienation, the pain of losing one's roots and torment of existence in-betweenness, while others celebrate the route instead of roots and embrace exuberantly hybridity.

Rootedness often associates with presumed wholeness and security, since it implies strong affiliation to a single locality. Rootlessness can appear as a manifestation of cultural dissolution and associates with search for identity, which oscillates between trying to get rid of one's root altogether and holding on to one's "origin" constantly through nostalgia. Mukherjee's writings of immigration emphasize the reinvention of identities and self-empowerment to gain multiple roots or affiliations.

To sum up, Mukherjee's writings of immigration reflect the following major points.

Mukherjee's writings of immigration do not dwell solely upon the common themes of immigrants' bewilderments, sufferings, rootless and limbo existence in the host country.

Mukherjee's major immigrant characters more often than not exhibit resilient and courageous attempts to overcome difficulties in sharply different cultures and get survival in the host country. The process often involves deconstruction of fixed identity and embracing of hybridity and fluid identities. Mukherjee's major immigrant characters also shun affiliation to a single "original" root by actively engaging in multiple cultural translations and transformations.

Mukherjee's presentation of immigration often subverts binary opposition and essentialist stance, be it colonial or narrow nationalist one. In this sense, Mukherjee's writings constitute what is called counter hegemonic discourse. The four novels studied in this book show Mukherjee's transition from decontextualization to re-contextualization in writings and Orientalism to cosmopolitanism in stance, which also reflect that Mukherjee's aesthetics of fusion matures gradually.

The book studies Mukherjee's writings of immigration mainly drawing on the theory of postcolonialism. In close reading, the book scrutinizes different construction of identities reflected in novels written in Mukherjee's immigrant phase of writing, which in a certain degree reflects the development and maturity of Mukherjee's aesthetics of fusion. Postcolonialism may be the best theoretical framework to be used in analyzing Mukherjee's novels of immigration.

As an academic discipline, postcolonialism's beginning may be traced back to the 1950s. In the 1980s and the 1990s, it gains momentum in development. Edward Said's *Orientalism* published in 1978, lays the foundation for postcolonial studies. Said studies the historical production of the Western discourse that constantly others the Orientals. In the othering of the Orientals and building of the West/East binary opposition, the West justifies its imperial domination and exploitation of the East. Said's theory of Orientalism is very influential and many other postcolonial scholars further the study of imperial power and the Orientalist discourse. Arif Dirlik argues that the Orientals participate in the construction of the Orient. Dirlik defines their participation, which involves a certain degree of agency, self-orientalization. Homi K. Bhabha questions Said's study of the Orientalist discourse for he believes that colonial discourse is far more complex than a mere Eurocentric construction. He introduces certain tenets of post-structuralism into postcolonial study. Drawing largely from ideas of Derrida, Mikhail Bakhtin, Frantz Fanon and Benedict Anderson, he defines many new terminologies, among which hybridity, mimicry, third space and ambivalence become very influential in postcolonial study. Among those terms, hybridity is central to Bhabha's thoughts. Bhabha first studies agency associated with hybridity in the discourse level, and then he moves on, together with other theorists, to study the agency of hybridity for immigrants in cultural translation. Theories of Orientalism, self-orientalization, hybridity and cultural translation will be employed to study the immigrant writing in Mukherjee's novels.

Besides, Foucault's theory of power, Derrida's theory of deconstruction, Judith Butler's theory of performativity, Spivak's theory of postcolonial feminism and other feminist thoughts, Fanon's critique of nationalism/nativism, Bhabha and others' theory of cosmopolitanisms and Kwame Anthony Appiah's theory of rooted cosmopolitanism will also be employed in order to elaborate on the identity formation and transformation of immigrants in Mukherjee's selected novels.

The book is divided into five parts, introduction, three main chapters, and conclusion. Introduction includes a brief summary of Mukherjee's literary achievements, personal migrant experience and unique position in migrant narrative. It also includes a literary review of Mukherjee studies both abroad and in China, theoretical framework and structure of the dissertation.

Chapter One applies theories of hybridity, Said's theory of Orientalism and Dirlik's theory of self-orientalization to analyze the self-assertion in metamorphoses in *Jasmine*. Migrating illegally from India to America, Jasmine goes through several stages of psychological metamorphoses. In metamorphoses, Jasmine demonstrates self-assertion in seeking agency in her hybridity and constantly self-orientalizing herself as tools of survival. Jasmine's self-assertion deconstructs fixity of identity, yet it is at the same time limited by her internalized Orientalist stance. The self-assertion in metamorphoses reflects Mukherjee's celebration of agency-seeking in hybridity, yet this celebration is often closely associated with dedication to full assimilation, namely Americanization. The self-assertion in metamorphoses and fluid identity construction reflects the Orientalist stance in Mukherjee's writing of immigration in this stage.

Chapter Two mainly applies theories of cultural translation, Derrida's theory of deconstruction, feminist thoughts and Foucault's theory of power to analyze the rebelliousness in transgression in *The Holder of the World*. Hannah, the protagonist of the novel, shows her rebelliousness in transgression of both gender and ethnic boundaries. She transgresses gender boundary by fighting patriarchal family structure and transgresses ethnic boundary by becoming a bibi of an Indian warrior. Besides, Hannah also liberates her female sensuality in various other ways. In transgression, Hannah rebels against both gender and ethnic roles forced upon her to realize her cultural translation. *The Holder of the World* is Mukherjee's rewriting of Nathaniel Hawthrone's *The Scarlet Letter*. The rewriting shows traces of Mukherjee's re-affirmation of Indianness while celebrating culture translation.

Chapter Three applies Fanon and other theorists' critiques of nationalism/ nativism, Bhabha and others' theory of cosmopolitanisms and Appiah's theory of "rooted" cosmopolitanism to analyze the self-reflection in migrancy in *Desirable Daughters* and *The Tree Bride*. Tara, the immigrant protagonist of the two novels, reflects upon different cultural affiliations of her two sisters and herself, namely ghettoization, nationalism and full assimilation. In critical self-reflection, Tara embarks on a roots search. In historical retrieval, Tara condemns the sins and trauma of colonialism and praises the strength of Indian culture and its people. The self-reflection in migrancy reflects the maturity of Mukherjee's writings of immigration, which gradually changes from an Orientalist stance to a rooted cosmopolitan one.

Conclusion part sums up the main ideas of the book. The identity construction and cultural reflection depicted in Mukherjee's immigrant phase of writing changes from Jasmine's self-assertion in metamorphosis, Hannah's rebelliousness in transgression to Tara's self-reflection upon different cultural affiliations. The writings of immigration in this stage also reflect the maturity of Mukherjee's aesthetics of fusion, changing from celebration of happy hybridity and fluid identity, to a tentative reaffirmation of Indianness, then to a more cosmopolitan perception of cultural fusion.

Chapter 1 Jasmine: Self-assertion in Metamorphoses

　　Jasmine is an undeniable success, which further establishes Mukherjee's literary status as a major immigrant American writer after the publication of the award-winning collection *The Middleman and Other Stories*. Despite its huge economic success and popularity among common readers, *Jasmine* is reviewed drastically differently among critics interpreting from different perspectives. On the one hand, some critics speak highly of the theme and the artistic significance of the novel, and elevate it almost to the status of a postcolonial canon. American novelist Alice Walker, one of the admirers, speaks highly of the literary achievement of the novel, "[t]his is a novel of great importance to any contemporary insight into ourselves as Americans in the midst of enormous social, political, and personal changes"[1]. Jill Roberts calls *Jasmine* Mukherjee's postmodern Bildungsroman, which in a way can be compared to Charlotte Brontë's *Jane Eyre*. Only this time it is set in a postcolonial scenario. Ralph Crane also praises Mukherjee's Bildungsroman that "traces the upward trajectory of an increasingly liberated woman"[2].

　　On the other hand, critics reading from feminist or postcolonial perspectives usually are more critical of *Jasmine*, perceiving it a typical representation that Orientalizes and stereotypes subaltern Indian women, but glorifies the freedom and status of women in America. Anu Aneja points out: "The text's desire to

---

　　[1] Bharati Mukherjee. *Jasmine*[M]. New York: Ballantine Books, 1989: I.
　　[2] Somdatta Mandal. *Bharati Mukherjee: Critical Perspective*[M]. New Delhi: Pencraft Books, 2010: 189.

give shape to the Orient through its own backward gaze seems to be in complicity with that imperialist position. The authority of perspective allows the narrator to construct a caricature of oppressed Indian womanhood"[1].

Besides, some critics from South Asia also criticize the detextualization of the novel, namely Mukherjee's slighting of social, racial and class reality in the novel, and question Mukherjee's bias as an upper-middle-class immigrant from India to the United States in representing third-world rural women, such as Jasmine. Especially many critics from India review *Jasmine* in a very critical way. They question the nature and the term of the novel's success in America.

Regardless of the mixed critical reviews, the publication of *Jasmine* is a landmark in Mukherjee's writing career. It signifies the further ending of Mukherjee's expatriate phase of writing, as sustained by Mukherjee's own comment on the novel, "[i]t was in writing that book that I transformed myself from being an expatriate to realizing I'm an immigrant ... There is no going back"[2]. The comment shows Mukherjee's strong desire to get "re-rooted" in her host country. Reflected in the novel, the protagonist Jasmine transcends Tara in *The Tiger's Daughter* and Dimple in *Wife* in that Jasmine takes more initiatives in her metamorphoses, both in actively seeking agency in hybridity and in sly submission in self-orientalization. The strong desire to survive in the host country is mainly shown in the deconstruction of fixed identity, introduction of fluid identities and the protagonist's positive attitude and willingness to adapt.

This chapter tries to analyze the self-assertion in metamorphoses in *Jasmine*. The protagonist's self-assertion is reflected in her seeking of agency in hybridity. Also at the same time, it is closely associated with the protagonist's purposeful self-orientalization, which proves instrumental in establishing herself in a strange land.

1.1 Hybrid Identity as Agency

Hybridity is a key term in postcolonial and cultural studies. However, the

---

[1] Somdatta Mandal. *Bharati Mukherjee: Critical Perspective* [M]. New Delhi: Pencraft Books, 2010: 188-189.

[2] Meera Ameena. Bharati Mukherjee[J]. *Bomb*, 1989(29): 26.

connotation of hybridity in postcolonial and cultural context has gone through several stages of the development.

"Hybridity" is a term developed from biological and botanical origins and in the nineteenth century. It gradually began to be used in linguistics and race theories. "Hybrid" has its origin in Latin, which refers to the offspring of a tame sow and a wild boar. In the nineteenth century it was initially used mainly as a biological term. However, with the modern colonial expansion, it was borrowed by racialist colonizers and thus became one of the major terms in racist theories. In the racist discourse, hybridity was considered to pose grave threat to the purity of race and social-political order, which would result in the degeneration of the white race and culture. Thus, hybridity assumed negative connotation and thereafter was used as a cultural term in a wider social context. Robert Young points out that in the nineteenth century:

> [T]he alleged degeneration of those of mixed race came increasingly both to feed off and to supplement hybridity as the focus of racial and cultural attention and anxiety. At the same time, however, as being instanced as degenerate, and, literally, degraded (that is, lowered by racial mixture from pure whiteness, the highest grade), those of mixed race were often invoked as the most beautiful human beings of all.[1]

These complex mentalities show the white colonizers' simultaneous desire and fear of the racial Other.

In the fight for national independence, Fanon and other theorists criticized the racial connotation of hybridity. In the 1980s and the 1990s, theorists in the postcolonial study began to further develop the connotation of hybridity. Bhabha studies the subversive nature of hybridity from language and cultural perspectives. In his theorization of hybridity, the agency associated with hybridity begins to assume academic attention.

In postcolonial studies today, there is no single and definite demarcation of hybridity. Bhabha, Stuart Hall, Paul Gilroy and Robert Young are often

---

[1] Robert J. C. Young. *Colonial Desire: Hybridity in Theory, Culture, and Race* [M]. London: Routledge, 1995: 15.

considered the authorities on hybridity theory. Besides, postcolonial feminists Lisa Lowe, Trinh T. Minh-ha and others have also contributed to the heated discussion of hybridity from varied perspectives.

Bhabha reintroduces and redefines the term hybridity and gradually forms his theory of hybridity. In his study of hybridity, Bhabha mainly employs Fanon's colonial psychoanalytical method, Bakhtin's polyphonic theory, and Lacan's mirror theory in formation of subjectivity. Bhabha maintains that colonial discourse is full of ambiguity and therefore is far more complex than previously assumed. In Bhabha's opinion, colonial discourse "produces the colonized as a social reality which is at once an 'other' and yet entirely knowable and visible"[1]. It results in colonial discourse's internal rupture and ambiguity, which makes the colonial authority lose its certainty of meaning. At this stage, Bhabha mainly explores the agency of hybridity in textual analysis of imperial discourse.

Later, Bhabha further develops the theory of hybridity to introduce the term "Third Space", which is a hybrid displacing space. Third Space denies the authenticity and originality of culture. Therefore, in Third Space, hybridity subverts discourse of authority and dominates. Bhabha's theorization of hybridity, unsettling binary and essentialist ways of thinking at the same time, is very influential in postcolonial studies.

Since the 1980s, Bhabha and other theorists of hybridity have diverted their studies of hybridity to the prevalence of migrations. They employ hybridity theory to study migrants, whose cultural identities are constantly in hybridization. Hybridization is the mixing of what is already a hybrid, since all cultures are not free of hybridization. Stuart Hall defines two understandings of cultural identity in "Cultural Identity and Diaspora" (1990): (1) a stable and relatively fixed identity that people usually assume when they live in the same culture for a rather long period of time; (2) migrants' identities that go through constant transformation because of the conflict between different cultures.[2] Hybridization is not an easy oscillation between two or more identities, but a

---

[1] Homi K. Bhabha. *The Location of Culture*[M]. London: Routledge, 1994: 70-71.

[2] Stuart Hall. Cultural Identity and Diaspora[G]//*Identity: Community, Culture, Difference*. Ed. Jonathan Rutherford. London: Lawrence and Wishart, 1990: 225.

tough process in which the migrant adapts, reinvents and reproduces different identities. Hall further points out that cultural identity is "not an essence but a positioning. Hence, there is always a politics of identity, a politics of position, which has no absolute guarantee in an unproblematic, transcendental 'law of origin'" [1].

Proponents of hybridity theory praise the deconstructive nature of hybridity and the agency associated with it. Hybridity emphasizes the affirmative presence of migrants and the ambivalent transformations experienced by both migrants and their host countries. In hybridization, migrants are capable of asserting their own agency. Agency, according to Barker, is commonly associated with "notions of freedom, free will, action, creativity, and the very possibility of change through the actions of free agents" [2]. By asserting agency in hybridity, migrants also change the dynamics of transformation in the dominant culture. Paul Gilroy also points out in his *The Black Atlantic* (1993) that hybridity is a major aspect of his so-called "the Black Atlantic", which connects local with global. Hybridity, with its agency, challenges and deconstructs essentialism in nationalistic and racial thoughts [3]. Barker also points out that "[c]ultural hybridity challenges not only the centrality of colonial culture and the marginalization of the colonized, but also the very idea of centre and margin as being anything other than 'representational effects'" [4].

Nowadays, hybridity still occupies the center of interests in cultural studies. Its "anti-essentialist" and "anti-integrationist" nature has been used by feminists in studying subjectivity construction of women in the postcolonial era. Postcolonial feminists Lisa Lowe and Trinh T. Minh-ha maintain that through cultural interactions, the Oriental migrants from the previously colonized countries unsettle the polarization of Occidental and Oriental, thus in a way prove the agency associated with hybridity. In a similar vein, Jania Sanga asserts

---

[1] Stuart Hall. *Colonial Desire: Hybridity in Theory, Culture and Race*[M]. London: Routledge, 1995: 226.

[2] Chris Barker. *Cultural Studies: Theory and Practice*[M]. London: Sage Publications Ltd., 2008: 234.

[3] Justin D. Edwards. *Postcolonial Literature*[M]. Hampshire: Palgrave Macmillan, 2008: 147.

[4] Chris Barker. *Cultural Studies: Theory and Practice*[M]. London: Sage Publications Ltd., 2008: 278.

that hybridity "implies a syncretic view of the world in which the notion of fixity or essentiality of identity is continually contested. The concept of hybridity dismantles the notion of heterogeneity, difference, an inevitable hodge-podge"[1].

The theorization of hybridity suggests its suitability for interpreting the self-assertion in metamorphoses of the protagonist in *Jasmine*. In this novel, hybridity is exemplified in the process of Jasmine's metamorphoses set in motion by her encounter of diverse cultures in various "contact zone". In hybridity, the protagonist seeks agency and get survived in the host country. The protagonist's embracing of hybridity deconstructs essentialized identity and thus in a way reconstructs subjectivity in varied ways.

Jasmine is narrated by the protagonist, Jane Ripplemeyer, twenty-four-year-old Indian immigrant, living presently in Iowa, the United States. The most striking feature of the novel is the metamorphoses of the protagonist, which deconstructs the fixity of identity and invokes emergence of cultural hybridity for both her and the societies she enters and leaves. The protagonist undergoes several stages of metamorphoses which are signified individually by identification of a new name: Jyoti in India her hometown, Jasmine when living with her husband Prakash, Kali when she kills her rapist, Jazzy when she is remade as an immigrant, Jase when she stays as a nanny in the house of the Hayeses, and Jane when she lives with the crippled banker Bud. According to Judith Butler, language and naming contribute to the subject's formation: "the use of language is itself enabled by first having been called a name; the occupation of that name is that by which one is, quite without choice, situated within discourse"[2]. With each naming, Jasmine shuttles between different identities.

It is noteworthy that transformation and naming is constantly employed by postcolonial women writers. For instance, Jhumpa Lahiri's short story collection *The Interpreter of Maladies*, which wins the 2000 Pulitzer Prize for Fiction, deals with transformations and naming. Also, in *Tripmaster Monkey*, Maxine

---

[1] Jania C. Sanga. *Salman Rushdie's Postcolonial Metaphors: Migration, Translation, Hybridity, Blasphemy, and Globalization*[M]. Westport: Greenwood Press, 2001: 75.

[2] Judith Butler. *Bodies That Matter*[M]. London: Routledge, 1993: 122.

Hong Kingston greatly alludes to metamorphoses represented by the image of a legendary monkey, Sun Wukong, in Chinese myth who can change into seventy-two forms. Linda Hutcheon points out that the strategies of transformation and naming associated with rewriting allow women writers "to contest the old—the representations of both their bodies and their desires—without denying them the right to re-colonize, to reclaim both sites of meaning and value"[1]. *Jasmine* is Mukherjee's effort to make a totally new representation of female immigrants. In Mukherjee's writing, the protagonist, capable of transformations, is no longer the stereotyped victim of dislocation. The novel reflects Mukherjee's perception at this stage that for migrants, the best policy is to get rid of fixed identity, assume fluid identity and seek agency in metamorphoses.

Each identity is always-already hybridized. As a subject of the newly independent postcolonial country India, the protagonist's hybridity begins early in age. In her upbringing, Jasmine is exposed to traditional Indian culture and values in her family and Western culture and values in her school. Born to a poor Indian family as the fifth daughter, the seventh of nine children, the girl's life seems doomed since it is quite unlikely that the father could gather enough dowries to marry her well. Her family members, especially her grandmother, taking the situation into consideration, always tries to bend the girl's strong will to make her more docile so that they could marry her off easily. The Indian value they attempt to input to achieve their goal is associated with the feudal Indian wife's self-abnegation. Self-abnegation is the definition of the ideal wife in the *Ramamyana* and in the story of Satyavan and Savitri[2]. Self-abnegation involves the denial of the wife's own interests to please the husband, which stands in sharp contrast to self-assertion and independence. The traditional Indian values and expectation of the family is suffocating. However, on the other hand, the girl is exposed to Western values and culture in school. The first person initiating the girl's desire of self-assertion is her school teacher, Masterji. Masterji, appreciating the girl's intelligence and beauty, lends piles of English

---

[1] Linda Hutcheon. *The Politics of Postmodernism*[M]. London: Routledge, 1989: 168.

[2] Emmanuel S. Nelson. *Bharati Mukherjee: Critical Perspectives* [M]. New York: Garland Publishing, Inc., 1993: 29.

books to her. Books in English such as *Shane*, *Alice in Wonderland*, *Great Expectations* and *Jane Eyre* are opening a brand new world for her. The early exposure to English literature and the influence of the modern and pro-Western Masterji in school profoundly contribute to the girl's fascination with the much advocated Western spirits of freedom and adventures.

Another important person that fosters the flame of Jasmine's self-assertion is her husband, Prakash. Growing up in a big city and being exposed to the Western culture makes Prakash a standard hybrid person in the postcolonial era. Prakash marries Jasmine out of love and will always prefer his wife to have her own judgments and exercise her will instead of acting like a slave to the husband and suffering from self-abnegation. Prakash treats Jyoti as an equal human being and is determined to get rid of feudalism in his family life. By giving Jyoti a new name "Jasmine", he intends for her to break off the past. Changing from Jyoti to Jasmine, the country girl goes through the first major hybridization and changes from a semi-feudal country girl to a liberated city woman. When her husband is killed tragically in a bomb, Jasmine resists a relapse into the stereotype of the feudal Indian widow wailing and mourning for the rest of her life. In an attempt to take control of her own life and commit sati on the campus of Prakash's prospective university, Jasmine immigrates to the United States illegally.

In America, Jasmine encounters cultural displacement and social discrimination. Bhabha, in discussion of the migrant's hybridity, points out that "such conditions of cultural displacement and social discrimination ... are the grounds on which Frantz Fanon ... locates an agency of empowerment"[1]. In cultural displacement and social discrimination, Jasmine seeks agency in hybridity to get survived in her host country.

Jasmine's first major metamorphose upon arriving at America is triggered by an attempted rape of her by the ship captain Half-face. On occasion of the horrible disaster, Jasmine demonstrates self-assertion by killing her rapist. Given his experience in Asia during Vietnam War, Half-face holds a typical Orientalist view about Asia and its people. In his perception, Asia is "the armpit of the

---

[1] Homi K. Bhabha. *The Location of Culture*[M]. London: Routledge, 1994: 8.

universe"[1], Asian men are "scrawny little bastards"[2], and Asian women, like Jasmine, are sexually appealing and should be obedient to become sex slaves for white men. In the Orientalist discourse, Oriental women are mysterious and yet sexually appealing and full of lust. They are silent and seem faceless all the time, yet they remain something or some territory expecting to be explored and represented by white men. Said thus analyzes French author Flaubert's narration of his experience and encounter with Oriental women:

> Flaubert's encounter with an Egyptian courtesan produced a widely influential model of the Oriental woman; she never spoke of herself, she never represented her emotions, presence, or history. He spoke for and represented her. He was foreign, comparatively wealthy, male, and these were historical facts of domination that allowed him not only to possess Kuchuk physically but to speak for her and tell his readers in what way she was "typically Oriental". [3]

Half-face's internalized stereotypes of the Orientals make him think that he understands Jasmine, could speak for her and thus takes the rape for granted. Jasmine, on the other hand, finds the violent crime outrageous, especially Half-face's defilement of her luggage, which contains items that connect her emotionally to India. In the bathroom, Jasmine goes through a sudden self-transcendence. With blood dripping from her sliced tongue, she staggers Half-face to death with a knife. Naked with her mouth open, pouring blood, her red tongue out, Jasmine demonizes into Kali, "death incarnated"[4]. Kali is the Hindu Goddess, often associated with death. In paintings and literary creations, she is often depicted as naked, fierce with gaping mouth. Despite her fierce appearance, Kali also represents the spirits of courage, rebellion and willingness to take control of one's own fate, which is in contrast with the spirits of submissiveness and accommodation represented by other more common docile goddesses. In modern age, many literary writers and critics have discovered that

---

[1] Bharati Mukherjee. *Jasmine*[M]. New York: Ballantine Books, 1989: 100.
[2] Bharati Mukherjee. *Jasmine*[M]. New York: Ballantine Books, 1989: 101.
[3] Edward W. Said. *Orientalism*[M]. New York: Vintage Books, 1979: 6.
[4] Bharati Mukherjee. *Jasmine*[M]. New York: Ballantine Books, 1989: 106.

goddess Kali is an interesting image for reflection and interpretation. Writers use the image of Kali in their writings representing female power, sexuality and liberation. Critics also try to shed new lights on the image of Kali in their interpretation of literary writings from feminist or other perspectives.

Facing the violence rape, Jasmine assumes the image of the ancient Indian Goddess Kali and resorts to the power of mythology to revenge her rapist. It's significant in that the action shows Jasmine's self-assertion and willingness to change. For Kali is self-assertive, and at the same time she does not have permanent qualities, which means she is very adaptable in her struggles against danger and odds, both qualities are advocated by Mukherjee. The moment of killing is a moment of violent transformation, and simultaneously it is a moment of manifestation of extreme self-assertion. Jasmine transfers from the devoted Indian wife who wants to commit sati after the death of her husband to a courageous and self-assertive woman who refuses to fall victim to the disaster of life. The transformation furthers Jasmine's hybrid identity. The violent event Jasmine experiences deconstructs and demystifies the stable identity for Jasmine. The killing of Half-face may be classified as an impulsive act of retaliation, but it definitely demonstrates Jasmine's individual agency. In confronting the man who oppresses and assaults her, Jasmine exhibits courage and strong will to take her own life into control. This strong will to be in control and not to fall victims to the circumstance help Jasmine's self-assertion in the process of hybridization.

Jasmine's self-assertion in violent transformation stands in sharp contrast with the withdrawal, self-denial and subsequent depression exhibited by Dimple, the protagonist of *Wife*, a novel written in Mukherjee's expatriate phase of writing. What set the two protagonists in the two novels apart are their different responses to cultural dislocation. The protagonist Dimple is both physically and mentally disillusioned and devastated in losing her old culture and fixity of identity after her immigration to America. Dimple seeks comfort in nostalgia whenever confronted with frustrations and difficulties. Jasmine, on the other hand, is self-assertive and never resorts to self-pitying or nostalgia, even facing the violent rape. The contrast in the portrayals of the protagonists in the two novel *Wife* and *Jasmine* also reveals Mukherjee's change in perception from the expatriate phase of writing to the immigrant phase of writing. In expatriate phase of writing, Mukherjee writes mainly about suffering in rootlessness, while in the immigrant phase of writing, Mukherjee advocates the assuming of agency in the struggle to survive in the host country. Self-assertion and assuming of fluid identity help immigrants overcome their isolation and frustration, which Mukherjee advocates strongly.

Jasmines embarks on her second major phase of metamorphose in the strange land and gains further agency after she is rescued by Lillian Gordon on the road. Lillian, a white American woman, never asks questions about origins or previous experiences of the immigrants that she helps and brings to her place. But she would not tolerate reminiscence, bitterness or nostalgia. She would prefer all those immigrants that she helps to let go of their past and be future-oriented. Lillian gives Jasmine a very common American name for girls: Jazzy. Mita Banerjee points out that "Jazzy" is "a generic generalization of the syncretism the migrant has come to resort to"[1] and "cultural specificities are merged into an endless series of 'Jazzy' simulacra, of 'Jazzies', which are uniform precisely in their syncretism"[2]. For the newly arrived immigrants to get survival in the host country, it is only natural that cultural belonging shows in a longing for the ordinariness, which allows them to mingle in the mainstream without being instantly set apart. Lillian also trains Jazzy to behave and dress like an American. The protagonist's identity further hybridizes under the coaching of Lillian, "I checked myself in the mirror, shocked at the transformation. Jazzy in a T-shirt, tight cords, and running shoes. I couldn't tell if with the Hasnapuri sidle I'd also abandoned my Hasnapuri modesty"[3]. In *Gender Trouble* (1990), Judith Butler asserts that identity is an effect, not a cause which comes into existence through performance, including "acts, gestures, enactments"[4]. The term "act" can be interpreted to include clothing, language, gestures, etc. Later, Butler's theory of performativity is

---

[1] Mita Banerjee. *The Chutneyfication of History: Salman Rushdie, Michael Ondaatje, Bharati Mukherjee and the Postcolonial Debate*[M]. Heidelberg: Universitätsverlag C. Winter, 2002: 243.

[2] Mita Banerjee. *The Chutneyfication of History: Salman Rushdie, Michael Ondaatje, Bharati Mukherjee and the Postcolonial Debate*[M]. Heidelberg: Universitätsverlag C. Winter, 2002: 243.

[3] Bharati Mukherjee. *Jasmine*[M]. New York: Ballantine Books, 1989: 119.

[4] Judith Butler. *Gender Trouble: Feminism and the Subversion of Identity*[M]. London: Routledge, 1990: 136.

further developed and used by theorists to study issues of ethnicity. Therefore, in this context, Jasmine's wearing of American clothes and assuming of American way of walking can be viewed as performance which is in essence her creation and embracing of new immigrant identity. In acting Americans, she welcomes her hybridity and gains agency from it.

The transformation from Jasmine to Jazzy is a huge step for the protagonist, which is in essence a transformation from the Western loving postcolonial subject to a more freely-spirited and self-assertive immigrant in a metropolitan center of the new Empire. Lillian observes the independent, adventurous, and self-assertive spirits in Jazzy which set her apart from other immigrants and encourages her to move on in the vast land of the United States and embraces her own hybridity. Lillian's influence on the protagonist is profound. Lillian becomes the spiritual mother for the transformed protagonist, who treasures her Christmas gifts of hand-knitted pink wool slippers "as a devotee might a saint's relics"[1]. Jazzy also writes in a letter about Lillian which shows her admiration for the old lady. For Jasmine, Lillian represents the best quality of the American characters.

The portrayal of the American woman Lillian stands in contrast to that of the protagonist's own mother, Mataji. Mataji is a very traditional Indian wife and mother, who conforms to the traditional Indian wife's code of conducts and totally yields to the hierarchical, classification-obsessed social structure. In her essay "American Dreamer", Mukherjee describes some particular Indian traditions for women that have been established for centuries: "in traditional Hindu families like ours, men provided and women were provided for"[2]. Therefore, it seems only too natural for men to rule in the house, and women labor to serve men and to be ruled. Also, Mukherjee discusses the Indian culture in which she lived as a child. She says that people did not speak of an "identity crisis" there and "one's identity was fixed, derived from religion, caste, patrimony, and mother tongue"[3]. Therefore, for many Indian women, they are destined to suffer in low status in the stratified societal and familial structure. Mataji is a typical example of such women who lack any female agency. She has

---

[1] Bharati Mukherjee. *Jasmine*[M]. New York: Ballantine Books, 1989: 121.
[2] Deborah Weagel. *Women and Contemporary World Literature*[M]. New York: Peter Lang, 2009: 80.
[3] Deborah Weagel. *Women and Contemporary World Literature*[M]. New York: Peter Lang, 2009: 81.

no final say when her husband is alive and her situation deteriorates after his death. Staying only in the company of other widows, she mourns for the rest of her life and never has the slightest intention of changing in life. She preaches to her daughter to stick to the fixed identity and live a miserable life of widowhood just like her. Jazzy struggles free from the influence of her mother and learns to appreciate the changes in her immigrant life and the fluidity of identities. Deconstruction of fixed identity and embracing of fluid identities is a major tool in the novel's depiction of immigrants' survival in their host country. Jasmine welcomes metamorphoses and hybridity, and gains agency in the process.

The protagonist's seeking of agency in hybridity also shows in her detest of expatriates' ghettoized lifestyle and nostalgia sentiments, which are exemplified by the Vadhera family in Flushing. Jasmine stays with the Vadhera family as a servant for five months. The Vadheras refuse any change even though they have migrated from India to the United States for years. In their ghettoized life, they stubbornly cling to the preexisting narrative of Indianness. The husband claims to be a professorji teaching in some university which no one in the family has any certain knowledge. The wife works in a sari store all days on their block and watches rented Indian films every night. The couple seldom goes out for they believe that it is totally unnecessary to waste the money when they have everything in the Indian ghetto. By everything they mean Indian food stores, Punjabi newspapers and Hindi film magazines and movies. The couple also follows an ancient Indian prescription for martial accord, the husband, "silence, order, authority"[1], while the wife, "submission, beauty, innocence"[2]. They expect Jasmine to follow Indian cultural and social codes as a humble widow. Jasmine is forced to replace American T-shirt and cords with plain saris and salwar-kameez outfits. The artificially maintained Indianness in the household is suffocating for the protagonist. Jasmine feels like a prisoner stuck in an imaginary brick wall, a prison cell, topped with barbed wire, unable to break free from the past or breaking into the future as she wishes.

What furthers Jasmine's disappointment and desperation in this limbo existence is that she finds out by accident that the much respected husband is not

---

[1] Bharati Mukherjee. *Jasmine*[M]. New York: Ballantine Books, 1989: 134.

[2] Bharati Mukherjee. *Jasmine*[M]. New York: Ballantine Books, 1989: 134.

a professorji at all, but an importer and sorter of human hair from India in the basement of Khyber Bar, BQ. The dealing of human hair is a very low profession in Indian culture, but the husband has no better options. In order to survive in the strange land, he has to work in a profession that he resents. He has sealed his heart as he labors. In refusing to adapt and change, he suffers from spiritual paralysis. Jasmine feels revulsion against this kind of clinging to the past which yields the migrants passive and pathetic in the "real life" in America. The coward clinging to the past runs against and contrasts strongly with Jasmine's self-assertion in embracing hybridity. In this novel, the Vadheras with their clinging to the past and refusal to adapt serve as a counter-example of the immigrants survival in the host country.

1.2　Self-orientalization as Tools

Jasmine's self-assertion in metamorphoses shows on the one hand in her seeking of agency in her hybridity, and on the other hand, in her purposeful employment of self-orientalization as tools to achieve her own aim, which is to survive and adapt to the host country. Many scholars have studied the instrumental nature of self-orientalization, among whom Dirlik makes the most significant contribution. Self-orientalization is developed from the theory of Orientalism. Orientalism refers to the discourse of the West's Othering of the East, which may or may not involve the collaboration of the Orientals. Self-orientalization definitely involves the Orientals' efforts to turn the Self into the Other. It may occur to people in the third world countries in pursuit of economic profits, or it may occur to the migrants in the metropolitan in an effort to adapt to the center.

Orientalism and self-orientalization are key theories in postcolonial studies. Edward Said explores Orientalism in his masterpiece *Orientalism* in 1978 employing mainly Antonio Gramsci's defining of hegemony and Michel Foucault's theory of discourse, knowledge and power. Said points out that the major Orientalist period was from 1815 to 1910 when entire institutions in Europe were dedicated to Oriental studies. The Oriental studies were Eurocentric in nature which was shown in the condescending Western attitude towards and the constant Othering of the Orientals. In the Orientalist discourse, the Orientals are often depicted as cruel, stupid, evil, cunning and dishonest in contrast to the kind, bright, upright and moral white of the Occidentals. In this binary construction, the Orientalists construct the West as the Self and the East as the Other, projecting all the negative and undesirable characteristics to the unknown Other. Orientalism works hand in glove with the imperial colonial expansion and exploitation. Said has never given a unique and definite definition of Orientalism. However, in *Orientalism*, there are multiple explanations of the connotation of the term. Orientalism is:

(1) "a Western style for dominating, restructuring, and having authority over the Orient"[1];

(2) "a manner of regularized writing, vision and study, dominated by imperative, perspectives, and ideological biases ostensibly suited to the Orient ... The Orient is taught, researched, administered and pronounced upon in certain discrete ways"[2];

(3) "a system of representations framed by a whole set of forces that brought the Orient into Western learning, Western consciousness, and later, Western Empire"[3].

Said's *Orientalism* is quite influential and lays the foundation of postcolonial study. Arif Dirlik in his book *Post-revolution Atmosphere* and other writings further develops Said's demarcation of Orientalism to involve a new term "self-orientalization". In Said's theory, Orientalism is the construction of the Orientals by the Europeans, with the Orientals silenced and losing any ability to represent themselves. However, Dirlik argues that on the contrary from the beginning, the Orientals participate in the construction of the Orient. Their participation may be defined as self-orientalization, which should be seen as a manifestation not of powerlessness but of agency. In Said's conceptualization of Orientalism, Power, specifically Euro-American political power, is central. Dirlik maintains that Orientalism is possibly a relation, involving not only the creation of the Orient by the Europeans but also the complicity of the Orientals.

---

[1] Edward W. Said. *Orientalism*[M]. New York: Vintage Books, 1979: 3.
[2] Edward W. Said. *Orientalism*[M]. New York: Vintage Books, 1979: 202.
[3] Edward W. Said. *Orientalism*[M]. New York: Vintage Books, 1979: 202-203.

The Orientals on some occasions engage in the exoticism of the Orient which would further marginalize the Orientals. And therefore, Dirlik proposes that the term Orientalism "needs to be extended to Asian views of Asia, to account for tendencies to self-orientalization which would become an integral part of the history of Orientalism"[1]. Dirlik views Orientalism as a product of "contact zone", a term first used by Mary Louis Pratt to describe social spaces where "cultures meet, clash and grapple with each other, often in contexts of highly asymmetrical relations of power ... as they are lived out in many parts of the world today"[2]. Therefore, Dirlik's demarcation of Orientalism is less antagonistic than that of Said's.

Dirlik touches upon other scholars' views of the positive side and the context-specific nature of self-orientalization, for instance, the reification of the Oriental culture into a commodity in the cause of global tourism. Therefore, self-orientalization may be exploited to serve the utilitarian purpose of the Orientals. However, Dirlik also points out the negative side of self-orientalization, "in the long run, self-orientalization serves to perpetuate, and even to consolidate, existing forms of power"[3].

Zhou Ning argues in a similar way and points out that through self-orientalization, "the East is enforced to confess the world order of West centralism and the binary opposition between the West and the East, that is, forwardness and backwardness, freedom and autocracy, civilization and barbarism. It further identifies superiority of the West and inferiority of the East and surrenders to the cultural hegemony of the West"[4].

To sum up, on an individual level, self-orientalization may be exploited by the Orientals for their own utilitarian purpose, which involves transformation and adaptation to the Western culture. However, the Orientals' employment of the

---

[1] Arif Dirlik. Chinese History and the Question of Orientalism[J]. *History & Theory*, 1996, 35 (4): 104.

[2] Mary Louise Pratt. *Imperial Eyes: Travel Writing and Transculturation* [M]. New York: Routledge, 1992: 496.

[3] Arif Dirlik. Chinese History and the Question of Orientalism[J]. *History & Theory*, 1996, 35 (4): 114.

[4] Mingguo Zhong. Self-orientalization and Its Counteraction against the Cultural Purpose of Gu Hongming in His Discourses and Sayings of Confucius[J]. *Theory and Practice in Language Studies*, 2012, 2 (11): 2417.

instrumental nature of self-orientalization may also be viewed as a manifestation of the Orientals' internalized Orientalist vein, which renders their agency in hybridity quite limited.

Jasmine's self-orientalization shows most prominently in her intimate relationship with her two white lovers, Taylor and Bud, when she caters to their stereotypical expectations of Asian women. In the relationship with Taylor, Jasmine's self-orientalization resides in her purposeful assuming of the roles as caregiver and comforter, first to the couple's daughter Duff, then to Taylor, after his separation from his wife. In the relationship with Bud, Jasmine deliberately explores her sexuality and exoticism. While staying with Taylor and Bud, Jasmine undergoes further metamorphoses to get survival by embracing the fluidity of identities and mobility of American life. In the two phases of Jasmine's transformation, self-orientalization becomes a means for Jasmine to fulfill her own desire and wanting to get adapted to American life. She demonstrates her self-assertion in her skillful and masterful manipulation of her own Oriental features.

Jasmine purposefully plays the roles as caregiver and comforter in her relationship with Taylor. Jasmine is introduced to the Hayeses to take care of their adopted daughter, Duff. The husband, Taylor, is a professor in Columbia University and the wife, Wylie, is a book editor for a publisher on Park Avenue. The first impression Jasmine gets from the couple is their casual, intimate American style. Jasmine falls in love with what Taylor represents to her, "a professor who served biscuits to a servant, smiled at her, and admitted her to the broad democracy of his joking, even when she didn't understand it. It seemed entirely American"[1]. Taylor's American lifestyle and casual manner contrast sharply with the self-importance and authoritative attitudes assumed by Vadhera, a false professor. Jasmine is attracted to Taylor's world, "its ease, its careless confidence and graceful self-absorption"[2]. Living with the Hayeses, Jasmine realizes that it is to be a coward to indulge in nostalgia and seal her heart, refusing to change and adapt. Jasmine absorbs the new ideas hungrily. In the Hayses' big apartment, Jasmine grows from a timid alien with a forged

---

[1] Bharati Mukherjee. *Jasmine*[M]. New York: Ballantine Books, 1989: 148.

[2] Bharati Mukherjee. *Jasmine*[M]. New York: Ballantine Books, 1989: 148.

American passport to an adventurous Jase. "Jase" is the name Taylor gives her. Jasmine likes it because it is associated with American carefree lifestyle and adventurous spirits. At this stage, Jasmine begins to determinedly cut off memories of and attachment to India and whole-heartedly accept American values and adventurous spirits. Jasmine's Indianness fades away quickly in her devotion to Americanness.

Under Taylor's guidance, Jasmine learns to enjoy her life in a very American way and American consumerism takes root in her. On her day off, Jasmine spends her week's salary to buy various staffs in stores along Broadway and even in the luxurious department stores. By living to the full of her life, Jasmine further cuts her Indian ties. She compares her old self and the new one. Jasmine believes that Jyoti, her old self, would have saved for she abides herself by the virtues of the goddesses in Indian mythology. However, Jasmine has killed her old self to be reborn and live anew. Jase, her new self, would spend her salary to please herself for she absorbs the American values and therefore would live for today. The transformation is quite radical, by living an American lifestyle like Taylor, Jasmine sees herself get-rooted for the first time in America.

Jasmine's self-assertion in the period of staying with the Hayeses is closely linked with her acceptance of the stereotyped Oriental women' roles as a caregiver and comforter. Wylie used to call Jasmine "caregiver" to Duff instead of maidservant. In the bitter separation from his wife, Taylor also expects Jasmine to be his caregiver and comforter. Fundamentally speaking, caregiver and comforter are the roles the Hayeses assigned to Jasmine. Jasmine accepts the roles willingly and more often than not she deliberately strengthens her roles through her behaviors. Taylor enjoys the family comfort provided by Jasmine and he is consoling himself with teaching Jasmine American stuffs without any intention of truly getting to know Jasmine's past. Jasmine always holds Taylor in a superior status for she treats Taylor as her mentor in adapting to America. The unequal footing of the relationship reveals Jasmine's internalized Orientalist perception. For Jasmine, the previous hostess Wylie is white, which also yields her more intelligent, more humorous, more confident, and a better match for Taylor. Jasmine believes that herself coming from a previous colony, could only learn things from Taylor, which follows that she would never become a soul mate for Taylor like Wylie, but could only remain a caregiver and comforter during the white hostess's absence. Although Jasmine believes that she has transformed from a timid alien into courageous and adventurous Jase, the patriarchal and colonial ideology still takes hold in her, which yields her self-assertion shadowed partly in self-denial of equal love and partly in lack of true confidence. To get survival, Jasmine utilizes the instrumental nature of self-orientalization. However, her obedient acceptance of the stereotyped roles to some degree can be designated as the limits of Jasmine's self-assertion, which often entices strong criticism from both feminist and postcolonial perspectives.

In the relationship with Bud, Jasmine also exploits self-orientalization as means. Jasmine is clearly aware of the fact that she is constantly viewed and treated as the exotic Other by Bud and people around him. Instead of being troubled by her subordinate position, Jasmine lives with the surrounding condescending gaze and sometimes even takes opportunities to flaunt her own exoticism. Her calm acceptance of the status as the Other and intentional Self-Othering serves as her means to assert herself and get survival in America.

Bud holds a typical Orientalist view towards Jasmine even before he meets her. Bud confesses to Jasmine later on that when his mother calls and tells him that an Indian girl is sent for a job, "he'd pictured a stick-legged, potbellied, veiled dark woman like the ones he'd seen fleeing wars, floods, and famines on television"[1]. Bud has never been to India before and his pre-perception is quite typical for the Western white exposed to the propaganda of neo-colonial and the Orientalist discourse. Said notes, "[o]ne aspect of the electronic, postmodern world is that there has been reinforcement of the stereotypes by which the Orient is viewed. Television, the films, and all the media's resources have forced information into more and more standardized molds"[2].

At first sight, Bud is stunned by Jasmine's beauty. Jasmine's extraordinary and exotic beauty attracts Bud so much that in order to date her, Bud divorces his wife Karin who has been married with him for more than twenty years and with whom he has two sons. Bud treats Jasmine as life-saver, whose exotic

---

[1] Bharati Mukherjee. *Jasmine*[M]. New York: Ballantine Books, 1989: 177.

[2] Edward W. Said. *Orientalism*[M]. New York: Vintage Books, 1979: 26.

beauty is so invigorating that he feels rescued from boredom of previous life. Jasmine is more clear-headed concerning her relationship with Bud. She is aware of the fact that she is the Oriental Other for Bud, whose attraction lies precisely in the mysterious and inscrutable Otherness, "Bud courts me because I am alien. I am darkness, mystery, inscrutability. The East plugs me into instant vitality and wisdom. I rejuvenate him simply by being who I am"[1].

Bud's perception of their relationship is also Orientalist in its nature. Firstly, Jasmine's being physically Eastern constitutes the greatest charm for him. To date Jasmine, is for him, in a sense, to conquer the unknown Other. The desire is both physically and emotionally. Bud's feelings for Jasmine constitute the Orientalist fantasy of conquering the mysterious East and its women. Secondly, Bud's desire for Jasmine is accompanied at the same time by the fear of Jasmine's origin and previous experiences. It is frightening for Bud to pry into the past of Jasmine; therefore, he always refrains from discussing it with Jasmine. Bud's fear does not escape Jasmine's observation, "he's always uneasy with tales of Hasnapur, just like mother Ripplemeyer. It's as though Hasnapur is an old husband or lover. Even memories are a sign of disloyalty"[2]. The desire and fear toward the unknown Other are quite typical of the mentality of the Westerners exposed to the Orientalist discourse. Bud gives Jasmine a new name, Jane. Jokingly, he calls her "Calamity Jane, Jane as in Jane Russell, not Jane as in Plain Jane"[3]. But Jasmine is aware that her genuine foreignness although attractive, actually frightens him and Jane is a role, like any other role that she has to play. Therefore, she collaborates in Bud's effort of shunning away her past. Jasmine's acquiescence to Bud's uneasiness about her past experiences shows Jasmine's yielding to the Orientalist discourse. In the Orientalist discourse, the Oriental women are sexually appealing to the White men, yet they remain silent and mysterious at the same time. To Bud, Jasmine's mysterious past contributes partly to her charm as the Oriental Other.

Jasmine's silent cooperation also reveals her determination to shun her past

---

[1] Bharati Mukherjee. *Jasmine*[M]. New York: Ballantine Books, 1989: 178.
[2] Bharati Mukherjee. *Jasmine*[M]. New York: Ballantine Books, 1989: 206.
[3] Bharati Mukherjee. *Jasmine*[M]. New York: Ballantine Books, 1989: 22.

to get re-rooted. After Bud is crippled in a shooting by a local farmer, Jasmine also assumes the role of an exotic temptress besides an obedient caregiver. "Bud may no longer be a whole man, but desire hasn't deserted him ... After I prepare him for bed, undo the shoes, pull off the pants, sponge-bathe him, he likes me to change roles, from caregiver to temptress"[1]. Jasmine's exploitation of her sexuality can be viewed in two different ways. On the one hand, the act can be viewed as an act of self-orientalization, which means that Jasmine is willing to cater to the sexual fantasy of the white man, Bud. Some critics in their studies criticize that Jasmine's self-orientalization in relationship with white men reinforce the Othering of the East by the West. "Jasmine reinforces the colonizer's project by figuring her activity as assimilation or commutation to her Other."[2]

On the other hand, this act can be viewed as Jasmine's liberation of sexuality and adaptation to new life. Brinda Bose observes: "In Mukherjee's fiction, a woman's sexual freedom often functions as a measure of her increasing detachment from traditional sexual mores and correspondingly, of her assimilation in the New World through her rapid Westernization/Americanization."[3] Jasmine frees herself from her previous identity as a de-sexed Indian widow to gain more liberty and get assimilated in American life. The re-discovery and exploitation of her own sexuality can also be viewed as Jasmine's attempt to take control and assert herself. Also, it may be viewed as a measurement of Jasmine's rapid Americanization.

Jasmine is aware of her position as the Other and she constantly plays the roles designated to her on purpose. It is fair to assert that she uses her own Oriental features and other people's Orientalist perception of her to achieve her own purpose of adaptation and re-rooting. Tandon comments upon Jasmine's flexibility and her manipulations of character roles to her own ends:

> Jasmine combines the force of the Hindu Trinity with her own uninhibited powers

---

[1] Bharati Mukherjee. *Jasmine*[M]. New York: Ballantine Books, 1989: 39.

[2] Kristin Carter-Sanborn. "We Murder Who We Were": Jasmine and the Violence of Identity[J]. *American Literature*, 1994, 66(3): 588.

[3] Emmanuel S. Nelson. *Bharati Mukherjee: Critical Perspectives* [M]. New York: Garland Publishing, Inc., 1993: 60.

of feminine creating wrath and sexual desire ... as the female Brahma, she is her own creator, pregnant with new life; as a caregiver, she matches Vishnu, the Preserver, as Shiva's counterpart Kali, she has killed the demon, half-face, her rapist. As Jane Ripplemeyer, she readily complies as the exotic other. In fact, the compliance is her ticket to American dream.[1]

The community also responds in two different ways to Jasmine's Otherness. Some treat Jasmine's Otherness with utter despise. Seeing the couple going out together, a young man shouts "whorepower" at Jasmine, "his next words were in something foreign, but probably Japanese or Thai or Filipino, something bar girls responded to in places where he'd spent his rifle-toting youth"[2]. The man's perception of Asian women as whores probably comes from his own experiences with Asian women in the Vietnam War or the stereotyped Asian women portrayed in Western media. This is one version of perverted distortion of the Eastern women, the subaltern Other. Other people view Jasmine as mysterious and full of unknown Eastern intelligence. The local farmers are full of awe towards Jasmine's foreignness and they are amazed to see Jasmine read aerograms written in the Indian language. To them, the alien knowledge that Jasmine possess, means intelligence. The awe that they hold towards Jasmine is due to lack of mutual knowledge and communication between the West and the East.

In nature, Jasmine is the unknown Other for the community, something to be desired for, to be conquered and at the same time to be feared. This kind of mixed feelings towards the Oriental Other shows most evidently in their neighbor Darrel. Darrel, a local farmer, shows strong interest in Jasmine and goes out of his way to please the mysterious Oriental princess. He grows Indian peppers and learns to cook Indian food in order to gain Jasmine's favor. When his farming business fails, he tries to persuade Jasmine to run away with him, "he wants to make love to an Indian princess"[3]. He wants to have his redemption and his

---

[1] Sushma Tandon. *Bharati Mukherjee's Fiction: A Perspective*[M]. New Delhi: Sarup & Sons, 2004: 160.
[2] Bharati Mukherjee. *Jasmine*[M]. New York: Ballantine Books, 1989: 179.
[3] Bharati Mukherjee. *Jasmine*[M]. New York: Ballantine Books, 1989: 192.

vitality back by having this mysterious Indian woman. To conquer the Other means so much to him that no wonder he goes crazy and eventually kills himself when Jasmine firmly turns him down.

The reason why Jasmine plays the roles assigned to her willingly is that she is never wavering concerning her own purpose, "I still think of myself as caregiver, recipe giver, preserver. I can honestly say all I wanted was to serve, be allowed to join"[1]. To "be allowed to join", namely to get accepted by the community and get re-rooted in American life, is the stated purpose for Jasmine. To achieve this purpose, Jasmine uses her own Oriental feature as tools. In self-orientalization, she endeavors to cater to the mainstream American views of Indianness. A typical example is that Jasmine always prepares spicy Indian foods for the Americans around her. A common kind of cultural reductionist view in Western countries is to epitomize Indianness by its spicy food. Jasmine observes that even though people make a show of fanning their mouths eating Indian foods, they are actually very fond of the spicy foods. They will get disappointed if there's not something Indian on the table. Bud's friends and family enjoy the exotic cuisine that Jasmine prepares not only because of its exotic specialty but also as a kind of transgression against American norm of sameness. Jasmine sees through the fact and she never fails to satisfy the fantasy of the people around her. In self-orientalizing herself, Jasmine is determined to please others to get accepted.

Sometimes Jasmine even resorts to exaggerated performance of the stereotyped Other in a mockery way. This is most evidently shown in her interview with Mary Webb. Mary Webb, a teacher of sociology or social work in the university, believes she has a retrievable life when she is an Australian aboriginal man. Since Jasmine comes from the East, Mary supposes Jasmine also believes in reincarnation. When Mary asks Jasmine the question "[d]on't you Hindus keep revisiting the world"[2], Jasmine consents without hesitation, "I am sure that I have been reborn several times, and that yes, some lives I can recall vividly"[3]. The answer is utterly a lie told just to meet Mary's

---

[1] Bharati Mukherjee. *Jasmine*[M]. New York: Ballantine Books, 1989: 190.
[2] Bharati Mukherjee. *Jasmine*[M]. New York: Ballantine Books, 1989: 113.
[3] Bharati Mukherjee. *Jasmine*[M]. New York: Ballantine Books, 1989: 113.

expectation. Cristina Emanuela Dascalu maintains that Jasmine's ready acceptance and eager performance of the Oriental stereotype in this occasion is an action of mimicry, which can be compared with the mimicry of some of Salman Rushdie's migrant characters [1]. Bhabha studies mimicry in Rushdie's novels and points out that "such repetition of the dominant stereotypes inscribed in a culture can become a mocking of the culture's discourse, can become a concrete position from which to attack that discourse"[2]. Cristina maintains that "by playing the part that Mary Webb has eked out for her, she (Jasmine) is exposing it as merely a part, a role, a lifeless stereotype with no depth"[3]. Jasmine's mimicry in this situation may be also viewed as a sly satire of the stereotyped American's perception of the Orientals. Jasmine's mimicry further evidences the instrumental nature of her self-orientalization.

Self-assertion is the primary feature for the protagonist of *Jasmine*. To settle down and get re-rooted, the protagonist seeks agency in hybridity and explores the instrumental nature of self-orientalization. Mukherjee also explains Jasmine's strong desire to survive and settle down in the host country and her assertion of agency. She explains:

> Jasmine's very open to new experience and optimistic about her outcome. Her attitude is: "Hey, you can't rape me and get away with it! You can't push me around! I'm here. I'm gonna stay if I want to, and I'm gonna conquer the territory." … Her Huck Finn-like gesture at the end of the novel would seem to be a bold assertion of agency.[4]

Jasmine's hybrid identity occurs in a space defined by Bhabha as the Third Space. The Third Space is closely associated with Bhabha's theory of hybridity. According to Bhabha, it is a space where the postcolonial subject is constructed

---

[1] Critina Emanuela Dascalu. *Imaginary Homelands of Writers in Exile: Salman Rushdie, Bharati Mukherjee, and V. S. Naipaul*[M]. New York: Cambria Press, 2007: 69.

[2] Critina Emanuela Dascalu. *Imaginary Homelands of Writers in Exile: Salman Rushdie, Bharati Mukherjee, and V. S. Naipaul*[M]. New York: Cambria Press, 2007: 69.

[3] Critina Emanuela Dascalu. *Imaginary Homelands of Writers in Exile: Salman Rushdie, Bharati Mukherjee, and V. S. Naipaul*[M]. New York: Cambria Press, 2007: 69.

[4] Rob Burton. *Artists of the Floating World: Contemporary Writers between Cultures*[M]. New York: America UP, 2007: 89.

anew. In *Jasmine*, hybridity is a cause for celebration and the Third Space is where the past is to be forgotten and the future is to be embraced. In hybridity and the Third Space's in-betweenness, Jasmine liberates herself from her fixed identity. The performativity nature of Jasmine's metamorphoses deconstructs the fixity of identity and stability of colonial discourse. Therefore, Mukherjee's use of bildungsroman in this novel can be viewed as a postcolonial counter-discourse, which runs against the idealized notion of individual maturity such as those depicted in canonized bildungsromans from Goethe to Dickens.

1.3 Mukherjee's Celebration of Fluid Identities

The publication of *Jasmine* marks Mukherjee's further moving away from the expatriate phase of writing to the immigrant phase of writing. The novel reflects Mukherjee's celebration of fluid identities. The celebration is shown in Mukherjee's severance of her Indianness to embrace Americanization. The celebration reveals Mukherjee's Orientalist stance in her aesthetics of fusion.

In her expatriate phase of writing, Mukherjee takes V. S. Naipaul, who is best-known for his writing of enigmas and dilemmas of expatriate experience, as her literary model. Although in some novels, Naipaul writes about immigrants' assimilation, it is fair to say that he always carries his own cultural heritage with him, which is reflected in the depiction of the suffering and limbo existence of his protagonists between two worlds. Mukherjee's earlier two novels, *The Tiger's Daughter* and *Wife*, run in the similar vein. Both Tara and Dimple, protagonists of *The Tiger's Daughter* and *Wife*, can be called typical expatriates, uncomfortable and alienated in both home culture and the foreign one. These novels reflect Mukherjee's experience as an expatriate living and writing in Canada. Mukherjee's frustration with expatriate experience is closely related to the Canadian government's promotion of mosaic multiculturalism. Mukherjee, among others, believes that instead of promoting ethnic unification on the basis of respect for equality, multiculturalism advocated by the Canadian government worsens the splitting of different ethnic groups and the pushing out of the colored by the white. Mukherjee once wrote an essay "An Invisible Woman" to attack the widely spread racism of Canadian society against immigrants. With her immigration back again to America from Canada in 1980 and her subsequent acceptance and appraisal of melting pot policy of American society, Mukherjee begins her immigrant phase of writing. In this phase of writing, Mukherjee advocates severance of home culture and full assimilation.

There are several reasons underlying Mukherjee's promotion of full assimilation which involves shedding most of her racial and cultural particularity in this period of time. First, Mukherjee's writing is largely formed by her background as an Asian American immigrant. Asian American immigrants, designated as the model minority, are often left out in the antagonist ethnic narrative of America, which according to the 2000 PMLA volume are largely framed by the black/white binary. More often than not, members of "the model minority" are dedicated to get assimilated and become successful. The writings of many Asian American writers, for instance, Alexander Meena, Vikrem Seth and many other second generation Asian American writers are certainly consciously or unconsciously formed by the narrative of "model minority". Mukherjee is just one of them. Second, different from African American literature, which has established itself in American mainstream narrative after so many years of struggle, Asian American literature has just begun to develop significantly after the 1960s. To gain their voices heard and attract more attention from both the academic circle and common readers, many Asian American writers, including Mukherjee, resort to detexualized metamorphoses which are originally a major metaphor in their own cultures. In the promotion of metamorphoses, the writers hope to get transformed and fully assimilated. Third, newly immigrating to America, Mukherjee is eager to establish herself as a major writer and suffers from her own anxiety of influence. She no longer wishes to be seen as one of those expatriate writers; therefore, assimilation writing may be a new direction that she can follow. The economic and academic success of *Jasmine* certainly in a way soothes her anxiety of influence.

Jasmine is the most important work at the beginning of Mukherjee's immigrant phase of writing. In this phase of her writing career, Mukherjee starts to admire Bernard Malamud as literary model by claiming that "[l]ike Malamud, I write about a minority community which escapes the ghetto and adapts itself to the patterns of the dominant American culture"[1]. Abraham points out that "the shift from Naipaul to Malamud as literary model signifies the transition from the exiled expatriate to the vibrant immigrant"[2]. Mukherjee's transition also reflected in her change from the portrayals of passive protagonists, like Tara and Dimple in *The Tiger's Daughter* and *Wife*, who are victims to the surroundings, to that of self-assertive one, like Jasmine in *Jasmine*, who fights bravely against odds to get adapted. Mukherjee strongly identifies with the protagonist of *Jasmine* and she confesses:

> Jasmine became the summary of my own emotions ... My Jasmine, or Mukherjee, have lived through hundreds of years within one generation, in the sense of and then coming out a world with fixed destinies, fixed cultures taking on culture which, for us, is without rules. I'm making the rules up as I go along, because, in many ways, I and my characters are pioneers.[3]

Mukherjee celebrates the immigrants' assuming of fluid identities and assimilation to new life and culture. In the process of assimilation and adaptation, the immigrants have to overcome setbacks and failures in their host country. What makes their efforts remarkable is their courage and perseverance to carry on with their new lives instead of seeking comfort in nostalgia. This process involves the complete severance of the home culture and acceptance of the host culture. Banerjee studies the severance of the home culture in her study. In her opinion, some postcolonial writers try to show in their works the fact that "the remembering of cultural belonging is now equated with an ossification of culture, an obsession with a certainty beyond retrieval"[4]. Mukherjee may be counted as one of those writers. In Mukherjee's perception, the attachment to the home culture curbs the immigrants' freedom to adapt. In Jasmine's case, it is

---

[1] Markose Abraham. *American Immigration Aesthetics: Bernard Malamud & Bharati Mukherjee as Immigrants*[M]. London: Author House Publishing, 2011: 52.

[2] Markose Abraham. *American Immigration Aesthetics: Bernard Malamud & Bharati Mukherjee as Immigrants*[M]. London: Author House Publishing, 2011: 52.

[3] Meera Ameena. Bharati Mukherjee[J]. *Bomb*, 1989(29): 26.

[4] Mita Banerjee. *The Chutneyfication of History: Salman Rushdie, Michael Ondaatje, Bharati Mukherjee and the Postcolonial Debate*[M]. Heidelberg: Universitätsverlag C. Winter, 2002: 35.

only fair to assert that the clinging to Indianness is harmful and cutting of Indian ties becomes a prerequisite for her survival in the host country.

To promote fluid identities, Mukherjee makes a clear cut with expatriate sentiments which she has depicted in her previous novels following the suits of exilic writers such as V. S. Naipaul. The expatriate sentiments are shown most evidently by the immigrants who live in ethnic ghettos years after their migration. In her immigrant phase of writing, Mukherjee shows more contempt than sympathy for the expatriates' ghettoized lifestyle for she believes that it does only harm to the immigrants' survival in the host country. In *Jasmine*, Mukherjee depicts the Vadheras' ghettoized lifestyle in the demeaning way. Dlaska holds the opinion that the purpose of Mukherjee's depiction of the Vadheras in *Jasmine* is to provide an example of pitfalls for the immigrants[1]. By sticking to the delusions of nostalgia and refusing any attempt of adaptation to the dominant host culture, the Vadheras create prisons in the heart and remain exiles living a pathetic life in a limbo world. To a certain degree, their sufferings are self-inflicted.

At the same time, Mukherjee disapproves of immigrant's hyphenation of identity which means to assume a new identity in the host country without giving up the previous identity in the homeland. This attitude is reflected most evidently from the portrayals of the half-failed assimilation of Jasmine's adopted son Du. Compared with Jasmine's genetic transformation, Du's transformation is hyphenated. Du is a Vietnamese refugee. Despite the memory of his traumatic life before coming to America, he tries to maintain his two identities, Vietnamese and American identities, at the same time, and thus in a way becomes a hyphenated Vietnamese-American. In her adaptation to American life, Jasmine cuts her ties with her past almost all together. Although Du is willing to adapt, he has no intention of severing his previous family connections and shows no hesitation in switching back to his previous identity as a Vietnamese. Therefore, Du's transformation is defined by Mukherjee as hyphenated one, against which she holds certain objections. Dascalu in her study analyzes the danger of hyphenated transformation on the individual's

---

[1] Andrea Dlaska. *Ways of Belonging: The Making of New Americans in the Fiction of Bharati Mukherjee*[M]. Vienna: Braumuller, 1999: 154.

subjectivity. In her perception, hyphenation involves only replacing one master with another and provides only the illusion of wholeness. In this sense, Du's transformation is half-failed. In contrast, Jasmine goes through genetic transformation and plays several roles. "Through her many character roles, what is put in doubt is not simply one particular cultural milieu, but the notion of a singular identity and a singular discourse generally"[1]. Therefore, Jasmine's transformation deconstructs fixity of identity and is more revolutionary compared with that of Du's. Mukherjee herself never welcomes the hyphenated labeling of Asian-American writer, rather she would insist being called an American writer of Bengali origin.

Mukherjee's designation of genetic transformation often involves abrupt and complete rupture with one's past. As stated by Jasmine, "[t]here are no harmless, compassionate ways to remake oneself. We murder who we were so we can rebirth ourselves in the images of dreams"[2]. This kind of rupture is so often associated with the use of violence that it becomes a leitmotif in *Jasmine* and many other works of Mukherjee. Scholars have made in-depth studies of the use of violence in *Jasmine*. Bose points out the pervasive use of violence in *Jasmine* and explains that "Mukherjee has shown violence as inescapable in 'the transformation of character', and that, if anything, the level of violence has gone up with succeeding novels"[3]. Samir Dayal observes that "violence is done to Jasmine at certain junctures of her life, but she is also an agent of violence in some other instances"[4]. Violence pushes Jasmine into abrupt metamorphoses. Jasmine's husband is violently killed by Sikh terrorism, which drives her to fly to America alone as a widow planning to commit sati there. Half-face's rape of her turns her to reincarnate as Kali in her revengeful killing of the rapist. The people around Jasmine are also changed by the violence inflicted by her. Bud's ex-wife describes Jasmine as a "tornado", by which she refers to the psychological violence Jasmine causes to the people around her.

---

[1] Critina Emanuela Dascalu. *Imaginary Homelands of Writers in Exile: Salman Rushdie, Bharati Mukherjee, and V. S. Naipaul*v[M]. New York: Cambria Press, 2007: 76.

[2] Bharati Mukherjee. *Jasmine*[M]. New York: Ballantine Books, 1989: 25.

[3] Emmanuel S. Nelson. *Bharati Mukherjee: Critical Perspectives*[M]. New York: Garland Publishing, Inc., 1993: 53.

[4] Frank Day. *Bharati Mukherjee*[M]. New York: Twayne Publishers, 1996: 114.

Jasmine goes through several stages of metamorphoses in violence. At the same time, she also changes the people and the environment around her. Therefore, in the context of *Jasmine*, violence can be categorized to some degree as catalyst, which leads to the realization of the complete and abrupt severance of the past.

At this stage of writing, Mukherjee is quite determined to sever her past, namely her Indianness in her effort of adapting to new culture. Critics such as Vijay Mishra have pointed out that "a writer such as Naipaul belongs to an early diasporic formation, called 'the diaspora of exclusion', while later Anglo-Indian writers, including Mukherjee and Rushdie, belong to a 'diaspora of border'" [1]. One major feature that separates these two generations of writers apart is that Naipaul always tends to look back to the old country, even in self-loathing, while Mukherjee is determined to cut the past, viewing dislocation as psychologically emancipating, where fluid identities will emerge in hybridity.

Meena Alexander, a South Asian American writer who writes of immigration in a similar way as Mukherjee, points out that the killing of old self to form new identity is originally a nineteenth-century mainstream belief exemplified by Ralph Waldo Emerson. She comments that "Ralph Waldo Emerson, transcendentalist and [nineteenth-century] philosopher of America, spoke of the American self as having no need of memory. He invoked life in the New World, cut free of the past, raised into the shining present"[2]. Although speaking for severance, Alexander herself does not decisively sever her past in writings like Mukherjee does. For example, in her masterpiece, *Manhattan Music*, which is also about the immigrants' re-rooting, Alexander emphasizes the importance of understanding the past in shaping one's present and future.

Mukherjee's severance of Indian ties at this stage of writing shows her own postmodernist stance against the certainty provided by clinging to a fixed identity but it also reveals the strong Orientalist stance in her aesthetics of fusion. Mukherjee's aesthetics of fusion rises out of her perception of immigrant experience. She once says:

---

[1] Bed Prasad Giri Butwal Nepal. Writing Back and Forth: Postcolonial Diaspora and Its Antinomies [D]. University of Virginia, 2006: 35.

[2] Meena Alexander. *The Shock of Arrival: Reflections on Postcolonial Experience* [M]. Boston: South End Press, 1996: 156-157.

> [1]t was not right to describe the American experience as one of a melting pot but a more appropriate word would be "fusion" because immigrants in America did not melt into or were forged into something like their white counterparts but immigration was a two-way process and both the whites and immigrants were growing into a third thing by this interchange and experience.[1]

Mukherjee's aesthetics of fusion develops gradually with her own writing. In her expatriate phase of writing, she writes in a way similar to that of V. S. Naipaul, mainly exploring the rootlessness of expatriates caught between two cultures. In this period of writing, she has not formed her unique perception concerning migrant issues. In her immigrant phase of writing, she gradually forms and develops her own aesthetics of fusion. The word "fusion" is used by her to emphasize the hybridity associated with migrancy. Although Mukherjee talks about the two-way process in which both the whites and the immigrants are growing into a third thing in their cultural exchange, in her writing she mainly explores the immigrants' one-way cultural hybridization to adapt to the host culture. The white's change is randomly touched upon in some of her novels but rarely fully elaborated. Therefore, it is fair to assert that reflected in Mukherjee's writing, the fusion is more often than not a one-way process, instead of a two-way process as emphasized by Mukherjee. Besides, Mukherjee's aesthetics of fusion may be extended to include the narrative technique and style of her novels, which are also a fusion of the Western and the Eastern writing traditions.

To sum up, there are several key points concerning Mukherjee's aesthetics of fusion reflected in *Jasmine*.

※ Self-assertion and fluid identity is central to Mukherjee's aesthetics of fusion. Self-assertion in metamorphoses, involves the breaking down of fixed identity and celebration of hybridity. The fusion involves Jasmine's one-way severance of Indian culture and whole-hearted embracing of American one.

※ Mukherjee's aesthetics of fusion is Orientalist in nature. In binary constructions, Mukherjee constantly privileges the Western culture over the Eastern one. The dichotomy of the Western and the Eastern cultures is reflected

---

[1] R. K. Dhawan. *The Fiction of Bharati Mukherjee: A Critical Symposium*[M]. New Delhi: Prestige Books, 1996: 130.

in many aspects of the novel, especially in the setting and characterization.

※ Mukherjee's aesthetics of fusion also involves the fusion of different narrative techniques and writing materials in both Western and Eastern writing traditions. Reflected in *Jasmine*, Mukherjee mainly follows Western narrative technique and style, while using certain Eastern materials.

Mukherjee distinguishes herself with her writing of immigration. Mukherjee once says that her American publishers strongly advise her to write exotic and nostalgic novels about India, "to be Vikram Seth or Amitav Ghosh, who churn out lively and controversial stories on exotic, superstitious, poor and god-fearing people of India, for rich Americans and Europeans" [1]. But Mukherjee sticks to the voice of her heart, believing that the finest novel evolves from a writer's personal obsessions. It is fair to say that self-assertion and fluid identities is at the core of her aesthetics of fusion.

According to Mukherjee, to get re-rooted, the immigrants should break away from fixity of identity and nostalgic feelings which prove to be detrimental to mental resilience. The immigrants should be devoted to forge new alliances in the friendly soil of the host country. In the process of getting re-rooted, an affirming self will emerge. In Mukherjee's aesthetics of fusion, the loss of one's old culture and severance of one's home ties is exhilarating. In this period of time, Mukherjee openly criticizes Indian culture and its hierarchy of caste, gender and family. Besides rejecting her Indian background, Mukherjee also rejects the Indian writing tradition and is eager to be admitted into the American writing tradition. She warmly embraces the American dream and has strong faith that America welcomes all immigrants, irrespective of their color and race.

At this stage, Mukherjee's aesthetics of fusion is Orientalist in nature. Reflected in the novel, Jasmine constantly contrasts Indian culture with that of the American one, with the former showing all its failings, therefore, setting off the latter in its perfection. Jasmine shows strong disliking for different aspects of her Indian cultural heritage. In her journey in America, Jasmine seldom talks about or recalls anything related to India in a positive or favorable light. Her rejection and revulsion of Indian modes of life is obvious and nothing in India

---

[1] R. K. Dhawan. *The Fiction of Bharati Mukherjee: A Critical Symposium*[M]. New Delhi: Prestige Books, 1996: 202.

seems to her liking. The violent society, the poor living condition and its ignorant people constitute the backwardness of the Orient. The dominate image of India haunting Jasmine is the stenchy dead dog in a river of her hometown. For Jasmine, homeland condenses into a pathetic picture and a stench. The backwardness of India makes her more determined to settle down in America and cut her ties with India.

The freezing of the East for eternity, contrasting with the ever developing and changing landscapes of the West reflects Mukherjee's typical Orientalist stance. There are also several other constructions of dichotomy within the novel. For example, the open-minded and caring Lillian Gordon is in contrast with Jasmine's own traditional and mourning mother, the humorous and loving Taylor is in contrast with the hypocritical and pathetic Vadhera. All of the dichotomic constructions aim to show the superiority of the Western culture to that of the Eastern one.

Mukherjee's Orientalist stance also shows in her unconsciously manifested consent to colonial ruling strategy, especially the education of English language and literature in India. Reflected in the novel, from her early childhood, Jasmine attaches great importance to the mastering of English. She admires her English teacher in school, and when the time comes for her to choose a husband, she sets the primary standard that her future husband must be good at English. Actually, Prakash wins her heart primarily by his fluent English and the mastery of Western machinery technique. When staying with the Vadhera family in Flushing, Jasmine feels dying partly because she is not allowed to use English in the household. Jasmine's somewhat excessive love of English actually reveals her internalized Orientalist stance. English teaching is closely related to the Empire's colonial rulings. English teaching in Indian became official and compulsory with the deepening of Britain's colonization in the nineteenth century. Thomas Babington Macaulay, the British historian and Whig politician, played a major role in introducing English and other Western concepts of education to India. He advocated the use of English as the official language and the medium of instruction in all schools. He once said, "We must at present do our best to form a class who may be interpreters, between us and the millions we govern; a class of persons, Indian in blood and color, but English in taste, in opinions, in morals and in intellect."[1] English teaching in India was a major step in achieving the "grand" imperialist goal of the Empire.

English teaching, together with the introduction of Western literature to India, serves the purpose of spreading the imperialist and Orientalist construction of the binary oppositions, namely the Self versus the Other, the West versus the East, the White versus the Black, with the privileging of the former over the latter. The imperialist and Orientalist construction works best when the oppressed internalize the system willingly and unconsciously, as shown in Jasmine's preferring of English over Indian native languages. Jasmine, born into a poor family and growing up in the countryside, unconsciously forms the concept that the mastery of English means something promising, namely the ticket to a better life. Jasmine's blindly held opinion does prove to be true in that the mastery of English does offer more opportunities in changing one's lot in life given the still prevailing influence of the new English-speaking imperialist countries in the world years after the decolonization of India. Jasmine's opinion also shows that the Orientalist construction is still deeply-rooted after years of political decolonization, which is a pathetic fact for the previously colonized.

Besides the learning of English language, Jasmine also reads English novels, *Jane Eyre* and *David Copperfield*, especially the American novel *Shane*. *Shane* is mentioned several times by Jasmine which shows the deep influence of the novel on her. *Shane*, written in 1949 by Jack Schaefer with the original name "Rider from Nowhere", is a Western novel advocating the spirit of adventure, mobility and toughness in territory expansion. The American novel might probably also inflame Jasmine's longing for the country of America, which is "founded on myths of mobility that disavow the histories of both the immobility of ghettoization and the forced dislocations of Asian Americans"[2]. Jasmine's self-assertion in metamorphoses closely associates with American mobility and Western frontier spirit, or in Mukherjee's term, "pioneering" spirit. In the end of the novel, Jasmine abandons the crippled Bud to head west

---

[1] Sushma Tandon. *Bharati Mukherjee's Fiction: A Perspective* [M]. New Delhi: Sarup & Sons, 2004: 155.

[2] Jana Evans Braziel & Anita Mannur. *Theorizing Diaspora* [M]. Malden: Blackwell Publishing, 2003: 151.

with Taylor. Jasmine's obsession with adventure and her journey towards the Western frontier closely echo the adventurous spirits of American myth and the new American imperialist's discourse of territory expansion.

The depiction of Jasmine's adventurous journey also reflects Mukherjee's own personal cultural orientation. Mukherjee explains that the reason for her to come back to America is that fact that America to her "is the stage for the drama of self-transformation"[1]. Mukherjee in this period of writing longs for her personal transformation. Mukherjee's severance of Indianness and celebration of transformation is very evident.

In *Jasmine*, Mukherjee also attempts to write in the American way. In this period of writing, she has abandoned British English and writing style, and begins to adopt American English and writing style. *Jasmine* resembles many American adventurous stories in style and narrative technique. In her strive to be admitted into the American writing tradition, Mukherjee distances herself from the influence of the Indian writing tradition by promoting the writings of American immigrant writers. Mukherjee uses Indian materials in *Jasmine*, but her narrative is rather Americanized. What is especially noteworthy is the narrative structure of the novel. There is no linear narrative line in the entire novel. The narrative shuttles between different temporal and spatial locations. It shuttles between the past and the present, and between different locations in India and America, ranging from Hasnpur to Jullundhar, Florida, Manhattan and Iowa. These shuttles parallel the shuttles of Jasmine's identities. The notion of shuttling also echoes with Gayatri Chakravorty Spivak's study of subaltern women. In her article "Can the Subaltern Speak?" Spivak asserts that "between patriarchy and imperialism, subject-constitution and object-formation, the figure of woman disappears, not into pristine nothingness, but into a violent shuttling"[2]. Spivak's "violent shuttling" refers mainly to the subjectivity of the subaltern women which are always suppressed by various discourses striving to speak for or represent them. The echoing of narrative shuttling between time

---

[1] Critina Emanuela Dascalu. *Imaginary Homelands of Writers in Exile: Salman Rushdie, Bharati Mukherjee, and V. S. Naipaul*[M]. New York: Cambria Press, 2007: 74.

[2] Gayatri Chakravorty Spivak. Can the Subaltern Speak? [G]//*Marxism and the Interpretation of Culture*. Ed. Cary Nelson. Urbana: University of Illinois, 1988: 227.

and space to that of Jasmine's shuttling between hybrid identities is no doubt the most dashing achievement in Mukherjee's narrative technique.

Mukherjee's portrayal of Jasmine's easy killing of the old self to invent the new one and her celebration of happy hybridity elicit strong criticism among scholars. According to them, the happy and epic mingling of the immigrants with the Americans often ignores or purposefully brightens up the real historical experiences of the immigrants. As Amindyo Roy points out that in *Jasmine*, the "epic theme" of assimilation elides the deep contradictions built within the space of postcoloniality, "[t]his experience is made possible as fictive construct by circumventing and suppressing the historical exigencies of the Third World immigration"[1]. The detextualization, namely the lighting of the immigrants' more material and traumatic transformation may be viewed as the biggest failing of the novel. Mukherjee's detexualization and lack of political dimension in writing reflected in *Jasmine* is in sharp contrast with many black and other ethnic women writers, for instance, Audre Lorde, Adrienne Rich and Toni Morrison, who in their writings attach great importance to material issues in daily life.

Some critics further point out the awkwardness of Mukherjee's position in her writing. They question whether Mukherjee, born into top caste, top family in India, educated in European and American elite schools and universities, socializing most of her life with the upper-middle class, is capable of representing or speaking for the subaltern women, like Jasmine. Actually, Spivak points out that it is always a tricky task to speak for the Other. "No perspective critical of imperialism can turn the Other into a self, because the project of imperialism has always already historically refracted what might have been the absolutely Other into a domesticated Other that consolidates the imperialist self."[2] Concerning Mukherjee's representation of the subaltern, Alpana S. Knippling argues that in her immigrant writing, Mukherjee sees herself as the colonial subject and the colonized Indian native simultaneously, balancing capriciously between the Self and the Other. In the novel, Mukherjee

---

[1] Sushma Tandon. *Bharati Mukherjee's Fiction: A Perspective* [M]. New Delhi: Sarup & Sons, 2004: 152.

[2] Gayatri Chakravorty Spivak. Can the Subaltern Speak? [G]//*Marxism and the Interpretation of Culture*[M]. Ed. Cary Nelson. Urbana: University of Illinois, 1988: 253.

constantly subjects the first-person narrator's narrative to the superior Orientalist gaze. As a result, there are constant ruptures in the text, which may lead readers to wonder whether they are the narrator's purposeful satirical self-depreciation or the author's accidental or careless slip of roles, from that of Jasmine to that of Mukherjee. Given Mukherjee's background, education and internalized Orientalist stance, these ruptures seem only natural to pop up here and there in the text. Besides, other Indian scholars also point out the wanting of Mukherjee's knowledge of Indian people from the low caste and the social class.

Despite the criticism of *Jasmine's* detextualization nature and performativity in the protagonist's metamorphoses, the novel successfully represents Mukherjee's promotion of fluid identity and self-assertion in metamorphoses. The agency associated with hybridity thus challenges the migrants' stereotyped role of victimization. The self-orientalization, although instrumental in getting survival, compromises the protagonist's self-assertion to a certain degree. In *Jasmine*, self-assertion in metamorphoses reflect Mukherjee's celebration of happy hybridity and deconstruction of fixed identity to embrace fluid ones. Therefore, Mukherjee's writing of immigration at this stage contrasts sharply with the writing of rootlessness which often involves the victimization of the migrants. However, in the writing of immigration, Mukherjee's promotion of severing the home culture and constant privileging the Western culture over the Eastern one reflects her evident Orientalist stance. The Orientalist stance with its constructions of binarisms is still an either/or ideology in nature. However, Mukherjee gradually changes her stance of aesthetics of fusion with the maturity of her writings.

Chapter 2 *The Holder of the World*: Rebelliousness in Transgression

The Holder of the World, published in 1994, is highly reviewed in the academic circle. For some critics the novel is a great success given its massive structure crossing three continents and overlapping several centuries. Amy Tan praises the literary achievements of the novel: "Once again, Bharati Mukherjee proves she is one of our foremost writers, with the literary muscle to weave both the future and the past into a tale that is singularly intelligent and provocative."[1]

However, the novel's rewriting of Nathaniel Hawthorne's *The Scarlet Letter* arouses much controversy among critics. Evidences of intertexuality between the two novels are abundant. Besides, the rewriting is further affirmed by the author herself. Mukherjee holds the opinion that by rewriting the American canonical novel, she can rewrite American national myth of origin. In an interview, Mukherjee explains that "this is a book about the process of history making, specifically about the 'American' way of making and remaking history"[2]. Critics hold sharply different opinions as to the true nature of this rewriting. Some critics hold the opinion that by rewriting the American canon, Mukherjee aims at being accepted by the mainstream American literary circle as one of the American writers with Bengali origin. Therefore, this rewriting is an attempt to

---

[1] Bharati Mukherjee. *The Holder of the World*[M]. New York: Alfred A., 1993: I.
[2] Bradley C. Edwards. *Conversations with Bharati Mukherjee*[M]. Oxford: Mississippi UP, 2009: 99.

reinforce and celebrate the American national myth of origin. Other critics believe that the novel is a kind of counter writing by the previously colonized in the postcolonial era, which is an attempt to deconstruct the American national myth of origin and give voice to the silenced colonized.

The Holder of the World reflects rebelliousness in transgression. Transgression is a boundary negotiation in hybridity which is closely related to cultural translation. In this novel, the white female protagonist, Hannah, travelling across three continents, constantly engages in cultural translations. The narrator, Beigh, is always in contemplation of the cultural translations that Hannah goes through and the term "translation" is even directly introduced in the narrative, "[m]any years later she called the trip (from Britain to India), and her long residence in India, her translation"[1]. Beigh observes that although the word "translation" with its connotation of change and adaptation may not exist in the time when Hannah lives, yet Hannah's travelling through three continents and more importantly her mental and interior voyage, changing from a Puritan maid, to an Old World wife and a bibi in India, may still be properly classified as "translation". "Bibi" is a term used by the white in Indian colony to refer to a native mistress of a white man.

The term "translation" derived etymologically from the Latin word *translatio*, "literally means to transfer, transport or remove from one person, place, time, or condition to another. It can imply transferal from the realm of ideas into the realm of words, and from one language or culture into another"[2]. Cultural translation has become a key concept in cultural study in recent years. The term is closely associated with postcolonial theorization of hybridity and is now often used to identify "the transformative dynamics that is forged by the interactions of different cultures"[3] from colonial to postcolonial contexts. Cultural translation is a form of hybridization, which is a process carrying over characteristics from one culture to another.

In *The Location of Culture*, Bhabha develops his theory of hybridity to

---

[1] Bharati Mukherjee. *The Holder of the World*[M]. New York: Alfred A., 1993: 104.

[2] Cosetta Gaudenzi. Exile, Translation, and Return: Ugo Foscolo in England [J]. *Annali d'Italianistica*, 2002(20): 217.

[3] Nikos Papastergiadis. *Cosmopolitanism and Culture*[M]. Malden: Polity Press, 2012: 136.

elaborate on cultural translation, cultural untranslatability, and cultural mistranslation. Bhabha points out that the notion of hybridity is closely associated with the idea of translation, for "if the act of cultural translation (both as representation and as reproduction) denies the essentialism of a prior given original or originary culture, then we see that all forms of culture are continually in a process of hybridity"[1]. In his perception, cultural translation may be the racists' strategy of assimilation or it may be the post-colonials' strive of culture survival. In recent years, Bhabha attaches much importance to the study of the migrants. He believes that "[t]he liminality of migrant experience is no less a transitional phenomenon than a translational one"[2]. The migrants are caught in-between nativism and assimilation. Bhabha maintains that in this in-between and hybrid space, cultural translation is against the fundamentalist urge to return to authenticity or postmodernist play of endless splitting. Bhabha argues that "[t]ranslation is the performative nature of cultural communication"[3]. Cultural translation is a borderline negotiation which records the disjunctive and transcultural experiences of the migrants. Further developing Bhabha's theory of cultural translation, Bery points out that "cultural translation may become the constructive resource for extending and negotiating identity"[4]. On an individual level, cultural translation refers to the transformation of the self that introduces fluid not fixed identities, challenges Orientalist view of Otherness and deconstructs binary construction in Western ideology. Translation, both literal and metaphorical, constitutes an important part in identity formation processes of the migrants. No wonder it is heatedly explored both in ethnic writings and cultural theories.

In her cultural translations, Hannah demonstrates rebelliousness in transgression, which Mukherjee advocates for the migrants. Compared fluid identity and self-assertion discussed in *Jasmine*, rebelliousness in transgression shows a more aggressive and bold gesture to deconstruct the constructions of

---

[1] Homi K. Bhabha. The Third Space[G]//*Identity: Community, Culture, Difference*. Ed. Jonathan Rutherford. London: Lawrence & Wishart, 1990: 211.

[2] Homi K. Bhabha. *The Location of Culture*[M]. London: Routledge, 1994: 224.

[3] Homi K. Bhabha. *The Location of Culture*[M]. London: Routledge, 1994: 228.

[4] Ashok Bery. *Cultural Translation and Postcolonial Poetry*[M]. New York: Palgrave Macmillian, 2007: 21.

binary oppositions to get re-rooted wherever one migrates.

2.1 Transgression of Gender and Racial Boundaries

The Holder of the World has two plots, the main plot and the subsidiary one. The main plot deals with the story of Hannah Easton, born in Brookfield, Massachusetts, the American colonies in 1670. Hannah is brought up by her devout Puritan adopted parents, Robert and Susannah Fitch. In 1692, she is married to an Irish wanderer Gabriel Legge and then travels to England and the Coromandel Coast of southeastern Moghul, India. As an inquisitive and energetic woman, she translates herself to adapt to the different cultures in her travelling and once even becomes the White bibi, the white lover of a Hindu raja.

The subsidiary plot deals with the story of the narrator, Beigh Masters, who is born in New England in the mid-twentieth century. Beigh is an asset hunter who is supposed to track down for her client a legendary diamond, the Emperor's tear. In tracing down the whereabouts of the diamond, Beigh becomes fascinated and obsessed with the travels and adventures of Hannah Easton. In Beigh's narrative, Hannah's cultural translations through three continents slowly unfold in the novel. In the spatial travels from American colony, to England, to Moghul India, and then back to America, Hannah also changes innerly, from a naive Puritan girl, to a lonely city housewife, to a passionate Salem Bibi, and later to a mature Precious-as-Pearl. In adapting to ever changing cultures, Hannah shows her rebelliousness in transgressions of both gender and racial boundaries to get re-rooted no matter in the West or in the East.

Transgression of gender and racial boundaries involves the deconstruction of binary oppositions. Derrida points out that Western metaphysics is based on a system of binary oppositions, within which there exist many invented terms function as centers. Within each opposition, the two opposing parties stand in sharp contrast to each other with one defined as superior to the other. For instance, within in the binary opposition, Self/Other, Self is defined as superior yet it has to be defined by the inferior Other.

Theorists and writers in the post-structural era are dedicated to challenge and deconstruct those binary oppositions in Western metaphysics. The binary oppositions under discussion in this novel are Men/Women and White/Black. A man recognizes himself/herself through negativity, that is through what the Other is and the subject is not, the binary oppositions are maintained. In her bold efforts of cultural translations to get re-rooted, Hannah transgressed gender and racial boundaries, thus subverted the hierarchal binary oppositions of Men/Women and White/Black.

Gender binary opposition, Men/Women, which is dichotomous and hierarchical, designates women to a subordinate and oppressed status for a long historical time, and forms the base of gender discrimination. Some feminists have found proofs that "gender discrimination may have begun with the biblical narrative that places the blame for the full of humanity on Eve, not Adam"[1]. The great philosopher Aristotle asserted: "The male is by nature superior, and the female inferior; and the one rules and the other is ruled."[2] Aristotle's ideas of gender discrimination contributed to the founding of patriarchal social system in Western society. Patriarchy literally means "the rule of the father", which may be defined as the social system in which the male predominates and controls while the female is subordinate and ruled. "Western civilization is pervasively patriarchal (ruled by the father)—that is, it is male-centered and controlled, and is organized and conducted in such a way as to subordinate women to men in all cultural domains: familial, religious, political, economic, social, legal, and artistic."[3] Passing down from generation to generation, the patriarchal system took roots. Under its influence, people began to believe that men are superior to women in nature. Later on, the Othering of women found more supports from other sources. Darwin announces that women are of a "characteristic of ... a past and lower state of civilization"[4]. Following

---

[1] Charles E. Bressler. *Literary Criticism: An Introduction to Theory and Practice*[M]. Upper Saddle River: Pearson Education, Inc.; Beijing: High Education Press, 2004: 144–145.

[2] Charles E. Bressler. *Literary Criticism: An Introduction to Theory and Practice*[M]. Upper Saddle River: Pearson Education, Inc.; Beijing: High Education Press, 2004: 145.

[3] M. H. Abrams & Geoffrey Galt Harpham. *A Glossary of Literary Terms*[M]. Beijing: Foreign Language Teaching and Research Press, 2010: 111.

[4] Charles E. Bressler. *Literary Criticism: An Introduction to Theory and Practice*[M]. Upper Saddle River: Pearson Education, Inc.; Beijing: High Education Press, 2004: 145.

Darwin's opinion, numerous other pseudo sciences help prove the superiority of men over women through comparing chromosomes, brain structure, and hormonal differences.

In the seventeenth century, although the status of women in colonial American was marginally better than those in the Old World, they were still in a minor and subordinate position. Madsen states in her study:

> The position of women in colonial America was determined by the hierarchal worldview of the Puritan colonists. As men deferred to God and His ministers, so women should defer to men. Puritans believed that the inferiority of women was a mark of original sin, manifest in physical weakness, smaller stature, intellectual limitations and a tendency to depend upon emotions rather than intellect. Women should be confined to the domestic sphere, nurturing children, maintaining the household and serving their husbands. John Winthrop, the first governor of the Massachusetts Bay colony, held that "A true wife accounts her subjection [as] her honor and freedom", finding contentment only "in subjection to her husband's authority".[1]

Hannah first exhibits rebelliousness in ripping herself off the patriarchal gender role forced upon her by her adopted father. After her father's death and her mother's elopement with a Nipmuc lover, Hannah is taken into the house of Robert and Susannah Fitch as the adopted daughter. Robert and Susannah are devout Puritans who are determined to bring up Hannah as an angle in the house. To bring up Hannah to become a "true wife", they keep close watch upon Hannah. Hannah's obsession with needlework or her occasional bursting into singing for desire is taken by the couple as signs of her wantonness in spirit. The adopted father tries relentlessly to correct her behaviors by reading and preaching from *The Bay Psalm Book*. Hannah is kept to stay at home most of the time with all her desire suppressed, living a suffocating life like a prisoner. Her suitor is declined directly by her father, with "no record of her feelings exists"[2].

Hannah is desperately in need of an escape from the strict Puritan ideals of

---

[1] Deborah L. Madsen. *Feminist Theory and Literary Practice*[M]. London: Pluto Press, 2000: 2.
[2] Bharati Mukherjee. *The Holder of the World*[M]. New York: Alfred A., 1993: 60.

humility, gratitude and meekness, from her adopted father's strict supervision and her adopted mother's constant caution of "moderation". Her first action of noncompliance and pursuit of independence shows in her hasty marriage to Gabriel Legge, who comes from London, claiming to be the son of a rich shipowner in the business of ferrying from the Old World to the New England. Hannah is thrilled to listen to Gabriel's sea-faring yarns, his stories of imprisonment by Turks, banishment to forests, brigands, highwaymen and pirates. Hannah's swift marriage to the apparently untrustworthy and inappropriate Gabriel reveals her strong desire to escape from the patriarchal Puritan family. The narrator Beigh analyzes that Gabriel Legge with his exhilarating tales of exotic adventure resembles to a large degree and in many ways the Nipmuc lover of Hannah's mother. Hannah's choice of a husband with wandering spirit also reveals the fact that unconsciously, Hannah still admires the boldness of her own mother to elope and therefore is not willing to submit herself to an ordinary domestic life.

By marrying herself off against her adopted parents' will, Hannah assumes that she has escaped from the patriarchal family structure. However, Hannah's condition has no improvement after travelling with her husband to the Old World. In the Old World, the requirements of women's homemaking skills that prevail are decidedly linked with submission and stupidity. "It was mandated that the wife should not outshine the husband in anything but parental wealth."[1] Hannah loses control of her property after marriage and has no freedom to choose a vocation outside her house. While Gabriel travels to the Orient in compulsion, Hannah is left lonely and confined to the only company of the bleak society of her fellow emigrants and repatriates who seek her out for the sake of nostalgia and consolation only. However, Hannah is different from her company in that she would rather adapt than indulge in nostalgia.

When the news of Gabriel's alleged death suddenly arrives, Hannah is determined to cut herself off the company of the expatriates and get re-rooted in the Old World. She defies the patriarchal society's doctrine of leading a gloomy and restraint life of widowhood by associating with common countrymen and seeking to take control of her own life. Soon, she gains herself a renowned fame

---

[1] Bharati Mukherjee. *The Holder of the World*[M]. New York: Alfred A., 1993: 71.

as a healer with her skills of healing scalped head. The local doctors solicit her to help on cases of head injury. People, treating her as a doctor, begin to visit her for poultices, for bone setting, and so on. Thus, she has changed from a sailor's widow to a woman blessed with healing powers. In the Old World, successfully gaining economic and social independence like a man, Hannah temporarily shakes off the patriarchal shackle as a woman. Her rebellious translation to get re-rooted in a sense deconstructs the Men/Women binary opposition. However, Hannah's attempt at transgressing gender boundary is cut short by Gabriel's sudden reappearance. In travelling to East India with her husband, Hannah makes further efforts to transgress gender boundary in her cultural hybridization and translation.

Hannah's rebelliousness in transgression of gender role shows most evidently in her breaking up with her husband in India because of her husband's infidelity in keeping a black bibi. For the white wives of the company factors, black bibis do not exist in the real sense. A bibi is an annoyance instead of a threat. The white wives tolerate their husbands' infidelity and seek consolation in their loneliness when their husbands are away with their bibis by subjecting bibis into a subhuman position. In their perception, bibis are mere cute little pets such as monkeys or birds (although considerably less trouble) that their husbands keep for pleasure and entertainment. They may be full of irresistible and overpowering sensuality, yet still they are quite beneath notice. The projection of bibis into a subhuman position is a typical example of the stereotyped projection of the Orientals in the Orientalist discourse. In their projection, the bibis are subhuman and at the same time they are temptresses with irresistible attraction. Cristina Emanuela Dascalu points out that the bibis are "stereotypes from the store of stereotypes that make up the shared colonial portrait of the native"[1]. The stereotypes reduce the Oriental women to a set of exaggerated and negative character traits. Bhabha discusses the nature of stereotype in colonial discourse:

> The stereotype is not a simplification because it is a false representation of a

---

[1] Critina Emanuela Dascalu. *Imaginary Homelands of Writers in Exile: Salman Rushdie, Bharati Mukherjee, and V. S. Naipaul*[M]. New York: Cambria Press, 2007: 82.

given reality. It is a simplification because it is an arrested, fixated form of representation that, in denying the play of difference (which the negations through the Other permits), constitutes a problem for the representation of the subject in signification of psychic and social relations ... For the stereotype impedes the circulation and articulation of the signifier "race" as anything other than its fixity as racism. We always already know that blacks are licentious, Asiatics duplicitous ...[1]

The stereotyping fixates the racial Other to a subordinate position, and thus strengthens the White/Black binary opposition. The stereotyped Other, bibis, also obediently subjected themselves to the projection of the white, "black bibis know their place"[2]. Most of them remain invisible in the shadows of white wives; therefore, white wives of factors could maintain a façade of happiness and stability of their families in spite of their husbands' numerous bibis and illegitimate children.

White wives in Indian colony are in an anomalous position: as the White, they are members of the rulers, but as women they are members of a powerless class. Underneath white wives' tolerance lies the code of female accommodation. As Hannah shrewdly observes, "[t]o accommodate meant to demonstrate an intention to please, even on occasion to yield, but with a view to establishing control"[3]. Also in colonies, "[a]ccommodation was synonymous with expatriate femininity"[4]. In patriarchal ideology, women's subordinance to men is sanctioned by divine decree: the Bible. Madsen explains that "[a]s God's agent, man as a sexual class has absolute power; this is traditionally exercised through the absolute monarch who has power over all his subjects; in turn, husbands have complete power over their wives"[5]. Therefore, it follows that women are to be ruled and controlled, and to please and accommodate their husband seem their destined obligations.

Hannah is well aware of the female code of accommodation but is rebellious

---

[1] Homi K. Bhabha. *The Location of Culture*[M]. London: Routledge, 1994: 75.
[2] Bharati Mukherjee. *The Holder of the World*[M]. New York: Alfred A., 1993: 133.
[3] Bharati Mukherjee. *The Holder of the World*[M]. New York: Alfred A., 1993: 132.
[4] Bharati Mukherjee. *The Holder of the World*[M]. New York: Alfred A., 1993: 134.
[5] Deborah L. Madsen. *Feminist Theory and Literary Practice*[M]. London: Pluto Press, 2000: 47.

enough not to follow. When Gabriel is caught naked with his bibi copulating in a cement bath tank in an explosion, Hannah decisively separates from her husband. Hannah shows her determination and rebelliousness in not yielding to the conventions held by most white wives about bibi keeping. For Hannah, the revelation of her husband's infidelity shatters her marriage definitively and "tolerance and patience and even a pragmatic tradeoff between luxury and uncertainty were no longer sufficient, no longer bearable"[1]. Hannah's decision to leave her husband is remarkable in her condition for the life of a single white woman in the East without economic substance and safety provided by a husband could be quite risky. However, with the help of her maid Bhagmati, Hannah begins to adapt to India and gradually realizes her cultural translations.

In defying her adopted father and her husband, both of whom are heads of patriarchal family, Hannah rejects gender roles assigned to her. Refusing to be a meek daughter and an accommodating wife, Hannah takes control of her own life like a man. In transgressing gender boundary, Hannah demonstrates her rebelliousness. The transgression of gender boundary rises out of Hannah's strong will to get adapted to cultures wherever she travels. In East India, to get re-rooted, Hannah also transgresses racial boundary.

Racial boundary is built on the binary opposition of the White/Black which is deeply embedded in racial thoughts. There is a long history of racial thoughts such as racial supremacy. Ancient Greek philosophers, such as Plato and Aristotle all held the opinion that the Greek were born superior to those of other race or origin. Aristotle even believed that people from some other races were mere "plant" or born slaves[2]. For a long period of time in European history, it was believed that different races belonged to different species and the hybrid, namely, the offspring of interracial intercourse, was doomed to become extinct for such mixture between different races was supposed to be fertile. The fear of degeneration and infertility caused by the hybrid, the offspring of interracial intercourse, led various white rulers to execute strict racial segregation. Therefore, in the Empire's colonial expansion, the promotion of racial hierarchy

---

[1] Bharati Mukherjee. *The Holder of the World*[M]. New York: Alfred A., 1993: 198.
[2] Aristotle. *The Politics*[M]. Cambridge: Cambridge UP, 1988: 17.

and prohibition of racial boundary crossing prevailed most of the time, except for a very brief period of time when some philosophers advocated the theory of "a drop of blood", which meant that the interracial breeding, with the white's drop of blood, would advance the civilization of the native in the colonies.

The theorization of racial thoughts began in the eighteenth century and it is fair to say that racial theories worked to substantiate racial convictions that preceded them. In the 1770s, J. F. Blumenbach, the German professor of natural history first classified the human races into twenty-eight varieties:

> He followed the Biblical account of man being descended from a single source, Adam and Eve ... The corollary of this was that he used the eighteenth-century thesis of degeneration to explain the differences between the races. This meant that the pure origin of man was the white male and that all other forms were deterioration from this ideal, on account of either gender or geography, or both. [1]

Although Darwin's finding that there was no fundamental distinction between species and variety refuted some racial thoughts, they gained more "scientific" supports in the nineteenth century. According to the study conducted by Young, the nineteenth century racial theory gained supports from and was proved by many different forms of science, "such as comparative and historical philology, anatomy, anthropometry (including osteometry, craniology, craniometry and pelvimetry), physiology, physiognomy and phrenology"[2]. Racial thoughts thrived and their influences extended to "theories of anthropology, archaeology, classics, ethnology, geography, geology, folklore, history, language, law, literature and theology, and thus dispersed from almost every academic discipline to permeate definitions of culture and nation"[3].

In its nature, racial theory is always manipulated as the tools of various rulers. It was developed most vigorously with British and European colonial

---

[1] Robert J. C. Young. *Colonial Desire: Hybridity in Theory, Culture, and Race* [M]. London: Routledge, 1995: 62.

[2] Robert J. C. Young. *Colonial Desire: Hybridity in Theory, Culture, and Race* [M]. London: Routledge, 1995: 88.

[3] Robert J. C. Young. *Colonial Desire: Hybridity in Theory, Culture, and Race* [M]. London: Routledge, 1995: 88.

expansion. Young points out that "[t]here is an obvious connection between racial theories of white superiority and the justification for that expansion"[1]. In support of the Empire's colonial expansion and rulings, the white followers of racial dichotomy and segregation exercised strict disciplines on any attempt of racial boundary crossing.

The Company factors in India are representatives of the disciplinary power, who guard against any racial boundary crossing through direct interruption or the surveillance gaze. Hannah shows her rebelliousness in defying the discipline and surveillance. In transgressing racial boundary, Hannah realizes her cultural translations and gets re-rooted in the Indian land.

Hannah's rebelliousness in spirit poses a great challenge to the patriarchal and racial authority in the Indian colony. Cephus Prynne, the Chief Factor, senses from subtle details as soon as Hannah arrives at India that she is not as malleable as an English factor's wife has to be. Hannah steps out of the boat, ignoring the steadying hands of her countrymen. Her bold gesture makes Cephus Prynne realize that the curbing of her spirit will be a tough task, requiring much more diligence and planning. The landscape and the natives greatly arouse the curiosity of Hannah and lure her to wander around in an attempt to get nearer to them. Hannah's attempt of getting connected with the natives raises the alarm and triggers direct intervention from the white male factors. The Second Factor, Higginbottham, coaxes and pleads with her: "Dear lady, do not stray ... I recommend you to the protection of your countrymen"[2]. The hidden massage of the pleading is that for white women, the natives are dangerous and only their countrymen, the white men, can protect them from the threats posed by the natives. In the Orientalist discourse, there are numerous rumors of white women easily falling prey to the desires of the lustful Orientals and getting raped or murdered by the natives in the colonies. Hannah might have ignored the warning of Higginbottham had the Chief Factor Prynne himself not intervenes. Hannah hears his grave voice all the way from the wharf. The voice warns Hannah that it hurts the Company's interests to let the natives see the white lady wander around

---

[1] Robert J. C. Young. *Colonial Desire: Hybridity in Theory, Culture, and Race*[M]. London: Routledge, 1995: 86.

[2] Bharati Mukherjee. *The Holder of the World*[M]. New York: Alfred A., 1993: 109.

at will, yielding to her self-indulgence. The Chief Factor's warning involves the supposed duty of the white in the colonies, which is to be the moral model for the natives in the Empire's mission of civilization. Restraint and not yielding to self-indulgence are important parts of the white's alleged superior morality.

Prynne goes on with his curbing of Hannah's free spirit by reminding her of the duty of a white wife in way of setting other factors' wives as role models. In his perception, the duties of factors' wives involve devotion to the well-being of their husbands, keeping their houses in order and raising their children in the Protestant religion. The preaching of the wives' duties which subjects women to a subordinate status is patriarchal in nature. Other factors' wives in India also internalize the roles they are supposed to play. In their houses, they are devoted to serve and please their husbands. Outside their houses, they are proud to be moral models for the uncivilized natives and at the same time they constantly keep the natives at arm's length in order to stay racially pure and superior. They are eager to turn Hannah into one of them. In fear of the fact that Hannah might be tainted because of her long residence in primitive New England, they keep close watch on Hannah, savoring their roles as guide and guardian to Hannah and constantly reminding her that she is a truly Englishwoman.

Besides being confined by direct admonishment in action, Hannah also becomes aware of the constant surveillance gaze. She once even catches Cephus Prynne in the action of "watching her". Jacques Lacan first uses the term "gaze" to describe the anxious state that comes with the awareness that one can be viewed. The gaze subjects the subject to an objective position with the loss of a certain degree of autonomy. In *The Birth of the Clinic*, Michel Foucault introduces the term "medical gaze" to account for the power dynamics between doctors and patients. In *Discipline and Punish*, he further explains that gaze is a kind of disciplinary mechanism used in prisons or schools. The surveillance and disciplinary gaze yield Hannah bound to the company of the factors and their wives, without any freedom to get translated and re-rooted.

However, Hannah's rebellious spirit is not smothered. In the relationship with her Indian maid, Bhagmati and later her Indian lover, the Raja, she transgresses the racial boundary and deconstructed the White/Black binary opposition that is maintained in racial discourse. Hannah's transgression of racial boundary first shows in her relationship with Bhagmati. Bhagmati is an Indian maid in Hannah's house and the bibi of the late Chief Governor, Henry Hedges. Due to the deep influence of the racial discourse, the other wives of the factors treat her as an invisible subhuman even though she serves them every time they pay visit to Hannah's house. However, Hannah shows a deep interest in her maid. To Hannah, Bhagmati is not the invisible Other, but a woman who is equal in spirit and could communicate with her even though Bhagmati speaks little English.

After befriended with Bhagmati, later on, Hannah begins to treat Bhagmati as her mentor in her cultural translation when she is cut off the company of the factors' wives after Gabriel's wandering off as a pirate. Bhagmati introduces Indian culture and history to Hannah through story-telling. Bhagmati's telling of Indian myth and epic vitalizes Hannah's urge to get re-rooted in the Oriental land. In their fleeing from the besieged enclave amidst war and typhoon, the mistress and the maid, the Occident and the Oriental, seem to change positions and roles in Hannah's crossing of racial boundary. "And now she was in a totally Hindu world. Bhagmati seemed no longer a servant. Perhaps she, Hannah was about to become one"[1]. Being rescued from the typhoon by Raja Jadav Singh, Hannah puts on the same sari as that of Bhagmati's when they stay in the Raja's fort. Bhagmati teaches Hannah the art of pleating and folding a sari. Sartorial transformation collapses the distance and erases the binary racial construction between Hannah and Bhagmati. The two women share their individual confidence. Bhagmati tells Hannah her personal experiences which bring Hannah to the sharp awareness that the Orientals are also living human beings instead of subhuman creatures or shadows in the background.

Bhagmati is a typical subaltern Indian woman who has suffered pathetically in the Indian feudal and patriarchal society. At the age of ten, she is disowned by her relatives after being raped. For in Hindu custom, an abused Hindu girl brings only shame to the family which fails to protect her. Thereafter, the twice victimized girl begins her vagrant life till she meets Henry Hedges, who is the first person to treat her with respect and real love. Henry renames her Bhagmati for her reborn self and he would dress in similar Indian clothes and share the

---

[1] Bharati Mukherjee. *The Holder of the World*[M]. New York: Alfred A., 1993: 220.

same space with her. The love which gives the subaltern woman hope for future is cut short by Henry's sudden death. Hannah is touched by the moving romance between Henry and Bhagmati which crosses the racial boundary and breaks social taboos. The racial boundary crossing romance also parallels that between Hannah's mother Rebecca and her Nipmuc lover, which leads Hannah to come to terms with her mother's elopement and abandonment of her in her early childhood. Hannah's sympathy for Bhagmati and her treating of an Indian maid as a mentor in her cultural translation show her rebelliousness in crossing the racial boundary.

Hannah's rebelliousness in transgression of racial boundary further shows in her relationship with Raja Jadav Singh. Hannah defies the White/Black binary opposition in racial discourse by falling in love with Jadav Singh and yielding herself subsequently to become a white bibi for the Indian warrior. Hannah's love for Jadav Singh is love at first sight. She is attracted at first by the physical beauty of the man, "the fine-grained luminosity of skin", and his manner, which resembles a true warrior with a kind of softness, "he didn't swagger like Gabriel; he didn't preen like Cephus"[1]. Also, Jadav Singh is quite accomplished in various fields. To Hannah, Jadav Singh is simultaneously "a shepherd and kind, cruel and kindly, a soldier, a musician, a voluptuary"[2]. The personal charm of the Indian warrior perceived by Hannah totally subverts the stereotyped image of the Oriental men. In the Orientalist discourse, "the Oriental male is seen as wily, fanatical, cruel and despotic"[3]. Hall points out that "[s]tereotyping reduces, essentializes, naturalizes and fixes 'difference'"[4]. In essence, the stereotyping of the Orientals marks the boundary between "Self" and "Other".

Furthermore, Hannah is conquered emotionally by the Raja's righteousness in personality. To Hannah, he is the first man really worth loving compared with those schemers who try in their selfish ways to "rescue" her. Those schemers are

---

[1] Bharati Mukherjee. *The Holder of the World*[M]. New York: Alfred A., 1993: 227.
[2] Bharati Mukherjee. *The Holder of the World*[M]. New York: Alfred A., 1993: 226.
[3] Chris Barker. *Cultural Studies: Theory and Practice*[M]. London: Sage Publications Ltd., 2008: 266.
[4] Stuart Hall, Sean Nixon & Jessica Evans. *Representation: Cultural Representations and Signifying Practices*[M]. London: Sage Publications Ltd., 1997: 258.

the white men who Hannah has encountered previously. Her husband Gabriel attracts Hannah to marry him by his fascinating adventure stories, while after marriage, often wanders around to satisfy his own wanderlust, leaving Hannah home alone bound by dutifulness of a wife. Gabriel even humiliates Hannah publicly with his infidelity when he is caught running naked with his bibi in an explosion. Chief Factor Prynne and Second Factor Higginbottham constantly keep Hannah under strict surveillance, claiming to protect her from being attacked by the natives and rescue her from being tainted by the wilderness of the subhuman Indians. However, they never really care about the well-being of Hannah. The hypocritical Prynne even tries on one occasion to sexually harass Hannah. In comparison, Jadav Singh is purer in heart and motive. Although he does not appear to be pious by the standards of Salem and the Coromandel, he is fighting a war against the Great Mughal according to the religious principles of his own. Therefore, besides the sexual bliss Hannah shares with Jadav Singh, she is also emotionally attracted to the man who is an artist, caregiver and justice dispenser. Hannah compares her previous life with the one with Jadav Singh and is determined to change and adapt to Indian life. Living with her husband Gabriel, she has to follow the wife's duties prescribed in the patriarchal society no matter in Salem or the Old World. Those do's and don'ts for the wife bind her behaviors and make her feel suffocated all the time. Living with Jadav Singh, she gets rid of wifely duties all together and does not have to care about the appropriateness of her own behaviors. Hannah realizes that here in India, she is no longer the same woman as she has been in Salem or London. She has changed from a wife to a bibi. As a bibi, Hannah is free to abandon the dutifulness of a wife and enjoy living for love. By yielding to the love for Jadav Singh and transforming to a bibi, Hannah transgresses the racial boundary and in a way subverts the racial discourse of the Occident's superiority.

Hannah's transgression reveals her wish to get re-rooted in India, which is of vital importance for her. For she does not want to live a life like other white men, who have no home, no going back and no staying on except clinging to the imaginary homelands. For Hannah, they are like ghosts, trapped between two worlds, unable to live a courageous life. Afraid of turning into one of them, living a ghostly life, Hannah is anxious to adapt and root herself in the new soil.

In her transgression to get culturally translated, Hannah also needs to resist the Othering process by the natives, for a white woman's presence in India, is part of the colonialist project. However, Hannah further demonstrates her rebelliousness through liberation of her female sensuality in an attempt to get rerooted in the new soil.

2.2 Liberation of Female Sensuality

Beside transgression of gender and racial boundaries, Hannah's rebelliousness also shows in her liberation of female sensuality in her re-rooting efforts. The liberation of Hannah's female sensuality in cultural translations celebrates hybridity and deconstructs the binary constructions in both patriarchal and racial discourses. The patriarchal and racial familial and social structure tries in every possible way to tame the female body. However, Hannah never gives up her rebellion in ridding herself of the sensual oppression. In the novel, Hannah's rebellion and her subsequent liberation of female sensuality is depicted in both implicit and explicit ways. Through embroidery and writing, Hannah gives vent to her suppressed desires; also, she realizes her sexual awakening in the romance with her Indian lover.

Through her embroidery and later her Memoirs writing, Hannah attempts to liberate her own sensuality and in a way to resist the gender and racial roles imposed upon her by patriarchal and imperialist power structure.

Embroidery is traditionally associated with femininity and is usually considered as an appropriate domestic occupation for women. However, embroidery in this novel functions as an important metaphor. Hannah's obsessive love of needlework is her way to get her voice heard. Starting from an early age, Hannah is particularly fond of sewing the beauty and the wildness of the landscape of America, "her needle spoke; it celebrated the trees, flowers, birds, fish of her infant days"[1]. The embroidery reflects her passion for life and love for beauty, which she inherits from her mother Rebecca. The passion tinged with wildness that Hannah tries so hard to suppress in her Puritan adopted parents' house finds expression in her embroidery.

---

[1] Bharati Mukherjee. *The Holder of the World*[M]. New York: Alfred A., 1993: 42.

Her adopted parents sense Hannah's passion from the wild landscapes that she embroiders and they try hard to smother it. The passion that is shown in Hannah's embroidery runs in contrary to the code of conformity for Puritans. Hannah's adopted parents, although impressed by Hannah's needlework skills, "feared the wantonness of spirit it betrayed"[1]. To correct it, the couple would chant and quote from *The Bay Psalm Book*, requiring Hannah to guide her own behaviors by those doctrines and principles, to pray for humility, gratitude, and meekness, to work diligently and stay humble. However, all their efforts to curb Hannah's wantonness of spirit and secretive disposition fail.

The passion and wildness in Hannah might come directly from the influence of her own mother Rebecca whose elopement with a native Indian is a rather unimaginable action for a white widow in her time. She represents to Hannah the boldness in spirit to cross the racial boundary and pursue her own happiness. Although Hannah never reveals the truth of her mother's disappearance to anyone, her mother's bravery and rebelliousness in satisfying her own desire and fulfilling her own happiness regardless of social and racial constraints must have influenced Hannah consciously or unconsciously. In her adopted parents' house, Hannah suffers a mysterious ailment which casts her in a doleful insomniac that keeps her in bed for weeks. In her spell, her mother Rebecca would step out of her memory and speak to her again, initiating her into a subversive alphabet, "A is for Act, B is for Boldness, C is for Character, D is for Dissent, E is for Ecstasy, F is for Forage, and I is for Independence …"[2]. The alphabet celebrates passion for life and rebelliousness, which is shown in the extravagance and ambiguity of embroidery that Hannah sews.

Hannah's sewing gets new significance after arriving at India. Hannah is overwhelmed by the sensuous India with its fecundity of nature and utterly different culture, which gives her new inspirations for sewing. She sews the landscape of India with passion. Besides, the narrator Beigh Masters also detects that Hannah's embroidery employs the same economy and native sophistication as the Moghul paintings which shows Hannah's adaptation to India even in subtle ways. Sewing is the main way for Hannah to express her emotions in an

---

[1] Bharati Mukherjee. *The Holder of the World*[M]. New York: Alfred A., 1993: 42.

[2] Bharati Mukherjee. *The Holder of the World*[M]. New York: Alfred A., 1993: 54.

ambiguous way and she matures mentally in her sewing. Baskaran and Mangaiyarkarasi point out that "[h]er embroidery is a metaphor of her thought process. It is a work towards self-realization and self-actualization"[1]. The embroidery shows that Hannah is transforming herself and going through cultural translations.

Hannah's embroidery also shows her love for both her mother country, America, and the host country of her migration, East India. Nalini Iyer points out that in Hannah's embroidery "landscapes of Massachusetts flora and fauna coexist with tropical Indian ones. Hannah's tales told by needlework also achieve a suspension of time in that these panels, like Keats's Grecian urn, are both static and dynamic in their tale telling"[2]. The equal love for both places show Hannah's strong will to get re-rooted wherever she migrates. It also reveals the fact that hybridization or cultural translations is a process that Hannah willingly embraces.

Besides employing sewing as an ambiguous way of expressing her sensuality, Hannah also shows a strong will to put pen to paper. When she is young, she keeps a diary and writes letters to friends and family members. In her old age she becomes a great storyteller, writing about her life experiences and remaking myth.

The narrator Beigh observes that Hannah's writing is very informative of the different cultures that she encounters. "Her written record is one long chronicle of discoveries, her curiosity extends to every branch of knowledge she ever had contact with."[3] While staying in England, Hannah keeps a diary of her daily life in the Old World, intended as epistles to a distant mother back in Salem. Part of her diary is later published as *London Sketches by an Anonymous Colonial Daughter*. Her letters are addressed from England to the nativists and expatriates, those who stay in Salem while dreaming of returning to England. Hannah, a shrew observer and keen commentator, compares the Old World with the New World. To her perception, the people of the Old World appear vastly

---

[1] G. Baskaran. Nature as Healer: An Eco-Critical Reading of Bharati Mukherjee's *The Holder of the World*[J]. *Language in India*, 2012(12): 390.

[2] Nalini Iyer. American/Indian: Metaphors of the Self in Bharati Mukherjee's *The Holder of the World*[J]. *Ariel*, 1996, 27(4): 36.

[3] Bharati Mukherjee. *The Holder of the World*[M]. New York: Alfred A., 1993: 76.

more excited and knowledgeable than those in the New World. Yet, Hannah criticizes the social hierarchy that prevails in the Old World, deeming it as false measures of value. At the same time, "she was no less shrewd in the skewering of colonial custom"[1]. Her letters, claims the narrator, offer a vigorous assessment of English life in the years of the Dutch King William III. After travelling to India, Hannah becomes fascinated with the sensuous and wild Indian land, which is in sharp contrast with Puritan America and static and hierarchal England. She keeps records of her travels and transformations there, her first encounter with the natives, her contempt of the white factors, and her later translations from the wife of an Englishman to a white bibi of a Hindu Raja.

Hannah's writing in a sense constitutes travel writing. Travel writing arouses wide interests in the academic circle in recent years. According to the study of Shao-pin Luo, "recent critical books on travel and travel writing cover a wide range of topics such as Orientalism and colonialism (Said, 1978; Lowe, 1991; Behdad, 1994), imperialism and globalization (Pratt, 1992; Kaplan, 1996; Clifford, 1997), and gender and sexual difference (Mills, 1991; Blunt, 1994; Grewal, 1996)"[2]. In travelling across continents, Hannah recreates herself, the process of which is reflected in her travel writing.

Hannah's writing reflects her innermost struggle and desire while staying in East India. Hannah finds herself in a rather complicated position in the Indian colony. On the one hand, as a woman, she is held in the subordinate gender position. On the other hand, as a white, she is temporarily held in racial superiority in imperial power structure. She is constantly curbed from going native, yet she is deeply attracted to the Indian land and its people, and therefore she is willing to adapt. The inner conflicts and transformation also show in the change of the style of her diary. Initially, Hannah keeps her Indian diary modeled on the diary kept by Gabriel in his capacity as a factor. Gabriel, although a man wild and restless in nature, keeps a diary in a cautious and practical way. He keeps the diary to record the summaries of daily business conducted in St. Sebastian, the Company's subordinate factory. Gabriel's

---

[1] Bharati Mukherjee. *The Holder of the World*[M]. New York: Alfred A., 1993: 75.

[2] Luo Shaopin. Rewriting Travel: Ahdaf Soueif's *The Map of Love* and Bharati Mukherjee's *The Holder of the World*[J]. *The Journal of Commonwealth Literature*, 2003(38): 77.

objective observation of life in the diary shows his concern for the Company's business in India and his distrust of the Chief Factor, with whom he is later on a bad term. To follow her husband's suit, Hannah's diary entries are initially of the order of events and the descriptions are cautiously impersonal. Gradually Hannah's diary changes from the practical and objective style to a more personal and emotional one. While Hannah struggles with the inner conflicts between dutifulness of a wife and her eagerness to adapt to her new surroundings, "the diary entries become more disorderly, more personal"[1]. Hannah's diary shows her fascination about the local culture and her suppressed desire to get rid of the fixed identity and get culturally translated.

The difference between Hannah's writing and that of her husband's also proves Sara Mills' assertion that female travel writing is quite different from those by male in that female writing has the more obvious tendency to present people as individuals.[2] Mills also asserts in her essay "Knowledge, Gender, Empire" that "knowledge produced within an imperial context are profoundly gendered"[3] and that "gender shapes the parameters of the possible texture structures within which writers construct their work"[4]. Hannah's will to pen as a way of rebellion shows more evidently in her attempt of memoirs writing in her old age. After returning to America with her illegitimate daughter, Hannah begins to write about her travelling and her romance with the Indian Raja. In her writing, she celebrates female sexuality. She writes so dashingly and movingly of sexual passion in her later years that her unique voice and writings cause quite a sensation in her time and place.

Writing which involves self-expression and self-development runs in direct conflict with the feminine subordination and repression advocated in Hannah's time. Even after two centuries, in the nineteenth century, women's will to pen was still strongly criticized. In 1844, Hannah More and Sarah Ellis in their

---

[1] Bharati Mukherjee. *The Holder of the World*[M]. New York: Alfred A., 1993: 124.

[2] Sara Mills. *Discourses of Difference: An Analysis of Women's Travel Writing and Colonialism*[M]. London: Routledge, 1991: 3.

[3] Sara Mills. Knowledge, Gender, and Empire[G]//*Writing Women and Space: Colonial and Postcolonial Geographies*. Eds. Alison Blunt & Gillian Rose. New York: The Guilford Press, 1994: 36.

[4] Sara Mills. Knowledge, Gender, and Empire[G]//*Writing Women and Space: Colonial and Postcolonial Geographies*. Eds. Alison Blunt & Gillian Rose. New York: The Guilford Press, 1994: 29.

widely circulated treaties of "women's mission" rendered women's writing "selfish, unwomanly, and unchristian"[1]. According to them, instead of writing, women should be "visiting the sick, fixing breakfast ... or general devotion to the good of the whole family"[2]. Hannah's writing is a rebellion against gender roles. Her will to pen also shows her eagerness to learn from different cultures. Later on, Hannah further liberates her sensuality in her sexual awakening in defiance of surrounding surveillance and disciplinary gaze.

Hannah's sexual awakening is a rebellion against the powers that control and discipline female bodies. In *Discipline and Punish: The Birth of the Prison* (1977), Michel Foucault points out that "in every society, the body was in the grip of very strict powers, which imposed on its constraints, prohibitions or obligations"[3]. The body becomes object and target of power, "attention then paid to the body—to the body that is manipulated, shaped, trained"[4]. Foucault's argument is that disciplinary power creates "docile bodies". Foucault states: "Disciplinary power ... is exercised through its invisibility; at the same time it impose on those whom it subjects a principle of compulsory visibility ... It is the fact of being constantly seen, of being able always to be seen, that maintains the disciplined individual in his subjection"[5].

Foucault deals with "Panopticism" in one chapter of the book. The term "Panopticism", meaning "all-seeing" is first used by Bentham. Bentham uses the term "Panopticon" to refer to a prison in which all of the prisoners have individual cells in a ring-like building and are subjected to be observed from a tower place at the hub of the ring. The prisoners are subjected to a gaze that they are constantly aware and could not return. The gaze forms a kind of disciplinary power. In *Ways of Seeing*, John Berger discusses the gender inequality caused by the male's gaze, "[m]en look at women. Women watched themselves being looked at. This determines not only most relations between men and women but

---

[1] Elaine Showalter. *A Literature of Their Own*[M]. Princeton: Princeton UP, 1977: 22.

[2] Elaine Showalter. *A Literature of Their Own*[M]. Princeton: Princeton UP, 1977: 22.

[3] Michel Foucault. *Discipline & Punish: The Birth of the Prison*[M]. Trans. Alan Sheridan. New York: Vintage Books, 1977: 136.

[4] Michel Foucault. *Discipline & Punish: The Birth of the Prison*[M]. Trans. Alan Sheridan. New York: Vintage Books, 1977: 136.

[5] Michel Foucault. *Discipline & Punish: The Birth of the Prison*[M]. Trans. Alan Sheridan. New York: Vintage Books, 1977: 187.

also the relation of women themselves"[1]. Marita once points out that gaze is not a tool or means that one uses; rather, it is the relationship in which someone enters and is aware, "[g]aze is integral to systems of power and ideas about knowledge"[2]. Gaze may achieve the effect of self-regulating if people are aware that they are being closely watched and yet not certain who or what is watching. For under this circumstance, people would voluntarily adjust and regulate their behaviors because of the awareness.

In both Salem and England, Hannah is constantly aware of the disciplinary gaze. She has to suppress all her sexual desire to remain docile. Travelling to East India, Hannah finds herself in another prison, suffering the constant modification and surveillance from the male factors and female associates. Her urge to fulfill her desire is suppressed forcefully and her body renders disciplined all along. The Chief Factor, Prynne, is a typical representative of patriarchal and imperialist disciplinary power. Assuming the moral and racial highland, he claims to be the protector of the white women in India by reminding them of their wifely duties and preventing them from going native. Hannah is keenly aware of the fact that the disciplinary forces personified by Prynne are on watch everywhere. Therefore, she has to repress her sensuality against her will. For Hannah, Prynne's sudden death constitutes a great degree of liberation from the gaze. She believes that Gabriel has killed Prynne and feels thankful to her husband. The evening after the body of Prynne is discovered, when Gabriel takes Hannah for a ride along the shore, "Hannah suddenly let go of her reins, twisted impulsively, violently, in her saddle, and kissed Gabriel"[3]. The compulsive expression of intimacy is the first stage of the liberation of Hannah's docile body and her sexual awakening.

Female sexuality is largely repressed in Hannah's time. Elaine Showalter points out in her study that there is a long history of repression of the so-called "animal" aspects of womanhood, which refers to the satisfaction of female sexuality. Madwomen are the incarnations of "the flesh, of female sexuality in

---

[1] Patricia Waugh. *Literary Theory and Criticism*[M]. Oxford: Oxford UP, 2006: 515–516.
[2] Marita Sturken & Lisa Cartwright. *Practices of Looking: An Introduction to Visual Culture*[M]. Oxford: Oxford UP, 2009: 103.
[3] Bharati Mukherjee. *The Holder of the World*[M]. New York: Alfred A., 1993: 160.

its most irredeemably bestial and terrifying form"[1]. Showalter states that there are several legends of imprisoned madwomen in Yorkshire and the legends in nature shows the patriarchal attitude toward female passion as wild and dangerous which has to be suppressed and punished. In defiance of social code, Hannah fully fulfills her passion and realizes her sexual awakening in her translation to a white bibi of her Indian lover, "[f]or fourteen days and thirteen nights the lovers abandoned themselves to pleasure"[2]. In their wooing and love-making, Hannah experiences the ecstasy which is denied to her previously.

The suppression and liberation of female sexuality is an often-explored theme in postcolonial writings. In Chinese American author Maxine Hong Kingston's memoir, *The Woman Warrior: Memoirs of a Girlhood Among Ghosts*, the first-person narrator Kingston is warned by her mother to temper her developing sexuality. The mother used to tell her the tragic story of her aunt who kills herself after indulging in her sexuality and giving birth to an illegitimate child. However, instead of learning from the lesson to temper her sexuality, Kingston decides to publish her aunt's story as a means to reclaim and liberate female sexuality. In postcolonial writings, female sexuality constitutes a major part in the construction of postcolonial identities. The liberation of female sexuality disrupts the stereotyped designation of patriarchal and racial roles, thus in a way free the subject from fixed identity.

In her sexual awakening and fulfillment, Hannah begins to understand her mother's elopement, which is previously considered by her as being shameful. Hannah realizes that her mother is probably the only woman she has known that could understand her feelings. Cristina points out:

> The story of Hannah's mother is not a repetition of a common colonialist fantasy concerning the native (the cultured woman who gives into the baser side of her nature and takes a foreign mate). Rather it is a moment of self-transformation, a transgression of the ordinary boundaries of culture that Hannah seeks to forget but

---

[1] Elaine Showalter. *A Literature of Their Own*[M]. Princeton: Princeton UP, 1977: 118.
[2] Bharati Mukherjee. *The Holder of the World*[M]. New York: Alfred A., 1993: 234.

understands in its fullness when she makes a similar transgression years later ...[1]

By becoming a white bibi of a Hindu Raja, Hannah exhibits her dedication to love and willingness to adapt. Hannah's becoming a bibi of an Indian warrior at the same time also "disrupted the dualism of the two separate cultures and put to play the point at which their boundaries meet"[2].

The awakening of Hannah's sexuality contributes to her strong desire to transform and get rooted wherever she migrates. After Jadav Singh is defeated and badly wounded in the battlefield, Hannah tries to persuade him to leave for America with her by giving examples of the transformations and adaptations she and others around her have gone through, "I was once a respectable married English lady and look at me now—a bibi in a sari. We can all change"[3]. Hannah's belief that "we can all change" is of ultimate importance in understanding the theme of the novel. This sentence reveals the underlying and unconscious motive of Hannah's rebelliousness in transgression—the willingness to change and adapt to a new place that one migrates, no matter one travels from the East to the West or from the West to the East.

The awakening of Hannah's sexuality also helps her form affections for India and its people, "I have come late in my life to the feeling of love. Love for a man, love for a place, love for a people"[4]. In transgression and sexual liberation, Hannah demonstrates rebelliousness to get re-rooted and shows love for all irrespective of their race and gender. The processes of Hannah's cultural translations, especially in East India, disrupt the imperialist discourse, which sets the European from the Indian, with the Indian as the Other.

The rebelliousness in transgression reflected in *The Holder of the World* deconstructs binary oppositions of the Men/Women and the White/Black. It evokes more vigorous shattering of fixed identity and brave embracing of fluid identities. In the process of cultural translations, the either/or binary

---

[1] Critina Emanuela Dascalu. *Imaginary Homelands of Writers in Exile: Salman Rushdie, Bharati Mukherjee, and V. S. Naipaul*[M]. New York: Cambria Press, 2007: 83.

[2] Critina Emanuela Dascalu. *Imaginary Homelands of Writers in Exile: Salman Rushdie, Bharati Mukherjee, and V. S. Naipaul*[M]. New York: Cambria Press, 2007: 83.

[3] Bharati Mukherjee. *The Holder of the World*[M]. New York: Alfred A., 1993: 256.

[4] Bharati Mukherjee. *The Holder of the World*[M]. New York: Alfred A., 1993: 268.

construction is replaced by the both/and ideology, which celebrates hybridity. The rebelliousness in transgression is bolder and subversive in nature to get re-rooted in the host country. Compared with self-assertion in metamorphoses reflected in *Jasmine*, the rebelliousness in transgression demonstrates the subtle change of perception in Mukherjee's aesthetics of fusion. Different from the total severance of Indianness reflected in *Jasmine*, Mukherjee shows her tentative reaffirmation of her Indianness in this novel, which involves her celebration of Indian cultural heritage and art achievements. This change shows Mukherjee's moving away from a total Orientalist stance to a more objective stance in balancing her Indianness and Americanness at the same time.

2.3 Mukherjee's Deconstruction of American National Myth of Origin

The Holder of the World is Mukherjee's attempt to rewrite the American founding myth, resembled by Nathaniel Hawthorne's romantic novel *The Scarlet Letter*. In her rewriting, Mukherjee successfully deconstructs the male, white American national myth of origin.

The canonic works of Hawthrone together with those of Melville, Poe and others in American literature construct a white, masculine American national myth of origin. Especially Hawthrone's *The Scarlet Letter*, with its canonic status and popularity among common readers is called by Lawrence Buell a "myth of American origin". In *The Holder of the World*, Mukherjee makes evident efforts to associate the novel with Nathaniel Hawthorne's romantic fiction *The Scarlet Letter*. She is so successful in her attempt that the intertextuality is readily recognized and valued by critics. In *The New York Times Book Review*, K. Anthony Appiah praises Mukherjee's rewriting: "and when, in the end, Bharati Mukherjee has hubris, the chutzpah, the sheer unmitigated gall, to connect her book, in Beigh's voice, with Nathaniel Hawthorne's novel *The Scarlet Letter* ... it is, I think, a connection she has earned. Nathaniel Hawthorne is a relative of hers"[1]. Therefore, Mukherjee's rewriting of *The*

---

[1] Alexandra W. Schultheis. *Regenerative Fictions: Postcolonialism, Psychoanalysis, and the Nation as Family*[M]. New York: Palgrave Macmillan, 2004: 53.

Scarlet Letter amounts to a rewriting of American national myth of origin. The intertextuality between the two novels shows the similarities in setting and characterization.

The Scarlet Letter is mainly set in the seventeenth century Puritan Boston, Massachusetts. In *The Holder of The World*, the protagonist Hannah is also born in the seventeenth century Massachusetts. Later in life, after travelling to England and East India, Hannah returns to Salem. Hannah's journey in life begins from Massachusetts and ends in it. The descriptions of the Puritan Massachusetts in the two novels are quite similar in its vast and wild nature, and depressing Puritan community with its pious believers and harsh doctrines governing people's behaviors.

The protagonists of the two novels, Hester and Hannah, are both women of rebellious spirits who would pursue love and fulfillment in defiance of the prevailing social codes of behaviors. At the beginning of *The Scarlet Letter*, Hester Prynne, is punished and shamed publicly because of the guilt of adultery. While at the beginning of *The Holder of the World*, Hannah has to witness the elopement of her mother Rebecca with a native Indian lover. Her mother's bold elopement in defiance of racial segregation must have influenced Hannah unconsciously. Later in life, Hannah shows her rebelliousness in transgressing racial boundary and transforming herself from a wife of a white man to a bibi of an Indian warrior. At the end of the two novels, both protagonists settle at the edge of the Puritan community with their "bastard" daughters. Yet with their straightness in character, both of them provide solace for people around them. They both gain respect and acceptance from the people who come to know them, Hester with her kindness and generosity, while Hannah with her scalp sewing skill and storytelling charm. Both protagonists share a great fondness for sewing, which becomes a vent of their inner passions.

> Hester Prynne had in her nature a rich, voluptuous, Oriental characteristic—a taste for the gorgeously beautiful, which, save in the exquisite productions of her needle, found nothing else in all the possibilities of her life to exercise itself upon ... To Hester Prynne, it [needlework] might have been a mode of expressing, and

therefore soothing, the passion of her life.[1]

Hannah's sewing is also an expression of her inner conflicts and desire, the wildness of which are detected by her adopted parents and the people around her. The strong will to get her voice heard leads her to write passionately about her romance in memories later in age, which is rather rare for women of her time.

Besides the similarities in setting and characterization, Mukherjee also endeavors to form intertextual connections between *The Holder of the World* and *The Scarlet Letter* in other aspects. In *The Scarlet Letter*, initially, Hester is forced to wear a scarlet "A" ("A" is a symbol of adultery and affair) on her dress as a sign of shame. But as the story developed, the scarlet letter "A" begins to assume the connotation of "Angle". In *The Holder of the World*, Mukherjee also tries to give special and quite opposite meanings to alphabetical letters. In her spells, Hannah hears her mother whisper subversive alphabet, "A" is for "Act", and "I" instead of standing for "Indian lover" is for "Independence". Mukherjee also plays with names in her novel. In *The Holder of the World*, the name of Hannah's best friend in childhood is Hester. Later Hannah names her Indian maid Hester, who has gradually become a bosom friend and mentor to her. Pearl is the name of Hester's daughter in *The Scarlet Letter*. In later years, Hannah comes to be called Pearl by the great Indian emperor and her daughter with the Indian lover is called Pearl Singh. When she settles down in Massachusetts with her daughter, they are named White Pearl and Black Pearl by the town people in their gossips.

In *The Holder of the World*, Mukherjee even boldly includes a character named Joseph Hawthorne, a boy of ten, who seems to enjoy Hannah's company, drawn by her stories of India that Hannah relates as she sews. The boy would supposedly become the grandfather of Nathaniel Hawthorne. At the end of novel, Mukherjee depicts an imaginary image of the great writer Hawthorne in the act of writing *The Scarlet Letter*, "he wrote his morbid introspection into guilt and repression that many call our greatest work. Preach! Write! Act! He wrote against the fading of the light, the dying of the old

---

[1] Nathaniel Hawthorne. *The Scarlet Letter*[M]. New York: New American Library, 1980: 61, 87.

program, the distant memory of a shameful, heroic time"[1]. In this way, even Hawthorne himself becomes a part in Mukherjee's rewriting of American myth of origin.

Mukherjee forms successfully in *The Holder of the World* the intertextuality with Hawthorne's *The Scarlet Letter*. The literary term "intertextuality" was first coined by poststructuralist Julia Kristeva in 1966. The term is used to "signify the multiple ways in which any one literary text is in fact made up of other texts, by means of its open or covert citations and allusions, its repetitions and transformations of the formal and substantive features of earlier texts"[2] Since its creation, the term has come to assume many meanings from different critics. Among many demarcations, the most influential ones include the definition given by Gerard Genette in his book, *Paratexts: Thresholds of Interpretation*. According to him, intertextuality refers to "a relation of co-presence between two or more texts, that is to say, eidetically and more often, by the literary presence of one text within another"[3]. As a writing technique of postmodern literature, intertextuality may be in the form of a reference or parallel to another literary work, or the adoption of a style, etc. Intertextuality is adopted by many postcolonial writers. Jean Rhys' novel *Wide Sargasso Sea* (1966) which contains textual references to Charlotte Brontë's *Jane Eyre* is a typical example. Only this time, the story is narrated from the supposedly mad woman Antoinette Cosway's point of view, thus it is a rewriting of the story of "the mad women in the attic". The rewriting reveals the racial and patriarchal oppression of a hybrid woman. It successfully deconstructs the imperialist and patriarchal discourse. This kind of postcolonial rewriting of Western canonical works constitutes what is in Edward Said's term "contrapuntal writing back". "Contrapuntal writing back", introduced by Said in his book *Culture and Imperialism*, refers to the native resistance of the colonial intellectuals, which "involves taking up the techniques and weapons of negation of the West, such as stereotypes of the lazy native or the noble savage, in order first to remake, and then eventually to

---

[1] Bharati Mukherjee. *The Holder of the World*[M]. New York: Alfred A., 1993: 286.

[2] M. H. Abrams & Geoffrey Galt Harpham. *A Glossary of Literary Terms*[M]. Beijing: Foreign Language Teaching and Research Press, 2010: 364.

[3] Gerard Genette. *Paratexts: Thresholds of Interpretation*[M]. New York: Cambridge UP, 1997: xviii.

transcend, them"[1].

Concerning the nature of Mukherjee's employment of intertextuality in her postcolonial rewriting, critics hold quite different opinions. Some critics believe that the "playing with the concepts of history, time and space"[2] and the mimicry of Hawthorne's tension building serve Mukherjee's purpose of writing in the postmodernist and yet American way. Frank Day points out that by associating her novel with *The Scarlet Letter*, Mukherjee is trying to achieve two goals. Firstly, she is hoping that the readers may consider the novel, with its strong intertexual features, to be in the tradition of American romance which is originally inaugurated by Hawthorne with his masterpiece *The Scarlet Letter*. Secondly, she is attempting to add the historical dimension to her novel.[3] The hidden message in Frank's comment is that Mukherjee is using the rewriting to gain acceptance by the West, winning herself a position in the literature of American tradition. In forming a parallel with the American canon, Mukherjee first attracts Western readers with something familiar, and then moves on to offer something exotic about India aiming at better commodifying her novel. Her catering to Western readers' unconscious and permanent desire for the Other amounts to what Edward Said called "latent Orientalism".

On the other hand, some critics believe that Mukherjee rewrites the American canon to subvert or deconstruct the American tradition. By contesting the founding myth of the United States, Mukherjee realizes her contrapuntal writing back. Newman argues that *The Holder of the World* is a postcolonial counter writing similar to *Wide Sargasso Sea*. *The Holder of the World* offers a different version of American myth of origin left behind by Hawthorne in his *The Scarlet Letter*. Newman claims that the novel "deliberately brings the two "spheres" together—postcolonial and American literature—upsetting institutional authorities in the process, crossing boundaries, and renegotiating the spaces of

---

[1] Patricia Waugh. *Literary Theory and Criticism*[M]. Oxford: Oxford UP, 2006: 352.

[2] Megan Obourn. *Reconstituting Americans: Liberal Multiculturalism and Identity Difference in Post-1960s Literature*[M]. New York: Palgrave Macmillan, 2011: 140.

[3] Frank Day. *Bharati Mukherjee*[M]. New York: Twayne Publishers, 1996: 129.

cultural authority"[1]. Other subtle details evidencing the nature of counter writing are also traced by critics. For instance, in the novel, an Indian fisherman's boy, witnessing Hannah and Legge's kiss on the shore later finds his way to William III's court in London, "[t]here he chanced upon John Dryden's *Aureng-Zebe* and was incensed by its Eurocentric falsity. That fisherman's boy composed his own heroic play, *The World-Taker*, in rhyming couplets as a corrective"[2]. By including this anecdote, Mukherjee gives a concrete example of postcolonial counter writing, which rises from dissatisfaction with Eurocentric falsity and aims at correcting it. In this sense, it seems rather partial to simplify Mukherjee's motive of rewriting to her eagerness to be admitted into the American writing tradition.

Mukherjee advocates history writing from the angle of the once colonized. At the end of the novel, Mukherjee vigorously expresses her hope in the switching of point of view, "Time, O Time! Time to tincture the lurid colors, time for the local understudies to learn their foreign lines, time only to touch and briefly bring alive the first letter of an alphabet of hope and of horror stretching out, and back to the uttermost shores"[3]. The appeal shows Mukherjee's desire to deconstruct the grand narrative of colonialism and reconstruct the colonial histories of the three continents. In her rewriting, Mukherjee rejects cultural purity and shows that hybridity perpetuates the beginning or origin of America. In undermining the white, male logocentrism shown in *The Scarlet Letter*, Mukherjee successfully deconstructs the American national myth of origin.

In the discussion about postcolonial theorists, Wang Ning asserts: "If we say that Said's postcolonial study starts with the criticism of Orientalism, then we can say Bhabha's postcolonial study starts with the deconstruction of national myth. To some degree, it is just the deconstruction of essentialist nature of nation that lays the foundation of Bhabha's postcolonial theory."[4] In a similar

---

[1] Judie Newman. Spaces In-Between: Hester Prynne as the Salem Bibi in Bhararti Mukherjee's *The Holder of the World*[G]//*Borderlands: Negotiating Boundaries in Post-Colonial Writing*. Ed. Monika Reif-Hülser. Amsterdam: Rodopi, 1999: 81.

[2] Bharati Mukherjee. *The Holder of the World*[M]. New York: Alfred A., 1993: 161.

[3] Bharati Mukherjee. *The Holder of the World*[M]. New York: Alfred A., 1993: 286.

[4] 王宁.叙述、文化定位和身份认同:霍米·巴巴的后殖民批评理论[J]. 外国文学, 2002, (6):48-55. (translated by the author of this book)

vein, Mukherjee's deconstruction of American national myth of origin may be viewed as the new beginning of her aesthetics of fusion. The post-structural deconstruction of binary oppositions and reaffirmation of Indianness reflected in the novel is quite remarkable.

In *The Holder of the World*, Mukherjee's tentative reaffirmation of her Indian cultural inheritance is partly reflected in the protagonists' constant appraisal of Indian natural beauty, artistic achievements and Indian people's righteousness in personality, and partly in Mukherjee's own employment of Moghul style in the narrative of the novel. This tentative reaffirmation of Indian culture forms sharp contrast with Mukherjee's utter celebration of American culture and derogation of Indian one reflected in *Jasmine*. The change in perception also shows Mukherjee's moving away from the Orientalist stance to a more objective and neutral stance concerning different cultures.

Mukherjee's reaffirmation of her Indianness is first reflected in the protagonist's appraisal of Indian natural beauty, its people and its artistic achievements. Upon arriving at India, the protagonist Hannah is attracted by the sensuous landscape of India and the art achievements of Indian culture. They attract her so much that she has to be constantly stopped by surveillance powers from going native. The description of the beauty of Indian nature and its artistic achievements perceived by Hannah is so luxurious and full of passion that it in a way reflects Mukherjee's rediscovered love for her homeland, India.

The Orientals in the novel are not corrupt, weak, or uncivilized as described in the Orientalist discourse. Instead, the main Indian characters in the novel, Hannah's maid Bhagmati and lover Jadav Singh, both show righteousness in personality. In contrast, many white characters are far more inferior in personality. The Chief Factor Mr. Prynne, generally considered by the white community as the very model of a British East India Company man in morality, is actually quite treacherous and deceitful, who is totally interest-driven regardless of moral concerns and literally dedicates himself to the pursuit of profit. The contrasts between the white and the native characters deconstruct the Orientalist's discourse in which the white are more righteous and the Orientals are deceitful. In this way, Mukherjee actually subverts the moral superiority of the white over the natives and the Orientalist construction of the binary opposition within which the white is superior to the black.

The narrator Beigh is generally considered the surrogate of Mukherjee. In her haunting for the whereabouts of the diamond, she constantly shows respect and admiration for the old Indian culture and its artistic achievements. Beigh is amazed with awesome at the art of the miniature painting named "The Apocalypse". The painting vividly portrays the beautiful landscape and the wild creatures, for instance, the leopards and tigers that roam in the grassland. Both the depiction of the contrast between the fertile Marblehead, a city in the northeast part of Massachusetts, and the sensuous India and Beigh's admiration for Indian artistic excellence reflect Mukherjee's celebration of her home culture.

Actually, Mukherjee once told her interviewers that the novel was inspired by an enigmatic Indian miniature that she viewed at Sotheby's in New York:

> [...] a 17th-century Indian miniature, a woman in ornate Moghul court dress holding a lotus blossom. The woman was Caucasian and blond ... I thought, "who is this very confident-looking 17th-century woman, who sailed some clumsy wooden boat across dangerous seas and then stayed there? She had transplanted herself in what must have been a traumatically different culture. How did she survive?"[1]

The image of the woman triggered Mukherjee to make a rather thorough study of "mercantile and military histories of India and the Puritan in the seventeenth century, Hawthorne's biography, tales of pirates, the development of medical knowledge, and Indian wars"[2]. Based on her study, Mukherjee writes the novel.

The miniature painting, which is "an art that knows no limit, no perspective and vanishing point, no limit to extravagance, or to detail"[3], also greatly forms the narrative style and technique of the novel. Mukherjee admits that the art of miniature painting inspires her narrative of history and reality from

---

[1] Marni Gauthier. Amnesia and Redress in Contemporary American Fiction[M]. New York: Marni Gauthier, 2011: 121.

[2] Judie Newman. Spaces In-Between: Hester Prynne as the Salem Bibi in Bhararti Mukherjee's *The Holder of the World*[G]//*Borderlands: Negotiating Boundaries in Post-Colonial Writing*. Ed. Monika Reif-Hülser. Amsterdam: Rodopi, 1999: 83.

[3] Bharati Mukherjee. *The Holder of the World*[M]. New York: Alfred A., 1993: 19.

different perspectives. The miniature painting, which can be accomplished within the size of a grain of rice, usually employs many different foci and centers, with different scenes portrayed at the same time and many stories told simultaneously. With its manipulation of shape and color, the miniature painting achieves its artistic excellence and is open to various interpretations among its viewers.

Jennifer Drake has made a thorough study of the feature of Moghul miniature painting. Moghul miniature painting is originally introduced to India by Islamic invaders and conquerors. In its vivid artistic way, this painting style signifies cultural clash and exchange. Jennifer compares this art with European ones.

> Unlike European medieval art, which shares some of the perspectival strategies of the miniatures but emphasizes God's-eye Christian narratives, and unlike Western painting during and after the Renaissance, which explores the visual organization of secular space from the perspective of a single viewer, Moghal miniature paintings gather stories together to create a multifocal field of vision, even as the different tableaux within each painting compete with each other for the viewer's attention.[1]

The multiple perspectives and the multifocal visions which fold into wholeness are the greatest artistic achievement of Indian miniature painting.

Mukherjee's reaffirmation of Indian culture also shows in her employment of Indian miniature painting technique in her writing. Mukherjee explains to her interviewer, "understanding this art (Moghul miniature painting) is really a matter of learning to see it in a different way. This is what I'm trying to do in my novels and stories. I want many stories going on simultaneously to distract, to crowd the reader's consciousness"[2].

In *The Holder of the World*, many stories are told at the same time and different perspectives are employed to form multifocal views. The novel is

---

[1] Jennifer Drake. Looting American Culture: Bharati Mukherjee's Immigrant Narratives [J]. *Contemporary Literature*, 1999, 40(1): 68.

[2] Bharati Mukherjee & Fred Bonnie. An Interview with Bharati Mukherjee [J]. *AWP Chronicle*, 1995, 28(2): 8.

multilayered. Beigh's search for the diamond mingles with Hannah's cultural translations. Everyday accidents are put together to rebuild the history of India and America several hundred years ago. Also, the same event is viewed and commented upon from different perspectives. The multilayered stories and different points of view give the novel features of metafiction and in a sense make it possible to be classified as a new historical novel.

The novel's features of metafiction include direct and self-reflective discussions about fiction writing and oral narrative. The boldest example is the allusion to Thomas Pynchon, a famous American novelist known for his "postmodernist themes and devices"[1]. Mukherjee discusses novel writing in the narrative, "[h]er (Hannah) life is at the crossroads of many worlds. If Thomas Pynchon, perhaps one of the descendants of her failed suitor, had not already written V., I would call her a V., a woman who was everywhere, the encoder of a secret history"[2]. The self-conscious reflection upon fiction writing draws readers' attention to the fact that fiction is an artifact. In the passage when Sita's story is told to Hannah by Bhagmati, Mukherjee comments upon the nature of orality, "[o]rality, as they say these days, is a complex narrative tradition. Reciters of Sita's story indulge themselves with closures that suit the mood of their times and their regions"[3]. The novel also includes different versions of the ending of Sita's story offered by different narrators, Bhagmati, Venn's mother Mrs. Padma S. Iyer, and Venn's friend Jay Basu, which further add to the uncertainty and playfulness of storytelling.

For Mukherjee, history is not a rigid construct. Her rewriting of history aims at deconstructing the hegemony of history writing and forming new conventions for history writing. Therefore, *The Holder of the World* may also be viewed as a typical postmodern historical novel, in which the author points out the fictionality of history writing. The narrator Beigh, viewing from her distinctive perspective, helps select historical data for her boyfriend to build the time-travelling machine. The history created by them is their version, for every time-traveler and builder of the time-travelling machine will create a different

---

[1] Brian McHale. *Postmodernist Fiction*[M]. New York: Methuen, 1987: 16.
[2] Bharati Mukherjee. *The Holder of the World*[M]. New York: Alfred A., 1993: 60.
[3] Bharati Mukherjee. *The Holder of the World*[M]. New York: Alfred A., 1993: 176.

reality. In this way, every one of them may assume the authority of historians. Mukherjee echoes postmodernism's privatization of history in the depiction of the building of the time-travelling machine, which reflects the fictional and whimsical nature of history writing. The novel reveals that "facts are not neutral, they have value. This is how a politics of difference interacts with history"[1]. In the novel, Mukherjee successfully achieves the aim of building what David Mura describes, "a discovery and a creation, as well as a retrieval, of a new set of myths, heroes, and gods, and a history that has been occluded or ignored"[2]. Mukherjee's postcolonial rewriting can be viewed as an attempt to set straight the misrepresentation in the grand narrative of imperialism, or to reveal the constructiveness of and the power play in the Orientalist discourse.

Different from *Jasmine's* decontextualization tendency, *The Holder of the World* shows Mukherjee's serious attempt of re-contextualization. Published in 1993, *The Holder of the World* is a novel with strong contextual relevance to the world situation at that time. Reflected in the novel, Mukherjee severely attacks the lust and greed that drive territory expansion of the ancient Moghul emperor and the exploitation of the British Empire in East India. Newman points out that "Mukherjee spots the gap in the story, the space in-between the Puritan tale of origins and the decline which Hawthorne describes—the space of imperial expansion and Eastern plunder which was the foundation of New England fortunes"[3]. Also, given the social context in the time of its publication, this novel can be interpreted as an implied attack on the jingoistic and imperialist policies in the wake of the Bush administration. Mukherjee once said, "I used two women characters, Hannah the pre-America American, and Beigh, the post-deEuropeanized American, to dramatize the need to redefine what it means

---

[1] Critina Emanuela Dascalu. *Imaginary Homelands of Writers in Exile: Salman Rushdie, Bharati Mukherjee, and V. S. Naipaul*[M]. New York: Cambria Press, 2007: 145.

[2] David Mura. A Shift in Power, a Sea Change in the Arts: Asian American Constructions[G]// *The State of Asian America Activism and Resistance in the 1990s*. Ed. Karin Aguilar-San Juan. Boston: South End, 1994: 204.

[3] Judie Newman. Spaces In-Between: Hester Prynne as the Salem Bibi in Bhararti Mukherjee's *The Holder of the World*[G]// *Borderlands: Negotiating Boundaries in Post-Colonial Writing*. Ed. Monika Reif-Hülser. Amsterdam: Rodopi, 1999: 78.

to be an 'American' in the 1990s"[1]. For the post-deEuropeanized America, what is more important in Mukherjee's perception is to deconstruct the binary and hierarchal constructions of the Men/Women, the White/Black, the West/East and curb its impulse of imperialist expansion. The criticism of war and plundering driven by lust and greed in the novel serves to warn the repetition of history in the contemporary world.

Mukherjee advocates that tolerance of cultural differences and love for all should transcend lust and will to power. The humanistic concern for all and the criticism of imperialist tendency in territorial expansion and exploitation show the budding of Mukherjee's ideas of cosmopolitanism, which echo Appiah's theorization of rooted cosmopolitanism.

The rebelliousness in transgression reflected in *The Holder of the World* shows new features of Mukherjee's writing of immigration. The novel shows the connectedness of lives dwelling in three continents. Appiah observes that "the novel advocates a 'vigorous' and even though maybe 'bitter fusion' of peoples"[2]. The fusion reflects Mukherjee's perception that people should transgress gender and racial boundaries to get re-rooted no matter migrating from the East to the West or from the West to the East. In fact, the rebelliousness in transgression reflected in *The Holder of the World* is of more significance since it is exemplified by a white woman's willingness to embrace hybridity, go through cultural translations and get re-rooted in the Eastern soil. In depicting the protagonist's rebelliousness in transgression, Mukherjee deconstructs the binary opposition in Western metaphysics, unsettling the patriarchal and racial discourses at the same time. Mukherjee's promotion of love for all and fusion of peoples aims at transforming an antagonist binary opposition to an all-embracing hybridity. This hybridity involves splitting and fluid identities instead of static and homogenous one. In the process of cultural translations, the migrants negotiate differences and reconstruct identities in a postmodern off-centered yet positive way rather than being stuck in the anguish of cultural dislocation and loss of certainty.

---

[1] Marni Gauthier. *Amnesia and Redress in Contemporary American Fiction*[M]. New York: Marni Gauthier, 2011: 131.

[2] Frank Day. *Bharati Mukherjee*[M]. New York: Twayne Publishers, 1996: 124.

Compared with the self-assertion reflected in *Jasmine*, the rebelliousness celebrated in *The Holder of the World* shows a bolder and more mature gesture of Mukherjee concerning migration. Regaining more confidence of her home culture, Mukherjee gradually moves away from a pure Orientalist and essentialist stance to embark on a new stage of writing.

Chapter 3　*Desirable Daughters* and *The Tree Bride*: Self-reflection in Immigration

Desirable Daughters and *The Tree Bride*, published in 2002 and 2004 respectively, are relatively recent works of Mukherjee. The two novels form a sequel and share the same narrator and protagonist, Tara Chatterjee. Both *Desirable Daughters* and *The Tree Bride* are warmly received and highly reviewed by critics. Some critics believe that Mukherjee eclipses all of the new young writers of South Asian origin in *Desirable Daughters*. Zaleski claims that "[o]nly a writer with mature vision, a sense of history and a long-nurtured observation of the Indo-American community could have created this absorbing tale of two rapidly changing cultures and the flash points where they intersect"[1]. *The Tree Bride* is deemed Mukherjee's best work to date for its successful fusion of "history, mysticism, treachery and enduring love"[2]. If *The Holder of the World* is Mukherjee's attempt to rewrite American myth of origin, then *The Tree Bride* may be viewed as Mukherjee's effort to reconstruct a national myth for India. In spite of the artistic achievements, till today, more than a decade after their publications, there are not many in-depth studies of the two novels.

Desirable Daughters and *The Tree Bride* show self-reflection upon different cultures in immigration. After years of immigration, the narrator Tara initiates a

---

[1]　Jeff Zaleski. Rev. of Desirable Daughters by Bharati Mukherjee[J]. *Publishers Weekly*, 2002, 249 (3): 62.

[2]　Jeff Zaleski. Rev. of The Tree Bride by Bharati Mukherjee[J]. *Publishers Weekly*, 2004, 251 (33): 41.

series of reflection as to different cultural affiliations and the strength of her homeland culture. The critical self-reflection can be read as a journey of self-discovery of the protagonist, Tara, which also reflects the maturity of Mukherjee's aesthetics of fusion.

In *Desirable Daughters*, Tara closely observes, compares and re-evaluates the different cultural affiliations of both her sisters' and her own. In self-reflection, she criticizes both Padma's ghettoization and Parvati's new Indian nationalism. However, at the same time, she comes to the realization of her own failure in full assimilation into America culture. In *The Tree Bride*, to write a book of her ancient ancestor, Tara embarks on a roots search back to India. In the depiction of her roots search, Tara lays bare the sins and trauma of the Empire's colonialism. At the same time, she reaffirms the strength of Indian culture and its people, represented by the Tree Bride. In self-reflection, Tara reorients herself in her cultural affiliation. As Mukherjee commented, "[i]n writing up history, she is going to reframe it, to tell herself a myth to survive by"[1]. Tara's self-reflection shows Mukherjee's own change of stance in recent years. Different from her celebration of American culture reflected in *Jasmine*, Mukherjee begins to further reaffirm the cultural strength of India, therefore; moving away from a thorough Orientalist stance to a "rooted cosmopolitan" one. This new turning may also be viewed as ushering in a new stage in Mukherjee's immigrant writing and marking the further maturity of her aesthetics of fusion.

3.1 *Desirable Daughters*: Reflection upon Different Cultural Affiliations

In *Desirable Daughters*, Tara and her sisters' identities are originally overdetermined, which means that their identities at birth are determined by the iron-clad identifiers of religion, language, caste, and sub-caste of India. Born into a top-caste, top-family in the late fifties and early sixties, Tara and her sisters' identities are fixed. The family, living in Calcutta, the commercial, cultural, and educational center of the country, belongs to Bengali Brahmin, the

---

[1] Judie Newman. *Fiction of America: Narrative of Global Empires* [M]. New York: Routledge, 2007: 152.

top category in the caste system in India. Besides being members of the top caste, the sisters also enjoy economic affluence because of their father's economic success.

Although three sisters share the same birthday and upbringings, their lives after their marriage take different tracks, as the narrator observes, the three sisters of the last generation of Calcutta high society were born into the same world, but from it, they have made their quite different and separate exits. Immigrated to America, Tara is determined to get fully assimilated into the host country. While her eldest sister Padma, who also immigrates to America, sticks to ghettoization and expatriate sentiments. Her second eldest sister, Parvati, living in India, is a representative of new Indian nationalists. The sudden appearance of an Indian boy who claims to be the illegitimate son of Padma forces Tara to get into more close contacts with her two elder sisters. In the process, Tara reflects upon their different cultural affiliations and identity construction. The self-reflection is very important for it signifies critical reevaluation and the maturity of the migrants concerning their cultural affiliations and identity construction. In self-reflection, Tara criticizes both the cultural affiliations of ghettoization and new nationalism.

The word "ghetto" originally comes from the Italian dialect ghèto, which means "foundry", a restricted Jewish residence in 1516. Later the word ghèto was borrowed into standard Italian as ghetto, with the meaning of "section of a city where Jews are forced to live"[1]. "From there it passed into most other European languages. Since the late 19th century, the meaning of ghetto has been extended to crowded urban districts where other ethnic or racial groups have been confined by poverty or prejudice."[2] Mutual help and support in ghetto may serve to some degree for the minority to survive in a formerly foreign place. Dwelling in close proximity to others who share their cultural background or upbringings, the immigrants may also get spiritual comfort from each other because despite differences within, they are all caught in an in-between world of

---

[1] "Ghetto". Merriam-webster Dictionary Online. Merriam-webster, 2014. Web. [2014-03-10]. https://www.merriam-webster.com/dictionary/ghettos.

[2] "Ghetto". Merriam-webster Dictionary Online. Merriam-webster, 2014. Web. [2014-03-10]. https://www.merriam-webster.com/dictionary/ghettos.

cultures.

But on the other hand, the negative aspects associated with ghettoization cannot be easily overlooked. As Verena Esterbauer points out that "[t]he formation of ghettos is a factor that, along with other preconditions, contributes to the problem of stereotyping a group of people. By deciding to lead a life in a ghetto-like area, the inhabitants seclude themselves from mainstream society, which contributes to their being looked at with suspicion"[1]. Ghetto represents the Other of the mainstream and assimilated society. Many dwellers of ghettos may be classified as expatriates, who refuse adaptation and assimilation. Reflected in *Desirable Daughters*, the inhabitants of the Indian ghetto seclude themselves from the vigorous life around them. They indulge in memories of the past and cling to an imaginary homeland that they could never return to.

Tara's eldest sister Padma, called Didi among sisters, is a representative of expatriates stuck in ghettoization who refuse any assimilation after years of immigration to the United States. Didi strongly opposes to Tara's Americanization and condemns Tara for becoming too self-engrossed and "American" in divorcing Bish. Didi on the other hand would rather model herself on Sita, Savitri, and Behalu, the virtuous and faithful wives in Hindu myths. Despite the fact that she has been living in America for more than ten years, Didi is determined to remain "Indian". She lives in an Indian ghetto with her husband Harish Mehta, and they socialize almost exclusively with the Indians. In Tara's eyes, in the nearly twenty-five years since Didi's immigration to the United States, she has become in many ways more Indian than before her immigration. Tara's description of Didi's house in New Jersey Indian ghetto is quite symbolic of the withdrawn mentality of Didi and her husband Harish, "[there was] no television, no books, no papers or magazines strewn on the tables. The house was kept cold and dark, uncluttered as a crypt, with halls sealed off and the curtains drawn"[2].

In the novel, many dwellers of ghettos shun contacts with real American life. Instead, they seek comfort in nostalgia and memory of their lost homeland.

---

[1] Verena Esterbauer. *The Immigrants' Search for Identity*[M]. Saarbrucken: VDM Verlag Dr. Mullter, 2008: 49.

[2] Bharati Mukherjee. *Desirable Daughters*[M]. New York: Hyperion Books, 2002: 174.

Didi's husband Harish locks himself at home, seldom venturing outside the house or communicating with others. He even has difficulty in carrying on a casual conversation with his sister-in-law, Tara. In the life of seclusion, he shows enormous interests in Bhattacharjee family's stories in the past. As Tara and Didi talk about the old days in India, he listens attentively by the side, "feasted on our nostalgia"[1]. To Tara, he lives a rather pathetic life, "[h]e was a man rooted in nostalgia, with no place to put it"[2]. Harish is surely not the only one in the ghetto who seals himself from the outside world. Didi's friend Mrs. Ghosal brings her grandparents and their servants to America. The new immigrants all have difficulties in adapting to American life. There are numerous cases of ill-adjustments. The most striking case is the cook who dies of frustration six weeks after his arrival at America since he cannot recognize the American vegetable and hates the taste of American foods. Mrs. Ghosal's Indian grandparents also rarely go out. By turning their places into a Calcutta museum, they believe imaginatively that they are still in Calcutta. These people are typical expatriates who seek consolation in indulging in their nostalgia and have difficulties in adapting to the new life. Although longing for the imaginary homeland, they have no courage to take action to return. For them, "the present experience of fragmentation is countered by an appeal to an unchanging country of origin which has been pickled in the migrant's mind"[3]. These people in the Indian ghetto hide in a construction of pure Indianness and their limbo existence fills Tara with despise.

The ghettoized mentality also shows in Didi's backward looking attitude and not letting go of the past. In public, she appears calm and gracious with faultless manners. But in private, when she is out of public attention, she seethes with bitterness. Didi bitterly blames others for ruining her life and is stuck in her illusion of the glorious past. In her own reflection, Tara criticizes Didi for her backward-looking attitude towards life, "[t]he fault line ran directly through my family, separating sister from sister, the forward-looking from the traditional

---

[1] Bharati Mukherjee. *Desirable Daughters*[M]. New York: Hyperion Books, 2002: 181.
[2] Bharati Mukherjee. *Desirable Daughters*[M]. New York: Hyperion Books, 2002: 181.
[3] Mita Banerjee. *The Chutneyfication of History: Salman Rushdie, Michael Ondaatje, Bharati Mukherjee and the Postcolonial Debate*[M]. Heidelberg: Universitätsverlag C. Winter, 2002: 101.

and the adaptable from the brittle"[1]. In comparison, Tara is more future-oriented in that she is not willing to dwell in nostalgia and would like to take responsibility for her own life. Tara doesn't blame others, not her dad or Bish, for making a mess of her own life and she believes that she has to bear the consequences of her own actions. Tara also realizes the impossibility of returning to the homeland that has changed while they are away, "I can't deal with modern India, it's changed too much and too fast, and I don't want to live in a half-India kept on life-support"[2]. Tara is completely aware of the fact that India is not the same one as preserved in the sisters' memory, while Didi still hangs on to her version of imaginary homeland.

In ghettoized life, Didi promotes her own ethnic Otherness to gain fame and profits. In the Indian ghetto, Didi is an icon of Indianness, who takes every chance to stress her ethnic roots, "[s]he is a 'multicultural performance artist' for local schools and community centers, staging Indian mythological evenings, with readings, slide shows, recitations, and musical accompaniment"[3]. Her efforts make her a celebrity. She owns her own brand of designs of saris and hosts Indian TV programs.

However, for some immigrants, the motive of stressing their ethnic roots is not totally out of their nostalgic feelings. They sometimes engage in commodification of their ethnic roots for fame or money which is totally irrelevant to cultural affiliations or identity construction. Kaplan points out in his study:

> ... instead of [pursuing] a spiritual or creative identity or profession, the immigrant is associated with less romantic forms of labor—even, simply, with purely material motives, ranging from physical survival to elite careerism. Neither political refugee nor exiled artist, the immigrant, in such a mystified and unified characterization, cannot participate in the terms of Euro-American modernism and cannot be recuperated or professionalized in terms of cultural production.[4]

---

[1] Bharati Mukherjee. *Desirable Daughters*[M]. New York: Hyperion Books, 2002: 133.
[2] Bharati Mukherjee. *Desirable Daughters*[M]. New York: Hyperion Books, 2002: 184.
[3] Bharati Mukherjee. *Desirable Daughters*[M]. New York: Hyperion Books, 2002: 94.
[4] Caren Kaplan. *Questions of Travel: Postmodern Discourses of Displacement*[M]. Durham: Duke UP, 1996: 110.

For example, Didi's promotion of Indianness focuses less on cultural production in artistic way than on material return. The display of ethnicity in the party thrown by Didi in Tara's honor proves just to be a marketing strategy to sell saris and jewelry. Also, Didi has plans for starting a TV show, which would be a vernacular soap opera from an Indian perspective for North American thirty something Bengalis. Didi claims that in the show she is going to cram in bits of those characteristic Indian things, "the shady stock deals, the corrupt accountants, the land scams in India, the anorexic girls, and the endless intrigue of the arranged-marriage market"[1], all of which would appeal to the taste of the Western viewers. Instead of presenting a relatively objective historical or modern version of India, Didi focuses on the Oriental materials that would intrigue the Western viewers. The deliberate catering to the taste of the Western viewers who seek to subject the Indian Other to their superior gaze shows Didi's tendency of self-orientalization in an attempt to gain economic success in America.

In reflection, Tara shows her sympathy and despise on the expatriates' ghettoized state of existence. Tara believes that it is a cowardly way of dealing with a new life and dismisses Didi as a liar and hypocrite. In Tara's perception, Didi's stubborn clinging to a version of India and to Indian ways is a cowardly way of dealing with a new life in the host country. And her "charming" Oriental accent and promotion of Indian clothes and foods strike Tara as hypocritical. For Tara, those who have difficulty in coping with their hybridity in America and seek shelter in their imaginarily authentic ethic life in the ghetto are actually cowards. Lacking the courage and audacity to move on renders them ghostly figures. Besides, those who commercialize their ethnic roots in ways similar to those of her eldest sister Didi are hypocrites. By self-orientalizing, they further strengthen the stereotyped image of the Orientals held by the Occidents, which is detrimental for the immigrants' adaption in the long run.

On the other hand, Tara also disapproves of her second elder sister's affiliation to narrow Indian nationalism. Many theorists have pointed out the danger of new narrow nationalism in the postcolonial era. Echoing Benedict Anderson's claim that nation is an imagined political community and nationalism

---

[1] Bharati Mukherjee. *Desirable Daughters*[M]. New York: Hyperion Books, 2002: 175.

is a cultural artifact, Bhabha, in *Nation and Narration* and other works, points out that nation is in a way narration and therefore quoting Fanon's idea, he believes that national consciousness rather than narrow nationalism should be promoted. In postcolonial theory, some critics have shown concern that "anti-colonial nationalism has been derivative of and complicitous with imperializing nationalism"[1]. Narrow nationalists' celebration of cultural authenticity and ethnic purity is similar to Orientalists' construction of binary opposition in theoretical mechanism, only replacing one superior in the hierarchy with another. Their objection to cultural hybridity and their adherence to fixity of identity are as narrow-minded and biased as those in the Oriental discourse. Spivak also points out that narrow nationalism, which is built on binary opposition and emphasizes essentialism and authenticity, is complicit with colonial discourse in nature. In Indian narrow nationalist discourse, the bourgeois "new women" are push to the front. With their sacrifice and endurance as mothers and wives, they are portrayed as preservers of Indian traditional value and cultural purity. In her discussion of women's role in nationalist projects, Deniz Kandiyoti argues that "[w]omen bear the burden of being 'mothers of the nation' (a duty that gets ideologically defined to suit official priorities) as well as being those who reproduce the boundaries of ethnic/national groups, who transmit the culture and who are privileged signifiers of national difference"[2].

Parvati is one of the new women. She strongly believes in narrow nationalist promotion of traditional value, cultural purity and takes pride in her exhibition of endurance and other virtue of women. Despite the Western education she receives, Parvati lives a rather traditional way of life. Parvati's family in India is hierarchical-structured, with the husband, Auro, as the head of the family and other family members constantly showing obedience and respect towards him. At home, Auro vents his unhappiness in career to his wife who is so determined to please him. Tara observes the feature of endurance,

---

[1] Gautam Premnath. Arguments with Nationalism in the Fiction of the Indian Diaspora[D]. Brown University, 2003: 3.

[2] Deniz Kandiyoti. Identity and Its Discontents[G]//*Colonial Discourse, Postcolonial Theory*. Eds. Patrick Williams & Laura Chrisman. New York: Columbia UP, 1994: 376-377.

sacrifice and self-denial in Parvati. Actually, the name "Parvati" is quite symbolic because in Indian myth, Parvati is another form of Shakti, the wife of Shiva, and the gentle aspect of Maha Devi, who usually appears in benevolence forms to please and entertain.

Mukherjee discusses the traditional status and role of Indian women in the memoir *Days and Nights in Calcutta*. According to her interpretation, most of the Indian women do not have strong personal ambition or inspiration. In most cases, the women need to form their individual identities initially in terms of their fathers and afterward in terms of their husbands and their communities[1]. Parvati defines herself in terms of her husband and her community. She has no life of her own. Her life revolves around governing the cook and servants at home, buying the food her husband prefers and keeping his clothes clean and crisply ironed. Tara observes that her life "is a life that preserves as much of the old ways as sanity permits"[2]. Parvati takes satisfaction in maintaining a household in traditional ways and within her reach upholds the mores of patriarchal family structure. Besides daily household chores, Parviti also has to entertain Auro's numerous relatives and family friends in their big flat. While Tara accuses them of taking advantage of Parvati, Parvati holds quite opposite view believing that it is her obligation to share her prosperous life with her in-laws and friends. Parvati gladly yields her personal world to the realm of customary relationships without feeling offended or intruded. The different stances held by the two sisters reflect their sharply different perceptions of social relationship. Tara's stance reflects her acceptance of the Western individualism, while Parvati's stance reflects a more traditional Indian view of social life.

Compared with those in the West, Indian tradition attaches more importance to familial relationships. For example, according to the study of Reiter, "[i]n most regions of India the so-called joint family is predominant. A joint family consists of several nuclear families which are connected through the paternal line of the family"[3]. The Indians are more accustomed to live in

---

[1] Clark Blaise & Bharati Mukherjee. *Days and Nights in Calcutta*[M]. Saint Paul: Hungry Mind Press, 1995: 204.
[2] Bharati Mukherjee. *Desirable Daughters*[M]. New York: Hyperion Books, 2002: 283.
[3] Verena Esterbauer. *The Immigrants' Search for Identity*[M]. Saarbrucken: VDM Verlag Dr. Mullter, 2008: 67.

extended families. Ravichandran and Deivasigamani point out in their study: "In India, the happiness of the individual is subordinate to the collective good of his/her community. More importantly, the role of women is to be supportive to their husbands in all circumstances. The individual needs and aspirations of women are not given due importance in what is essentially a patriarchal society."[1] In her constant endeavor to please and entertain, Parvati gives up her own needs and aspirations.

Cultural purity is promoted in the discourse of narrow nationalism. Parvati takes pride in preserving the imagined cultural purity of India. Tara's frank questing about the illegitimate child of their eldest sister offends her for such a question put the honor of the high-caste Bhattacharjee family in doubt, which is quite unacceptable and unimaginable for Parvati. Her first response is that "all those crazy (American) soap operas ... putting bad ideas into susceptible minds"[2] and she blamed American culture for Tara's drifting away from Indian traditions.

Therefore, Parvati constantly urges Tara to move back to India for she believes that Tara's hybridity in America is dangerous. In her opinion, to restore ethnic and cultural purity, Tara should end her American adventure and return to India. Parvati warns Tara of the pitfalls in staying longer as an immigrant in America, "... your child isn't American or Indian and if you stay there any longer, you won't be either"[3]. Parvati's insistence on the ethnic and cultural purity reflects the mindset of new narrow nationalists. By sticking to an essentialist and imaginary cultural purity, they turn away from the hybridity of the world reality.

Postcolonial new narrow nationalism is often under criticism for it often benefits a small elite group, who are, in Spivak's opinion "instrumental in changing the geopolitical conjuncture from territorial imperialism to neocolonialism"[4]. Elite nationalists often work in complicity with neocolonialism.

---

[1] M. Ravichandran & T. Deivasigamani. Immigration and identity in Bharati Mukherjee's *Jasmine* and *Desirable Daughters*[J]. *Language in India*, 2013(15): 552.

[2] Bharati Mukherjee. *Desirable Daughters*[M]. New York: Hyperion Books, 2002: 96.

[3] Bharati Mukherjee. *Desirable Daughters*[M]. New York: Hyperion Books, 2002: 66.

[4] Gayatri Chakravorty Spivak. *In Other Worlds: Essays in Cultural Politics*[M]. New York: Methuen, 1987: 245.

Parvati and her husband are representatives of such elite nationalists in the postcolonial India. They live on the fifteenth floor of a spectacular high-rise in Bombay because of Auro's career success in a multinational corporation. Tara admits that with a solid marriage, Parvati lives a far more luxurious life in India than the other two sisters in America. Parvati and her husband enjoy their luxurious life brought about by the expansion of multinational corporations, which carry with them cultural neocolonialism in the postcolonial era. While at the same time, they advocate the preservation of Indian nationalism. They promote ethnic purity while shunning any association with the poor living in huts. The paradoxes render their nationalists' claims rather hypocritical.

Both ghettoization and narrow nationalism in their refusal to embrace hybridity are essentialist and in line with binary construction. Only this time, they appoint the new Other. Ghettoization, with its close association with expatriate sentiments, treats the overwhelming mainstream culture as the Other. Narrow nationalism, by reversing the binary construction of the West/East, establishes the West as the Other. Both binary constructions elicit antagonism and exclusion, which is detrimental for the immigrants in the long run. Therefore, in self-reflection, Tara is critical of the narrow-mindedness and essentialism of both cultural affiliations. However, at the same time, Tara also comes to face her own disillusion of full assimilation.

Full assimilation in immigration is usually referring to a one-way process by which the immigrants fully accept the language and/or culture of the host country. For the immigrants, in the course of cultural assimilation, they usually give up their original cultural attributes and heritage. Therefore, in full assimilation, in the end, the immigrants become to fully resemble and therefore indistinguishable from the members of the host country. Full assimilation for the immigrants is usually driven by a strong desire of upward mobility in the host country.

There are large-scale Jewish immigrations into America in the period between the 1880s and the 1920s, and South Asian immigration into America in the early 1960s. Those immigrants composed a large percentage of the so-called "model minority" who attach great importance to fully assimilation into mainstream American culture. Narrator Tara may be designated as one of the immigrants who are dedicated to full assimilation. However, after years of endeavor, in self-reflection, Tara realizes that her dream of full assimilation has turned into an illusion. Although she tries to rid herself off Indianness and endeavors to be considered a recognized member of her host country, Tara still fails to get fully assimilated into American culture. She finds herself caught in an in-between world. Tara confesses her bewilderments confronting two cultures and her identity crisis:

> There was a time when I could identify faces from any north Indian state ... now my radar was down, I couldn't distinguish Muslims from Hindus anymore. I wasn't even one hundred percent sure of Bengalis. I felt as though I were lost inside a Salman Rushdie novel, a once-firm identity smashed by hammer blows, melted down and reemerging as something wondrous, or grotesque.[1]

Jopi Nyman argues in his study that this smashing down of fixed identity is at the same time the formation of hybridity, defined by Homi Bhabha as a way of negotiating the past and the present:

> Such assignations of social differences—where difference is neither One nor the Other but something else besides, in-between—find their agency in a form of the "future" where the past is not originary, where the present is not simply transitory. It is, if I may stretch a point, an interstitial future, that emerge in-between the claims of the past and the needs of the present.[2]

Tara makes a clear break from her previous identity, yet she then has difficulty in becoming part of any collectivity.

The strongest opposition Tara holds against Indian culture is its fixedness in identity construction, promotion of cultural purity and social segregation. A person's identity in India is largely determined by the caste, the family, the community, the social class, the language at birth or in early childhood. In

---

[1] Bharati Mukherjee. *Desirable Daughters*[M]. New York: Hyperion Books, 2002: 195-196.
[2] Jopi Nyman. *Home, Identity, and Mobility in Contemporary Diasporic Fiction*[M]. New York: Rodopi B. V., 2009: 206.

India, a person is lost in the phantom of social hierarchy and networking with slim chance of boundary crossing or transgression. The love affair between Padma and Ronald Dey in their youth ends in failure exactly because of the fixity of identity and social hierarchy. They are not blessed by both families to get married because they do not belong to the same caste and community. Mukherjee explains in her essay, "Indian tradition forbade inter-caste, inter-language, inter-ethnic marriage. Bengali tradition discouraged even emigration; to remove oneself from Bengal was to 'pollute' true culture"[1]. In reflection, Tara strongly attacks the social segregation and holds sympathy towards Padma for her failed love affair. Tara believes that it is unreasonable and cruel to separate people with lines drawn between castes and classes. The infinity of lines, ever-smaller lines, and ever-sharper distinctions forbid love across castes and classes. Didi is a typical example of "girls of good family" who put caste duty and family reputation before love and passion.

After the immigration to America, in getting rid of her Indianness and fully assimilated into America, Tara divorces her husband, Bish. The couple is originally arranged to get married by their families. Arranged marriage, common in India, aims at preserving the so-called cultural purity and social fixity. The couple barely knows each other before their marriage and lives an unhappy marriage life in spite of Bish's tremendous economic success. Sticking to the rather old-fashioned Indian perception of love and marriage, Bish tries to maintain a typical patriarchal family structure with everything in his firm control. Tara recalls that to Bish, love is synonymous to responsibility and honor. To love is to provide for parents and family, contribute to good causes and community charities, and gain recognition for hard work and honesty. Bish stays put mentally in traditional Indian ways despite his Western education and a decade of living in America. For instance, in Bish's perception, "America made children soft in the brain as well as the body, it weakened the moral fiber"[2]. In order to steer his son through the pitfalls and temptations of the American life, he even manages to build a community school similar to those in India in

---

[1] Bharati Mukherjee. Beyond Multiculturalism: Surviving the Nineties [J]. *Journal of Modern Literature*, 1996, 20(1): 30.

[2] Bharati Mukherjee. *Desirable Daughters*[M]. New York: Hyperion Books, 2002: 154.

an attempt to raise his son in Indian ways. It is fair to say that Bish is an expatriate in his refusal of full assimilation. On the contrary, Tara is an immigrant who is anxious to get fully assimilated into the host culture. Tara's willingness to cut her past and adapt to American culture stands in sharp contrast with Bish's patriarchal ideology and adherence to Indian culture and tradition. The couple's sharply different perceptions and orientations finally lead to the failure of the marriage.

After the divorce, Tara is free to fulfill her dream of full assimilation. She begins her new life in a rather American way. She buys and redecorates her own house, raises her son Babi as a single mother, and gets a live-in lover, Andy. Andy is a Hungarian immigrant to America, who resembles Jasmine in *Jasmine* a lot in his attitude of severing all ties to his past in order to get fully assimilated. Andy never has deep interest in Tara's Indian past and he strongly opposes Tara's digging into the past. In a similar way, although he visits his friends from homeland now and then, he seldom talks about his previous experiences before immigration to America. He is quite Americanized in spirit, although he talks a lot about Buddhism and Zen. Cutting all his connections with his past, he is determined to seize the day and enjoy himself. For him, past experiences and home culture are to be shunned and forgotten. It is only natural that when Tara becomes obsessed with getting connected once more with her past, Andy breaks up with her immediately.

For Tara, full assimilation is quite a different case. In the first few years after her divorce, Tara enjoys her Americanization. She wears jeans and behaves just like an independent American woman would do. Getting rid of fixity of Indian identity, she enjoys her anonymity in American life, "I am not 'Asian', which is reserved for what in outdated textbooks used to be called 'Oriental', I'm all things ... I thrive on this invisibility. It frees me to make myself over, by the hour"[1].

However, Tara gradually realizes that it is not always so easy to get fully mingled with the Americans. People never stop asking questions about India or casting curious glances upon her Oriental appearance. The daily Othering process fixes Tara as the permanent Oriental Other, without any real sense of belonging.

---

[1] Bharati Mukherjee. *Desirable Daughters*[M]. New York: Hyperion Books, 2002: 78.

Tara feels sick of being an outsider and having to explain India to Americans all the time. The constant frustrations force Tara to doubt the possibility of full assimilation, "I am convinced. I don't belong here (America), despite my political learning; worse, I don't want to belong"[1]. Tara comes to the realization that she dwelled in a liminal space, "[m]aybe I really was between two lives"[2].

The bombing of Tara's own house in California symbolizes the failure of Tara's full assimilation. Tara is deeply attached to the new home that she buys and redecorates after divorce. She watches it grow from demolition to completion with a kind of maternal tenderness that a mother feels towards her baby. In *The Politics of Home*, Rosemary George examines the role of homes in gendered identity construction, arguing that "home is a way of establishing difference ... along with gender/sexuality, race, and class, [it] acts as an ideological determinant of the subject"[3]. Tara's new home cannot be compared with those of her father's and Bish's in term of magnitude. However, the home is of vital importance for the identity construction of Tara. The homes of Tara's father and Bish constitute what Rosemary George refers to as "private sphere of patriarchal hierarchy, gendered self-identity, shelter, comfort, nurture, and protection"[4]. It is at her home, for the first time in her life that Tara is not under control of patriarchal leaders, father and husband, and is free to construct her own identity. By getting rid of the fixity of identity, Tara tries to escape from the constraints of Indian community and culture. The American-styled home represents an American ideology of freedom and full assimilation. However, the freedom and full assimilation symbolized by the home is smashed down by the Indian ethnic terrorists' bombing.

In self-reflection, Tara realizes that full assimilation which carries with it the derogation of one culture and preference of another may not be the best policy for immigrants. Tara compares Andy's American style recklessness and

---

[1] Bharati Mukherjee. *Desirable Daughters*[M]. New York: Hyperion Books, 2002: 79.
[2] Bharati Mukherjee. *Desirable Daughters*[M]. New York: Hyperion Books, 2002: 251.
[3] Rosemary Marangoly George. *The Politics of Home: Postcolonial Relocations and Twentieth-Century Fiction*[M]. Cambridge: Cambridge UP, 1996: 2.
[4] Rosemary Marangoly George. *The Politics of Home: Postcolonial Relocations and Twentieth-Century Fiction*[M]. Cambridge: Cambridge UP, 1996: 1.

evasion of burden with Bish's Indian virtue of sacrifice and duty honoring. Gradually, Tara comes to the realization that each culture may have its merits and defects, and cultures do not necessarily conflict with each other. Different cultures may coexist and complement each other, such as the spiritualism of the East may well serve to balance the liberalism of the West.

After Tara's disillusion of full assimilation, she begins to see more clearly the ugly sides of American life, the open drug market in the street, murders and terrorist attacks associated with materialism, etc. To seek spiritual redemption and a reference point for solutions, Tara takes her son Rabi with her and returns to her parents' place back in India. As a second-generation immigrant, Rabi is an English-only American who is born and growing up in America entirely except for occasional and brief visits back to India. Therefore, Rabi is quite American in spirit despite his Indian appearance. He firmly sticks to his American identity, feeling that he belongs to America and holds a rather low opinion about Indian culture. Rabi constantly criticizes his mother's Indian radar, her Indian way of distrust towards others, and her roundabout Indian way of communication. However, when he stays for a longer period with his grandfather in India, he begins to see the virtue of Indian culture. Tara's father believes in the orthodox Hinduism. After his retirement, to achieve his spiritual elevation, he moves to a remote countryside, spending most of his time in direct communication with God and reading Indian books. Rabi finds his grandfather's Indian way of meditation and reading fascinating. And the grandfather is willing to introduce Indian cultural heritage and tradition to his rather Americanized grandson. Gradually, Rabi learns to respect the Indian culture and becomes "engrossed by the saint's lectures, sayings, and religious verses"[1], from which he gains strength and insight. Rabi's appraisal of Indian culture is quite significant in that it is not a returning to Indian culture from the American one, but rather it is symbolic of the fusion of the two cultures.

Tara's disillusion of full assimilation carries with it profound significance. For full assimilation, namely Americanization in this novel, in nature is the privilege of one culture, American culture, over another, Indian one. This privilege is still in line with the Eurocentric binary construction. The binary

---

[1] Bharati Mukherjee. *Desirable Daughters*[M]. New York: Hyperion Books, 2002: 297.

construction leads to cultural exclusion and antagonist cultural conflicts. Therefore, full assimilation could be as detrimental as ghettoization and narrow nationalism for the immigrants' adaptation. Tara's self-reflection concerning different cultural affiliations shows that openness to different cultures and transcendence of essentialist attitudes are of vital importance for the immigrants to get settled down in the host country.

3.2 *The Tree Bride*: Criticism of Colonial History and Re-evaluation of Homeland Culture

Clifford points out that "ethnic writing often becomes an act of retrieval ... It is often an intentional reconstruction of a textual identity, an act of conscious self-fashioning performed from the margins"[1]. In the sequel to *Desirable Daughters*, Mukherjee writes about roots search in *The Tree Bride*. In retrieval, the novel reflects in-depth self-reflection with the protagonist Tara renegotiating her identities in a larger context.

In writing a book about her ancestor, the Tree Bride, her namesake great-great aunt, Tara Lata, the narrator Tara embarks on a roots search. By piecing clusters of episodes and fragments together, Tara writes mainly about events that happened during and after the Indian Independent Movement. Tara's writing involves a confluence of self-reflection and a strong sense of history. In the act of writing, Tara, being an observer and an organizer of events into narrative, gains more insights about her own immigration. With its strong autobiographical features, the novel also reflects Mukherjee's contemplation about decolonization and how it illuminates the immigrants' present conditions.

Decolonization could be a long process. In *The Wretched of the Earth*, Fanon defines decolonization as "a process of thorough social transformation that disorganizes the stratified social hierarchy beyond the nationalist party's capture of the state from the colonizer"[2]. Lisa Lowe in her study sheds light on postcolonial writers' interest in history writing:

---

[1] Krystyna Zamorska. Ethnic Fictions: Cultural Mediations in Contemporary American Writing[D]. The City University of New York, 2006: 5.

[2] Lisa Lowe. *Immigrant Acts*[M]. London: Duke UP, 1996: 107.

If we understand "decolonization" as an ongoing disruption of the colonial mode of production, then Asian American writing performs that displacement from a social formation marked by the uneven and unsynthetic encounters of colonial, neocolonial, and mass and elite indigenous cultures that characterize decolonization. These material pressures produce texts that resist the formal abstraction of aestheticization that is a legacy of European modernism and a continuing feature of European postmodernism. In this sense, the writing of the "decolonizing novel" takes place necessarily by way of a detour into the excavation of "history" ... [1]

Digging into history, the narrator Tara tries to build a bigger picture of Indian culture during and after the Indian Independence. In writing about decolonization, the modern Tara gains a better understanding of the sins and traumas of colonial ruling and the strength of Indian culture and its people represented by the Tree Bride; therefore, she can be in a better position to get re-rooted in the modern metropolis.

In her roots search, Tara condemns sins and traumas caused by the Empire's colonial rulings. The first major sin of British colonial ruling that Tara digs out is the Empire's economic exploitation of Indian colony and the sufferings that it causes. For example, Tara points out that to support economic exploitation, the British policies aggravate famines which lead to the death of millions of natives:

> It was the wealth of India that underwrote the industrial and commercial prosperity of England ... In the nineteenth century, twenty-five million Indians were allowed to starve because India's "excess" harvests were shipped to England. Commodity brokers were encouraged to hoard and speculate ... Recurrent starvation was blamed on Indian laziness, on their beastly, fatalistic religion, their money-lending banias and corrupt Brahmins, and it served as the ultimate colonial sanction.[2]

According to scholars, under British rule, incidence of severe famine was on the rise in India, especially in the late eighteenth and the nineteenth centuries.

---

[1] Lisa Lowe. *Immigrant Acts*[M]. London: Duke UP, 1996: 108.
[2] Bharati Mukherjee. *Desirable Daughters*[M]. New York: Hyperion Books, 2002: 45.

Besides weather and crop conditions, British colonial policies and responses to famine in a large degree deteriorated the situation. A typical example is that in the 1877—1879 famine, Lord Lytton, the governing British Viceroy in India, strongly opposed relief and instructed his subordinates to discourage relief works in every possible way. He believed that the situation was not severe enough for opening a relief work. Scholar Mike Davis terms the famines of the 1870s and the 1890s "Late Victorian Holocausts", which reflects the British government's ferocious policies and vices in dealing with the famines in India.

The cold-blooded sins committed to the colonized by the colonizer with the purpose of maintaining long-term colonial ruling proves outrageous. By digging into the colonial history, the modern Tara lays bare the sins of colonialism. Holding up the lamp of civilization, the British colonial ruling in India caused more disasters by skimming away economic profits and leaving the Indian colony in poverty and its native people devastated. According to the study conducted by Davis:

> There was no increase in India's per capita income from 1757 to 1947. Indeed, in the last half of the nineteenth century, income probably declined by more than 50 percent. There was no economic at all in the usual sense of the term ... Moreover in the age of Kipling, "that glorious imperial half century" from 1872 to 1921, the life expectancy of ordinary Indians fell by a staggering 20 percent, a deterioration in human health probably without precedent in the subcontinent's long history of war and invasion.[1]

In colonial ruling, the Empire cruelly harnessed the natives to scramble for wealth. Tara sees through the true nature of colonial ruling and writes down her newly gained insight, "[a]ll the could-have-beens and should-have-beens of history, the best of the East meeting the best of the West, etc., shrink from grandeur to petty profit-taking"[2].

Tara further studies the trauma of British colonial ruling and its subsequent

---

[1] Mike Davis. *Late Victorian Holocausts: El Nino Famine and the Making of the Third World*[M]. London: Verso Books, 2001: 311-312.

[2] Bharati Mukherjee. *Desirable Daughters*[M]. New York: Hyperion Books, 2002: 48.

Partition. During the period of the British colonial ruling, the colonizer set one group of the colonized against another, aggravating the already existing caste and class segregation in India to facilitate their imperial ruling and exploitation. Scholars have explored the trauma of the Partition in 1947. Urvashi Butalia points out that in the Partition "an estimated one million people died from violence, malnutrition, and disease; twelve million people were displaced; acts of 'sexual savagery' were committed against approximately 75,000 women thought to have been kidnapped and raped; and thousands of families were divided, losing their loved ones as well as all of their land and possessions"[1].

In both Indian and Pakistani cultures, the Partition and the violence associated with it is a major national trauma, which has recently become a major theme in postcolonial literature. Chaman Nahal's *Azadi*, Anita Desai's *Clear Light of Day*, and Amitav Ghosh's *The Shadow Lines* all explore the Partition and its trauma. In fact, there is already a monograph named *The Theme of Partition in Indian English Novels: A Select Study* dedicated to the study of the theme of the Partition in novels. The relocation caused by the Partition affects millions of Indians both physically and mentally. The Partition and the following relocation are considered as one of the major causes of the sense of loss and displacement that haunt so many previous colonized in the postcolonial age. In reflection, Tara realizes that Muslims are not to blame for the large scale of relocation in India and the Partition has already begun long before the ending of the British colonial ruling. To rule the large population in Indian colony with its troops and realize its economic exploitation, the British government employs divide and rule colonial policy:

> Thirty thousand British bureaucrats and "factors" were able to rule ten thousand times more Indian by dividing Muslims from Hindus, Persian Zoroastrains from Muslims, Sikhs from Hindus, and nearly everyone, including Hindus, from castes like lazy Brahmins and money-grubbing banias ... But behind gymkhana doors, all of us, martial races or not, fair-skinned or dark, were referred to as niggers.[2]

---

[1] Urvashi Butalia. *The Other Side of Silence: Voices from the Partition of India*[M]. Durham: Duke UP, 2000: 3.

[2] Bharati Mukherjee. *Desirable Daughters*[M]. New York: Hyperion Books, 2002: 44.

Caste in India is a birth-ascribed, interdependent, and hierarchically ranked system which is usually associated with a traditional occupation. According to the study of Gerald D. Berreman, "[t]he rationale which justifies the system is both religious and philosophical, relying upon the idea of ritual purity and pollution to explain group rank, and upon the notions of right conduct (dharma), just deserts (Karma), and rebirth to explain the individual's fate within the system"[1].

Under British colonial ruling between the late nineteenth century and the early twentieth century, the British government worked closely with higher casters in their administration and control of the colony. The British colonial strata working in combination with the traditional caste system, further segregated Indian society, which led to the almost impossibility of individual social mobility and the silencing of the lower casters in social affairs. This system worked well to serve the purpose of British colonial ruling by buying out some colonized to support and collaborate with the colonizer and divide the colonized from within. The resulting social stratification and fixity of individual identity troubled and afflicted the previously colonized even decades after their gaining of national independence.

Ambreen Hai argues in his study that "postcolonial narrative is ... a trauma narrative ... its function is to reclaim agency both by remembering belatedly, and by trying to heal, to undo that trauma by recalling in a public venue—but in the mode of the personal—the violence of nation formation"[2]. In *The Tree Bride*, Tara digs into the colonial history to gain insight for the future. In her case, agency is also gained by seeing through the hypocrisy and cruelty of a specific racist colonizer, Vertie Treadwell. Treadwell is appointed District Commissioner of Mishtigunj in 1930 and returns to England after the Partition in 1947. He comes from a family which has become prosperous because of colonialism and from an early age, he is soaked in the Empire's civilization propaganda. He would listen to the stories of the Empire's territorial expansion in

---

[1] Gerald D. Berreman. Race, Caste, and Other Invidious Distinctions in Social Stratification[J]. *Race Class*, 1972, 13(4): 389.

[2] Ambreen Hai. Border Work, Border Trouble: Postcolonial Feminism and the Ayah in Bapsi Sidhwa's Cracking India[J]. *Modern Fiction Studies*, 2000(46): 388.

India, the Straits and East Africa. He would lament on the backwardness of the British colonies and assume that it is his responsibility or burden to serve the Empire to civilize the colonies. He would envision that he, in his glorious mission, would defend the British garrison and bring order and dignity to the ignorant and ungrateful Orientals.

In his post as DC of Mishtigunj, Treadwell is determined to carry out the civilization missions. He assumes that the Crown would be ruling India forever and therefore keeps a meticulous record of weather data and names every living thing in his district, every fruit, flower, every crawling, flying and swimming creature, in at least three languages. He believes that "only through the Adamic naming process can a conqueror be at ease and expect compliance from his subject"[1]. Said discusses the nature of this kind of knowledge in *Orientalism*:

> Under the general heading of knowledge of the Orient ... there emerged a complex Orient suitable for study in the academy ... for theoretical illustration anthropological, biological, linguistic, racial and historical theses about mankind and the universe ... the imaginative examination of things Oriental was based more or less exclusively upon a sovereign Western consciousness out of whose unchallenged centrality an Oriental world emerge, first according to general ideas about who or what was an Oriental, then according to a detailed logic governed not simply empirical reality but by a battery of desires, repressions, investments, and projections.[2]

Orientalism is, according to Said, "the corporate institution dealing with the Orient"[3], while the production and control of knowledge is in the center of the "institution". The colonizers wield the power to name and define, with the ultimate goal to rule and control. Looma has also pointed out that "through the 'objectivity' of observation and science, European penetration into other lands is legitimized"[4]. Treadwell's "scientific" recording and naming is the mechanism of the "institution" at work.

---

[1] Bharati Mukherjee. *The Tree Bride*[M]. New York: Hyperion Books, 2004: 174.
[2] Edward W. Said. *Orientalism*[M]. New York: Vintage Books, 1979: 7,8.
[3] Edward W. Said. *Orientalism*[M]. New York: Vintage Books, 1979: 482.
[4] Ania Loomba. *Colonialism/Postcolonialism*[M]. New York: Routledge, 1998: 61.

Treadwell also tries in various other ways to promote the so-called manly virtues of the White, namely, discipline, rigor, and morality. Pramod K. Nayar points out that the colonial civilizing intervention is often two-folded: material-technological and moral, "[t]he first aimed at a radical and visible change in the condition of the native cities, economy, the infrastructure and the institutions. The second aimed at a change in belief systems, native ways of thinking, 'character-building' of the natives and such 'abstract' domains"[1]. Treadwell tries to accomplish the character-building of the natives by promoting cricket in India. He believes that through introducing cricket wherever he is appointed as a colonial official, he can promote manly virtues, such as healthy competition, respect for rules, modesty in victory, dignity in defeat, etc. Cricket was originated in England in the sixteenth century. In the eighteenth century, it gained more popularity and gradually developed to be the national sport of England. Treadwell introduces cricket to India as an attempt to build the so-called manly virtues of the natives. However, all his efforts fail due to the natives' refusal to cooperate wholeheartedly.

Treadwell blames the Indian's ungratefulness for the ending of British colonial ruling. Especially, Treadwell holds grudge against those "first-class hypocrites" that the Empire creates, who come to England to receive Western education and then return to India, using their knowledge in fighting against the Empire. For Treadwell, Mohandas K. Gandhi is a typical example of this kind of hypocrites. The withdrawal of the Empire's colonial ruling in India deals a heavy blow on Treadwell. The most unacceptable part to Treadwell is that the Indian National Independent Movement against the Empire is led by the natives who received Western education and use their knowledge in throwing over the Empire's ruling. Treadwell laments "we created these clever little Ariels and they used our own laws and language against us"[2].

Bitter with resentment and remorse, Treadwell ends his career as a colonial officer in India and returns to England in 1947. However, during his service years in India, his homeland has gone through tremendous changes and become

---

[1] Pramod K. Nayar. *Postcolonialism: A Guide for the Perplexed*[M]. New York: Continuum, 2010: 37,38.

[2] Bharati Mukherjee. *The Tree Bride*[M]. New York: Hyperion Books, 2004: 178.

much hybridized with immigrants from various countries. One day, in his walk, Treadwell seeing an Indian boy playing cricket with others in the village of his upbringing, becomes very angry that those Indians who he considers subhuman could enjoy life in his homeland with his people. The hybridity exasperates him so such that when the Indian boy yells at him to pick up the ball that lies accidently at his feet, Treadwell decides to teach him a lesson. He picks up the ball, "took a few running steps in the manner cricket had intended, rotating his arm like a propeller blade and launching it"[1]. The series of exaggerated and overstretched gestures cause him to fall and drop paralyzed into unconsciousness. The mocking depiction of the incident satirizes the Empire's idealizations of its manly masculinity and national values.

 Treadwell's hypocrisy and brutality in carrying out his civilization mission in India is further revealed in his imaginary conversation with Winston Churchill during his coma in old age. Treadwell holds strong racist opinions about the natives. For him, the Indians are "debased savages"[2], who are stuck in childhood and need constant guidance from the white. Beneath Treadwell's seemingly benevolent Orientalist stance lies the cruel profit-grabbing desire for the Empire. For instance, in time of Indian famine, Treadwell follows Mister Coughlin's order and burns tons of rice rather than distributing them as relief to the starving Indians just for the purpose of keeping the Indians from getting lazy in their future laboring for the Empire.

 Also, in his ruling district, Treadwell carries out strict racial segregation to maintain the racial hierarchy and purity. For him, racial and cultural hybridity is intolerable and the reverse assimilation of the white into the natives must be punished. This is the exact reason why Treadwell brutally executes John Mist, the founder of the town Mishtigunj where Tara Lata dwells for her life. John Mist, although born white, has gone totally native in India. He severs his ties with the white and forges an alliance between Mussalmans and Hindus. He learns to communicate in native languages and quits speaking English. John Mist's transformation is a typical example of "reverse assimilation", which refers to the White's going native and assimilating into the culture of the East. Mist's

---

[1] Bharati Mukherjee. *The Tree Bride*[M]. New York: Hyperion Books, 2004: 176-177.

[2] Bharati Mukherjee. *The Tree Bride*[M]. New York: Hyperion Books, 2004: 200.

reverse assimilation violates the racial hierarchy Treadwell works so hard to maintain that he orders the execution of John Mist by accusing him of a killing in self-defense which happened fifty years ago.

  Treadwell's wickedness and lacking of any manly value is shown in his scheming and cunning way to get the Tree Bride killed. Treadwell plans to kill the Tree Bride after he finds out that she is in active support of the nationalist movement for India Independence, which would jeopardize the British colonial ruling in India. However, the Tree Bride is revered as a goddess by the local people, which makes it rather difficult and tricky for the British authorities to get rid of her. To achieve his goal, Treadwell sets her up in a rather calculating way. He first pays a visit to her in a rather benevolent manner. In their conversation, he learns that she is quite interested in the works of George Orwell, some of which are officially banned in the colony. After the visit, Treadwell sends the Tree Bride as gifts Orwell's the then banned novel *Burmese Days* and a magazine containing Orwell's "A Hanging" in secret, which she accepts with appreciation. Soon after, Treadwell orders her arrestment and execution with the possession of proscribed literature on the top of arrest warrant. Treadwell brags conceitedly to the imaginary Churchill in retrospect, "I knew she possessed them, because I had been their purveyor"[1]. Treadwell is a typical colonial ruler, who would scheme and kill brutally in maintaining the ruling and exploitation of the Empire in its colony. The unconscious and imaginary conversation with the Prime Minister, Winston Churchill, brings his scheming and brutal nature into light.

  In *The Tree Bride*, there is no linear narrative of the Empire's history of colonial ruling in India and no full account of the brutal suppressions of the Indian Independence Movement. Instead, the novel contains episodes and scenes which lay bare the atrocities committed by British troops and police against Indian nationalist fighters and unarmed villagers in the district of Mishtigunj. The novel juxtaposes two figures, the colonial ruler Vertie Treadwell and the legendary Tree Bride, Tara Lata. In the depiction of Treadwell, the hypocrisy, brutality and exploitative nature of the colonizer is revealed and strongly attacked. In the portrayal of the heroic figure, the Tree Bride, the vision, open-

---

[1] Bharati Mukherjee. *The Tree Bride*[M]. New York: Hyperion Books, 2004: 209.

mindedness, generosity, courage and tenacity of the Indian people are affirmed.

Tara Lata gets to be known as the Tree Bride after her child groom is killed by the snakebite in her child wedding ceremony and her father formally marries her to a tree, which is a bold and visionary decision intended to save her from the miserable prospect of becoming a widow who brought bad luck to the family. In her whole life, she seldom sets foot outside her house. Yet, she wins herself love and reverence, and turns herself into a goddess figure among the natives with her strength of character, her vision, open-mindedness, generosity, courage and tenacity. In reflection, the modern Tara believes that the Tree Bride represents the best quality of Indian culture and national strength.

Tara Lara's vision is first shown in her realization that education is of ultimate importance in founding a national consciousness and winning national independence. In the colonial period of time, the Empire limited the education to the native elites only and deprived Indian people from lower social classes and castes of the opportunity to receive education. Besides, the Empire had enforced English as the "language of command" replacing both Persian and Sanskrit as the official languages in Indian colony. As a result, English instead of the native languages was taught to the elites in India and at the same time English literary works were promoted, while Indian literature was often dismissed as worthless. Lord Macaulay's "Minute on Education" in 1935 was a benchmark work of the Empire's educational policy in colonies. Macaulay advocated that English should be taught in India and English literature should also be introduced for:

> The dialects commonly spoken among the natives of this part of India contain neither literary nor scientific information, and are moreover so poor and rude that, until they are enriched from some other quarter, it will not be easy to translate any valuable work into them ... a single shelf of a good European library was worth the whole native literature of India and Arabia.[1]

Actually, Macaulay's promotion of English language and literature aimed at creating surrogates for the Empire among the natives, especially among the

---

[1] George Anderson & Manilal Bhagwandes Subedar. *The Development of an Indian Policy (1818–1858)*[M]. London: G. Bell, 1921: 113.

elites, who would acquire the tastes and value system of the Empire and cooperate willingly with the white in the colonial ruling. Narrator Tara observes, for Macaulay, the British adventurers who embraced Hindu and Muslim practices might not be loyal any more. On the contrary, it was easier to control natives who were desirous of the English language and Western values and turned into surrogate Englishmen. In his work, *The Gift of English* (2009), Alok Mukherjee points out that the colonial system uses English education "as a way of imposing and reinforcing their dominance"[1]. The Tree Bride sees through the nature of English education and endeavors to correct it.

Tara Lata masters three different languages and is well-versed in both English and Indian literature. Although Tara Lata is open-minded to absorb knowledge from both the West and the East, she is clearly-minded not to cooperate with British colonial ruling mechanism. She is visionary to see the importance of the natives' education in the founding of the independent nation. Therefore, since her youth, Tara Lata has begun her mission of spreading education to her countrymen, "she'd trained all her servants to read and write and then she'd sent them out into the villages to teach five others"[2]. She regards the education of the natives as a way to preserve the fine quality of Indian culture and raise national consciousness among the natives. In order to spread literary reading materials to more common villagers, she turns her house into a veritable printing press. Her spreading of education and literature helps the natives around her understand more deeply the tyranny of the colonial ruling, the preciousness of freedom and the importance of Indian national independence.

For Tara Lata, the education of English language and literature opens her mind and serves the counter purpose of that desired by the Empire. Occasionally, she tries to use the Master's tool in the fight against the Master. In conversation with Treadwell during his first visit to her house, Tara purposefully mentions the novel *Burmese Days*. The novel, set in the 1920s, the last days of the Empire's ruling in Burma, contains fierce criticism on the exploitative nature of colonial ruling and other dark sides of the British Raj. Besides, the author George Orwell himself has served as an imperial policeman in Burma in the

---

[1] Pramod K. Nayar. *Postcolonialism: A Guide for the Perplexed*[M]. New York: Continuum, 2010: 51.
[2] Bharati Mukherjee. *The Tree Bride*[M]. New York: Hyperion Books, 2004: 212.

1920s. Therefore, the novel may be considered to have been written from an Empire insider's point of view against its own policies. Tara Lata mentions the book to Treadwell in an attempt to solicit him to reconsider the Empire's cruel deeds and tyrannical policies in India. Tara's attempt, although fails, is a very smart move in trying to turn the colonizer round.

The modern Tara also appreciates the open-mindedness and generosity of the Tree Bride. Tara Lara constantly breaks social hierarchy, class and caste segregation, "her house was open to all"[1]. She treats all country men as equals and provides help for whoever needs regardless of social status. Local people no longer see her as a rich, high caste virgin widow, but as "a teacher of literary, distributor of grains, and occasional oracle on subjects of Indian freedom and communal harmony"[2]. In order to support Gandhi's Salt March, the Tree Bride donates her buried dowry gold. Her donation is so generous that it arouses the attention of the Congress officials. They are amazed to learn that a remote village has contributed more to the national liberation movement than some of the richest cities. The Tree Bride's open-mindedness and generosity win her reverence and veneration. In the eyes of the natives around her, she has become a goddess to pray to in time of difficulty and need.

Tara Lara also demonstrates courage and tenacity in her active participation in the Indian Independent Movement. With narrator Tara's digging into history and weaving together fragments and episodes, the Tree Bride turns from a hazy folkloric figure into a fighter in the struggle for freedom and liberation. Echoing Gandhi, Tara Lara says, "No boy is too young, no sudra too poor, no woman too weak, to fight for the freedom of India."[3] She stands up bravely to accuse the British colonial authorities of the atrocities committed by British troops and police against unarmed villagers in the district of Mishtigunj. She keeps records of the brutal killings and constantly searches for an outlet to expose the colonial sins to the world. Her activities draw the attention from the colonial authorities. Eventually, she is set up by the colonial officer Treadwell which leads to her subsequent imprisonment and mysterious death there. However, her courage and

---

[1] Bharati Mukherjee. *The Tree Bride*[M]. New York: Hyperion Books, 2004: 255.
[2] Bharati Mukherjee. *The Tree Bride*[M]. New York: Hyperion Books, 2004: 255.
[3] Bharati Mukherjee. *The Tree Bride*[M]. New York: Hyperion Books, 2004: 61.

tenacity inspire so many around her to dedicate to the cause of decolonization.

Tara Lata represents the best quality of Indian culture and its people. In conjuring up the life story of the Tree Bride, modern Tara realizes that under colonial rulings, true communication between the two great cultures of the world, the English culture and the Bengali culture, is impossible. In order to maintain its colonial rulings and continue its exploitation, the Empire promotes racial ideas and the Orientalist discourse which runs against cultural fusion and adds to the adversity between different cultures. The Tree Bride is put to death because of her efforts in preserving Indian culture and founding an independent nation which would be in a position to communicate on equal footing with other nations in the world.

Besides it is equally harmful to shun communication between cultures in today's world which is becoming so connected and globalized. In Tara's reflection, getting rid of imperialism and racism, and stressing openness towards different cultures should be recommended. At the end of the novel, Tara returns to Kashi to conduct a cremation for the Tree Bride. By liberating the soul of her ancestor, Tara believes that she also comes to term with a phase of history and two cultures. To sum up, the novel deepens the dimensions of immigration literature by the means of illuminating the present by reflecting upon history.

The self-reflection in immigration represents further maturity of Mukherjee's aesthetics of fusion. The self-reflection is quite critical. In self-reflection, to get better re-rooted in the host country, the immigrant protagonist compares different cultural affiliations and resumes her faith in the strength of her homeland culture. The protagonist realizes that expatriation in ghettoization, narrow nationalism, as well as full assimilation with their essentialist bias cannot lead to true fusion of cultures and peoples. Condemning sins of colonialism and terrorist attacks rising out of ethnic hatred, the protagonist begins to promote multiple cultural affiliations and openness to cultural differences, which echoes with thoughts of cosmopolitanisms.

3.3 A New Turn in Mukherjee's Writing of Immigration

Recent years witness a new turn in Mukherjee's aesthetics of fusion. Her relatively recent novels *Desirable Daughters* and *The Tree Bride* show self-reflection in immigration. The autobiographical protagonist Tara begins to re-evaluate different cultural affiliations, which reflect Mukherjee's more serious self-reflection of her own stance and cultural affiliation after years of living in America as an immigrant writer. Reflected in her novels, besides being still strongly contemptuous of expatriate sentiments, she becomes more critical of the pitfalls of narrow nationalism's appeals for ethnic purity and cultural originality. What is most noteworthy is that Mukherjee begins to realize the impossibility of full assimilation which she advocates so strongly in her early years of immigrant writing. In the two novels, the protagonist's repeated frustration and failure in attempting to get fully assimilated into America reflects Mukherjee's own disillusion with full cultural assimilation. Besides, in the two novels there appears the recurring leitmotif of roots search. In her roots search, the protagonist Tara reviews sins and trauma of British colonialism and begins to see the strength of her own culture and people. The promotion of connectedness between cultures and openness towards cultural differences reflects Mukherjee's assuming of a rooted cosmopolitan stance in her aesthetics of fusion.

In the time of writing the novel *Desirable Daughters*, Mukherjee has been dwelling and writing in America for about three decades. Having successfully established her status as a major American writer and freed herself largely from anxiety of influence, Mukherjee has begun to seriously reflect upon different cultural affiliations. *Desirable Daughters*, with its strong autobiographical features, evidently reflects Mukherjee's self-reflection.

Desirable Daughters has the strongest feature of being an autobiographical novel in characterization. The protagonist and narrator Tara Chatterjee bears strong resemblance to Mukherjee in cultural background and upbringing. Mukherjee also confirms the resemblance in an interview: "I also have two sisters. I'm playing with author-protagonist relationship in ways that I haven't before. I think it's because I want to write an autobiography, but I just can't bring myself to. You created masks."[1] The three sisters Tara, Parvati and Padma in the novel strongly resemble Mukherjee, her younger sister Ranu, and

---

[1] Verena Esterbauer. *The Immigrants' Search for Identity* [M]. Saarbrucken: VDM Verlag Dr. Mullter, 2008: 81.

another sister Mira in life experiences and cultural affiliations. Like Tara and her sisters in the novel, Mukherjee and her sisters also come from top caste and top family in India. However, after adulthood, the three sisters begin to represent three different ways of belongings. Ranu stays in India and has become in Mukherjee's words, "the ideal modern Indian womanhood"[1], while Mira and Mukherjee both migrate to America. But Mira and Mukherjee are quite different in that Mira sticks to expatriate sentiments, while Mukherjee openly advocates assimilation into the host culture. In *Desirable Daughters*, in self-reflection, the protagonist Tara considers Parvati's nationalist stance as too narrow-minded, while Padma's expatriate sentiment as pathetic and profit-driven in nature. However, at the same time, Tara has to face her own disillusion of full assimilation. To a large degree, the protagonist Tara's perceptions reflect those of Mukherjee's. In Mukherjee's opinion, the new narrow nationalist status, in Ranu's case, although hard earned, still carries with it so many visible or invisible constraints. In today's hybrid world, narrow nationalism, with its promotion of cultural purity and essentialism, bears many resemblances to the Eurocentric racial discourse. In nature, it is still a binary construction, only this time, the West and the White are projected as the Others. Ghettoization is what Mukherjee deplores. In ghettoized life, viewing expatriate sentiment as a sign of integrity, some inhabitants resist change and adaption. Their behaviors are, in Mukherjee's words, "using the Old Culture as a shield against the New"[2]. In discussing this kind of cultural affiliation, Mukherjee once takes her sister Mira as an example. Mira, who has stayed in America since 1960, refuses to adapt and thus suffers in nostalgia for an imaginary homeland. In her short article of memoir, Mukherjee writes, "I recognize Mira's pain as real. I understand her survivor's need of nostalgia for a homeland she doesn't have to live in and experience the gritty aggravations of every day. But ... her expatriate stance of stubborn resistance to America seems a sad waste"[3].

---

[1] Bharati Mukherjee & Suzanne Ruta. Decoding the Language: Bharati Mukherjee Tells Suzanne Ruta Some of the Stories behind "Desirable Daughters"[J]. *The Women's Review of Books*, 2002(19): 13.
[2] Claudine Chiawei O'Hearn. *Half and Half: Writers on Growing Up Biracial and Bicultural*[M]. New York: Pantheon Books, 1998: 78.
[3] Claudine Chiawei O'Hearn. *Half and Half: Writers on Growing Up Biracial and Bicultural*[M]. New York: Pantheon Books, 1998: 79.

While criticizing both narrow nationalism and ghettoization, Mukherjee apparently reconsiders full assimilation. Novels written in Mukherjee's early immigrant phase of writing reflect her strong urge to get assimilated into one culture (American culture) while severing the other one (Indian culture) totally. While in her more recent novels, for example, *Desirable Daughters* and *The Tree Bride*, Mukherjee depicts disillusion of full assimilation. Mukherjee explains that "the point is not to adopt the mainstream American's easy ironies nor the expatriate's self-protective contempt for the 'vulgarity' of immigration. The point is to stay resilient and compassionate in the face of change"[1]. To stay resilient and compassionate in the face of change is closely associated with Mukherjee's aesthetics of fusion. To get re-rooted in the host country, one has to take a courageous attitude to break fixed identity, cross boundaries in binary constructions and remain open to cultural differences.

Interestingly enough, in her early expatriate phase of writing, Mukherjee has also written a novel called *The Tiger's Daughter* with the protagonist similarly named Tara. After the publication of the novel, it is widely acknowledged among critics that the protagonist Tara is an autobiographical representation of the author herself. It would be rewarding to compare the journeys both protagonists made back to India after staying in America for many years as immigrants. The two Taras view the journeys and the Indianness quite differently, which reflects Mukherjee's change of perception concerning migrancy in more than thirty years of writing. In *The Tiger's Daughter*, everything associated with Western culture is portrayed in a bright light, while Indian cultural heritage and traditions are more often than not associated with backwardness, conservatism and negative connotations. Drawing to the end of the novel, Tara realizes that the only solution for all her predicaments is to get assimilated into America and cut all her Indian ties. While in *Desirable Daughters*, after a series of setbacks in her full assimilation into American culture, the protagonist Tara returns to India to seek strength to carry on with her life in the metropolitan center. In this novel, Indian culture, especially the fine quality of its people is viewed in a more positive light. The contrast between

---

[1] Claudine Chiawei O'Hearn. *Half and Half: Writers on Growing Up Biracial and Bicultural*[M]. New York: Pantheon Books, 1998: 79.

the two Taras' perceptions reflects Mukherjee's changed attitude towards assimilation. In early immigrant phase of writing, Mukherjee advocates assimilation, while in recent years, she has become to be more objective and critical concerning assimilation.

Mukherjee discusses her writing of the immigrants' journeys back home and roots search in *Desirable Daughters* in an interview,

> I wanted to go back to the beginning of the story from a very different perspective in that last paragraph of the book, back to the crowds, to the vendors and the children in 1879. The scene hasn't changed, the people, the sounds haven't changed, but the narrator suddenly realizes, "This is my heritage in ways that I never understood, never cared about, and I have to make sense of it and put it down in writing."[1]

In writing down the immigrants' roots search anew, Mukherjee advocates the value of one's home culture, while at the same time emphasizes the importance of tolerance and openness to different cultures.

The leitmotif of roots search continues into her next novel *The Tree Bride*. Roots search is a commonly explored theme in literary writings. Saul Bellow's *Herzog* and V. S. Naipaul's Indian trilogy are typical texts. Roots search in history retrievals can help the previously colonized build their national consciousness, but it can also be detrimental. Bhabha once quotes Fanon's criticism:

> Fanon recognizes the crucial importance, for subordinated peoples, of asserting their indigenous cultural traditions and retrieving their repressed histories. But he is far too aware of the dangers of the fixity and fetishism of identities within the calcification of colonial cultures to recommend that "roots" be struck in the celebratory romance of the past or by homogenizing the history of the present.[2]

---

[1] Bharati Mukherjee & Suzanne Ruta. Decoding the Language: Bharati Mukherjee Tells Suzanne Ruta Some of the Stories behind "Desirable Daughters"[J]. *The Women's Review of Books*, 2002(19): 13.

[2] Homi K. Bhabha. *The Location of Culture*[M]. London: Routledge, 1994: 9.

The roots search of the protagonist in *Desirable Daughters* and *The Tree Bride* does not aim at finding an essentialist myth of origin or fixing her identity to a single place. In the roots search, Tara strongly criticizes the imperial violence in the colonial past and ethnic terroristic attacks in the postcolonial era. In her roots search, Tara deconstructs the fixedness of identity construction, gains further agency in her hybridity and forms a more open-minded attitude towards cultural differences.

Mukherjee's writing of roots search does not aim at reflecting the anguish of alienation as in Bellow's *Herzog*. Instead, the roots search traverses locality to favor multiple cosmopolitan affiliations. The return of the native in the roots search sees different pictures. In his three India books, *An Area of Darkness*, *India: A Wounded Civilization*, and *India: A Million Mutinies Now*, to celebrate rootlessness, Naipaul depicts India in a very demeaning way and sees mainly degrading sides of India culture and its people. On the contrary, in *Desirable Daughters* and *The Tree Bride*, to advocate re-rooting, Mukherjee portrays India in a quite positive light. Her protagonist sees and values the strength in Indian national consciousness, which will sustain the immigrants to get better re-rooted in the cosmopolitan centers. Therefore, to sum up, the roots search in Mukherjee's novels loses its fixed spatial sense in abstraction and becomes efforts to gain sustaining strength in one's multiple affiliations. The return to the roots symbolizes new departure and new arrival, which celebrates multiplicity of identities across space and time.

Critics have found the similar turn in roots search in other immigrant writers' writings. For instance, in Chen Xiaohui's study of Chinese American women writers, he analyzes Jade Snow Wong's writing of roots search in her novels. Jade Snow Wong, also known as Connie Wong, is one of best first generation Chinese American writers, well-known for her two autobiographical novels, *Fifth Chinese Daughter* and *No Chinese Stranger*. Jade Snow Wong's first autobiographical novel *Fifth Chinese Daughter* dealing with the protagonist's identity construction contains many derogative depictions of Chinese culture and tradition. It is often under fierce criticism for its Orientalist stance. However, in the second autobiographical novel, *No Chinese Stranger*, Jade Snow Wong writes about the protagonist's roots search back to China. The depiction of the roots search shows Wong's appreciation for Chinese culture and tradition. In their more mature writings, immigrant writers' reaffirmation of their homeland culture shows their multiple cultural affiliations, to the cultures of both their homeland and their host country. The openness to different cultures and multiple cultural affiliations are in line with thoughts of cosmopolitanism, especially those of rooted cosmopolitanism.

The term "cosmopolitanism" originally refers to a kind of ideal and utopian status of global citizenship. Socrates used the term in his avoidance of traditional political engagement and promotion of examining himself and others. The Cynics and the Stoics also adopted the term as their motifs. In his exile, Diogenes of Sinope, the founding father of the Cynic movement in Ancient Greece once claimed, "I am a citizen of the world"[1]. The Stoics also promoted the concept of cosmopolitanism to represent a spiritual sense of interconnectedness and an aesthetic interest in difference.

The concept of cosmopolitanism evolves over time. In modern time, Rousseau, Kant and Marx all express their cosmopolitan ideas, with Kant's ideas being most widespread and influential. The German philosopher Immanuel Kant uses the term cosmopolitanism in his promotion of global peace and equal rights to all human beings. However, Derrida points out that Kant's cosmopolitanism is exclusive towards the foreigner in nature. In Derrida's interpretation, Kant's cosmopolitanism welcomes the stranger, a citizen of another country, but only on the condition that he is here to pay a visit not to stay.

William Barbieri argues that cosmopolitanism rebels against the sovereignty of individual country's territorial ruling. Therefore, besides being impractical, the promotion of cosmopolitanism will definitely result in the erasure of differences between nations and diversity between cultures. The resulting overall homogeneity is detrimental to the basic well-being of human beings.

Barbieri's opinion is important because it reflects the widely-held perception in the nineteenth and the twentieth centuries that cosmopolitanism is in direct conflict with national sovereignty. Caren Kaplan argues that cosmopolitans' non-affiliation and nomadism can be viewed as an assertion of power. Those

---

[1] Nikos Papastergiadis. *Cosmopolitanism and Culture*[M]. Malden: Polity Press, 2012: 81.

European cosmopolitans "wander and travel at will, become 'native' in 'foreign' lands while retaining their identity and power as Europeans"[1]. To sum up, the traditional European demarcation of cosmopolitanism always carries with it the Eurocentric overtone and the West's desire to conquer the world.

In contemporary cultural studies, there is a resurgence of interest in the concept of cosmopolitanism which is not totally Eurocentric in nature any more. In the introduction to *Cosmopolitanism*, Bhabha et al. assert that the study of cosmopolitanism with its growing importance involves some of most challenging problems in academic research and political practice. Yet, till now, there is no systematic school of theory concerning cosmopolitanism.

Important works published in the area of studies include Kwame Anthony Appiah's "Cosmopolitan Patriots" (1997), Charles Beitz's "Cosmopolitan Ideals and National Sentiment" (1983), *Cosmopolitanism* (2002) edited by Carol A. Breckenridge et al. *Cosmopolitics: Thinking and Feeling Beyond the Nation* (1998) edited by Pheng Cheah and Bruce Robbins, and Nikos Papastergiadis' *Cosmopolitanism and Culture* (2012), etc.

There are so many different strands of cosmopolitanism theory nowadays that Bhabha et al. propose in their study that "cosmopolitanism be considered in the plural, as cosmopolitanisms"[2]. Bhabha et al. sum up some common features and grounds for cosmopolitanisms. Firstly, the boom of cosmopolitanism studies is not without sound reasons. The deepening of globalization and increasingly frequent culture contacts in contemporary world demands the theoretical study of cosmopolitanism and naturally draws people's attention to it. Secondly, it is commonly agreed that in contemporary world, refugees, migrants and exiles, instead of adventurers and colonizers, are representatives of cosmopolitans. They are the "citizens of the world". Thirdly, contemporary cosmopolitanism studies differ sharply from the previous ones and tend to be more interdisciplinary. Bhabha et al. point out that cosmopolitan practices have begun to be considered as mixtures of things and disciplines that are supposed to be pure and unmixed previously. In its hybridization,

---

[1] Inderpal Grewal, Caren Kaplan & Robyn Wiegman. *Transnational America*[M]. London: Duke UP, 2005: 43.

[2] Homi K. Bhabha, et al. *Cosmopolitanism*[M]. Durham: Duke UP, 2002: 8.

cosmopolitanism, which celebrates plurality and inclusivity, is a rebellion against modernity. Therefore, it may be fair to say that the trace of deconstruction tendency in the heart of contemporary cosmopolitanism studies casts doubts upon the fact that cosmopolitanism is a creation of Europe and its Enlightenment. Walkowitz points out that those contemporary cosmopolitanisms actually are linked to other critical practices. They also celebrate "double-consciousness, comparison, negation, and persistent self-reflection"[1].

However, there is also strong criticism against some form of contemporary cosmopolitanisms. As Cheah and Robbins point out that "[i]n postcolonial contexts, Frantz Fanon and others (in a criticism echoed by Rob Nixon against V. S. Naipaul, and Tim Brennan against Salman Rushdie) dismantled a certain kind of free-floating comprador cosmopolitanism as undermining the will to 'national vocation' and Third World struggles to decolonize"[2]. Robbins criticizes the rootless cosmopolitanism which highlights detachment, and the free floating mobility without material affiliation to any locality. In his opinion, the ironic detachment of Naipaul does not reflect the true spirit of cosmopolitanism. Robbins promotes over-lapping presence, allegiances and locatedness, instead of non-allegiance, detachment and rootlessness. Robbins maintains that today's actually existing cosmopolitanisms should be "a reality of re-attachment, multiple attachments, or attachment at a distance"[3].

Among the various strands of contemporary cosmopolitan theory, Kwame Anthony Appiah's cosmopolitan thoughts are quite representative and insightful. In his article "Cosmopolitan Patriots", Appiah praises cosmopolitan patriots and promotes the so-called "rooted cosmopolitanism". He further explains that in his term "rooted cosmopolitanism", "rooted" means to be loyal to one local society (or a few) that one counts as home, as Gertrude Stein once said, "America is my country and Paris is my hometown"[4]. Appiah holds the view that

---

[1] Rebecca Walkowitz. *Cosmopolitan Style: Modernism Beyond the Nation* [M]. New York: Columbia UP, 2007: 2.

[2] Pheng Cheah & Bruce Robbins. *Cosmopolitics: Thing and Feeling Beyond the Nation* [M]. Minneapolis: Minnesota UP, 1998: 358.

[3] Pheng Cheah & Bruce Robbins. *Cosmopolitics: Thing and Feeling Beyond the Nation* [M]. Minneapolis: Minnesota UP, 1998: 3.

[4] Pheng Cheah & Bruce Robbins. *Cosmopolitics: Thing and Feeling Beyond the Nation* [M]. Minneapolis: Minnesota UP, 1998: 91.

patriotism is not incompatible with cosmopolitanism and in this way he greatly extends the scope of patriotism and cosmopolitanism. Appiah maintains that in today's world of ever enhancing mutation and complexity, it is difficult for people who travel far and often to focus their affinities and passions only on a single place. Therefore, openness and multi-affiliations should be promoted. Appiah argues that humanism treats the Other equally regardless of cultural differences, while cosmopolitanism welcomes the Other just because of the differences. The humanists tolerate the differences in cultural communication by putting them aside, while the cosmopolitans hold the opinion that it is sometimes exactly the differences which make cultural communication a rewarding experience.

In his monograph *Cosmopolitanism: Ethics in a World of Strangers*, Appiah further develops his theory of cosmopolitanism. After briefly reviewing the development of cosmopolitanism in history, Appiah proposes two ideals of cosmopolitanism: universal concern and respect for legitimate difference. Praising his own father as a fine representative of rooted cosmopolitan, Appiah maintains that his father maintains multiple affiliations. He always sees himself belong to part of the place that he is born or dwells and a broader human community, without seeing any conflict between local partialities and a universal morality. In Appiah's cosmopolitanism theory, cosmopolitanism is not regarded as exalted attainment. The idea that human beings need to learn to develop habits of coexistence in the human community, just like in national communities, is the starting point of cosmopolitanism. In Rob Wilson's opinion, Appiah's theorization of "rooted cosmopolitanism" and "cosmopolitan patriotism" represents "embrace of liberal self-invention ('the tool kit of self-invention') and global mobility ('take your roots with you')"[1]. In its heart, such cosmopolitanism embraces openness to otherness while at the same advocating strong affiliation to locality, sometimes more than one place.

To sum up, Appiah's theorization of rooted cosmopolitanism covers the following major points:

(1) Rooted cosmopolitanism's promotion of universal concern and respect

---

[1] Pheng Cheah & Bruce Robbins. *Cosmopolitics: Thing and Feeling beyond the Nation* [M]. Minneapolis: Minnesota UP, 1998: 355.

for legitimate difference rises from the realization that cultures are widely and deeply connected. Since the cultural connectedness is everywhere and is deepening, a cosmopolitan should be open-minded and display more respect to cultures other than his own. For cosmopolitans, "conversation" across boundaries and between people from different places is of vital importance. The term "conversation" is used by Appiah in metaphorical sense. Besides, Appiah also points out that we should not always expect a promise of final agreement in this kind of cultural conversation. Also, the connectedness between cultures deconstructs the division between "the West and the Rest; between locals and moderns; between a bloodless ethnic of profit and a bloody ethnic of identity; between 'us' and 'them'"[1].

(2) A rooted cosmopolitan has a strong sense of national or local affiliation. He may be loyal to one local society (or a few) that one counts as home. The cultural affiliation the cosmopolitan cherishes may be to his home culture or the host culture, or both ones at the same time. Compared with a rootless migrant who would like to be a citizen of the world, a rooted cosmopolitan cherishes strong love for his home, which may both be the place where he is born into or the place where he chooses to settle down. The strong affiliation to locality more often than not renders the cosmopolitan more concerned about social and cultural context. This kind of concern makes a rooted cosmopolitan distinctively different from other types of cosmopolitans who indulge in nomadism. Yet the affiliation and contextual concern is quite different from that of narrow nationalism in its openness. A rooted cosmopolitan tries to balance cosmopolitanism and rootedness at the same time.

In *Desirable Daughters* and its sequel, *The Tree Bride*, narrator Tara's self-reflection upon different cultural affiliations and re-evaluation of colonial history and homeland culture reflects Mukherjee's rooted cosmopolitan consciousness. In the two novels, narrator Tara may be defined as a typical contemporary cosmopolitan who travels widely and frequently. Her communication with her sisters across spaces and her roots search across time all reveal the connectedness between cultures, peoples and countries which erases the boundary of place and

---

[1] Kwame Anthony Appiah. *Cosmopolitanism: Ethics in a World of Strangers* [M]. New York: W. W. Norton, 2006: xxi.

simultaneity of time.

The connectedness shows to different degrees and in different ways in the novels. First, it is shown in connections between peoples from different cultures. Although the three sisters dwell miles apart and are quite differently affiliated, they are all connected in an intimate and traditional way as members of their parents' family. In her roots search, Tara forms her connection to her name sake ancestor, the legendary Tree Bride, in whom she reaffirms the strength of Indian culture and its people. In Tara's roots search, her doctor in America Victoria Khanna, also known as Victoria Alexandria Treadwell, finds her connection to India through her ancestor Treadwell. Even criminal networks are becoming globally connected. The Indian Dawood gang has members in America, who are responsible for the bombing down of Tara's American house. The connectedness between people from different cultures also shows the hybridity of world culture today.

Second, the connectedness is shown in connections of world economy. Bish's computer system which makes him a millionaire is one that facilitates communication and strengthens connections between people. His corporation which includes its headquarters in America, an assembly plant in Bangalore, a marketing army in Bombay, and a start-up in Bangladesh, shows the connectedness of global economy.

Third, the narrative structures of the two novels also echo the spirits of connectedness. In discussing the writing of *Desirable Daughters*, Mukherjee says that "the aesthetic strategy of the book was using the width of the field—of history, geography, diaspora, gender, ethnicity, language—rather than the old-fashioned long, clean throw"[1]. In both *Desirable Daughters* and *The Tree Bride*, the storylines, seemly centering on the story of the narrator Tara, are constantly interrupted by other stories and digressions to other directions. Newman comments that "the reader is passed from story to story across a broad geographical and historical sweep; the narrative passes from one controller to another, at times appearing to be misdirected or displaced, with the story

---

[1] Judie Newman. *Fiction of America: Narrative of Global Empires*[M]. New York: Routledge, 2007: 156.

moving forward through changes of direction, side-passes, misdirections and feints"[1]. The narrative which ranges widely across time and spaces, involves many different levels of side connections and horizontal moves. Narrator Tara's story is often interrupted by others' stories. Tara claims that she is writing a novel about her experience and it seems that some parts of the novels are excerpts cut from the novel that Tara is writing. Mukherjee demonstrates her artistic maturity in weaving different stories through various connections to form a complete narrative which centers on the affiliations of the immigrants and attitudes towards cultural differences.

In a very realistic and artistically mature way, Mukherjee elaborates on the connectedness between cultures, peoples, histories, and spaces which defies any appeal to originality. Tara's individual history is connected to the lives of other people and in the process of roots search, what matters more is not the cultural originality but a "looking for the join"[2]. In his masterpiece *A Passage to India*, E. M. Forster also writes about connection between the West and the East, namely the British and the Indians. Reflected in the novel, Forster is anti-colonialism, anti-imperialism and seeks a solution to cultural conflicts through connections between cultures and people. However, Forster's depiction of connectedness in modern time is different from that of Mukherjee in contemporary world in that Forster is Eurocentric in his narrative and basically his vision of connectedness is quite gloomy. Said points out the patronizing attitude of Forster in his depiction of India in *A Passage to India*. In Said's opinion, Forster's portrayal of the East follows and echoes with the Orientalist discourse. In *A Passage to India*, the East with its "vastness, incomprehensible creeds, secret motions, histories and social forms" constitutes the uncivilized and mysterious Other to the civilized and modern West[3]. In writing about the connectedness between cultures and peoples, Forster further reveals his Orientalist stance. Benita Parry points out that in the novel, Forster presents the confrontation of the "civilized mind" of "the modern West" with "the primitive

---

[1] Judie Newman. *Fiction of America: Narrative of Global Empires*[M]. New York: Routledge, 2007: 156.

[2] Homi K. Bhabha. *The Location of Culture*[M]. London: Routledge, 1994: 18.

[3] Edward W. Said. *Culture and Imperialism*[M]. New York: Vintage Books, 1993: 241.

memories dormant in man"[1]. Therefore, the real connection is only illusionary or in Forster's perception a "not yet" thing.

On the contrary, Mukherjee's writing of connectedness reflects a rooted cosmopolitanism stance. Besides, Mukherjee is certainly more positive about the fusion of cultures and peoples. To deal with the ever-enhancing connectedness in today's world, Mukherjee advocates cosmopolitan ideas of respect and tolerance towards cultural differences. Reflected in the novels, the Tree Bride who is open-minded to different cultures is depicted in a very positive way and may be designated as a true cosmopolitan in spirit. In contrast, the Dawood gangs are strongly criticized for their terrorist activities which rise out of Hindu-Muslim ethnic antagonism and hatred. Tara's roots search makes her further realize the importance in respecting and tolerating cultural differences in cross-cultural communication and offers her the strength and insight to get re-rooted in the metropolitan center.

Besides openness to cultural differences, Mukherjee also promotes that cosmopolitans should learn from those differences. In the epigraph of *Desirable Daughters*, Mukherjee includes a Sanskrit verse, which is adapted by Octavio Paz and translated into English by Eliot Weinberger:

> No one behind, no one ahead
> The path the ancients cleared has closed.
> And the other path, everyone's path,
> Easy and wide, goes nowhere.
> I am alone and find my way. (Epigraph)[2]

In an interview, Mukherjee explains that the verse embodied "the globalization that we really want to prize ... that we can take from each other's heritages what we need and sew it together into our heritage"[3]. The respect and willingness to learn from each other's cultural heritages begins with the recognition that

---

[1] Benita Parry. *Delusions and Discoveries: Studies on India in the British Imagination 1880–1930* [M]. Los Angeles: California UP, 1972: 294.

[2] Bharati Mukherjee. *Desirable Daughters* [M]. New York: Hyperion Books, 2002: Epigraph.

[3] Judie Newman. *Fiction of America: Narrative of Global Empires* [M]. New York: Routledge, 2007: 154.

human beings are different and cultures are connected. Mukherjee's opinion echoes Appiah's notion of cosmopolitanism. In Appiah's interpretation, cosmopolitanism carries with it in the heart the recognition that people are different and therefore there is much to learn from the differences. The ever-enhancing connectedness between culture and people makes it much more significant for individuals to show respect and openness in cultural communications.

Mukherjee's promotion of openness also echoes what Bhabha et al. advocate in cosmopolitanism, "ground our sense of mutuality in conditions of mutability"[1]. In the two novels, the protagonist Tara is quite open-minded in valuing both Indian culture and American culture. The Tree Bride, though seldom leaves her house in her entire life, is also open-minded and more than willing to absorb cultural heritages from both the East and the West. Newman points out that although the Tree Bride is immobile in the home, "the world came to her"[2]. Therefore, it is fair to assert that both Tara and the Tree Bride are cosmopolitans in spirits. The characterization of both Tara and the Tree Bride reflect Mukherjee's open-mindedness towards and willingness to learn from cultural differences, which are in line with the spirits of cosmopolitanism.

The two novels also reflect Mukherjee's love and affiliations both to her host country, America and her homeland, India. The double love and affiliations are in line with Appiah's promotion of rooted cosmopolitanism. Reflected in the novels, Tara is a cosmopolitan loving her new home America, which is shown in her constant efforts in getting assimilated. Even suffering from a series of setbacks and coming to the realization of the impossibility of full assimilation, Tara is still dead set to adapt and get re-rooted. Yet at the same time she begins to reaffirm the cultural heritage of her homeland India, which is shown in her enthusiasm in digging out the past in her roots search. The two novels strongly attack colonial sins and traumas, and praise the strength of Indian culture and its people. In an interview discussing the writing of *Desirable Daughters*, Mukherjee strongly criticizes the violence and sins of British colonial ruling in

---

[1] Carol A. Breckenridge, et al. *Cosmopolitanism*[M]. Durham: Duke UP, 2002: 4.
[2] Judie Newman. *Fiction of America: Narrative of Global Empires*[M]. New York: Routledge, 2007: 154.

India:

> I was born in 1940, which means that I was witness to colonial brutality ... It touched everyone's life. And I also remember—in flashes of image—famine victims, which must have been during the 1943 famine. My father organized food lines. We were constantly being told, even as children, that the famine was manipulated by the Raj, that they were siphoning off food for the British Army. This is the kind of violence by osmosis I ingested.[1]

The criticism reflects Mukherjee's patriotic ideology for her homeland, India. Besides, by digging into the past, one can often gain insight of the present and the future. Mukherjee's discussion of colonial sins in the last several centuries also shows her concern for the neo-colonial tendency demonstrated by the Western powers in today's world of globalization. The topic of neo-colonization in globalization is fully explored in her newly published novel, *Miss New Indian*.

Moving from happy celebration of hybridity in *Jasmine* to serious recontexualization in more recent works, the nature of Mukherjee's aesthetics of fusion also changes. In self-assertion reflected in *Jasmine*, Mukherjee advocates whole-hearted assimilation to the host culture, namely, American culture. In self-reflection reflected in more recent years of writing, Mukherjee shows her openness and affiliations to both American and Indian cultures. The change reflects the development and maturity of Mukherjee's aesthetics of fusion, moving from an Orientalist stance to a rooted cosmopolitan one. In emphasizing the connectedness of human life in globalization, advocating adaptability to where one migrates, promoting cultural hybridity and at the same time, respecting and loving the cultures of both homeland and host country, Mukherjee further deconstructs fixity of identity and blurs the boundary of single affiliation in pursuit of rooted cosmopolitanism.

---

[1] Bharati Mukherjee & Suzanne Ruta. Decoding the Language: Bharati Mukherjee Tells Suzanne Ruta Some of the Stories behind "Desirable Daughters"[J]. *The Women's Review of Books*, 2002(19): 13.

Conclusion

With the recognition in the academic circle and popularity among common readers, Mukherjee has successfully established her status as a major writer in American immigrant writings. In her immigrant phase of writing, by distancing herself from the influences of exilic writers and affiliating herself with other immigrant writers, Mukherjee has moved away from the aloofness of expatriation to concentration of the depictions of immigration. Her major novels in this period represent a quite distinctive and unique strand in postcolonial writings. Mukherjee's depiction of the immigrants' courageous transformation and adaptation to get survival in the host country, stands in sharp contrast with rootedness and rootlessness.

This book studies four of Mukherjee's novels, *Jasmine*, *The Holder of the World*, *Desirable Daughters* and *The Tree Bride*, written in her immigrant phase of writing. In transformation, transgression and settling down, the immigrants in these novels changes from being assertive and rebellious to become more self-reflective. The book also tries to trace the change of Mukherjee's aesthetics of fusion in her immigrant phase of writing.

Jasmine reflects self-assertion in metamorphoses. The protagonist Jasmine, migrating from her poor homeland in Hasnapur, India to the vast Western frontier of America, goes through several stages of metamorphoses each signified by identification of a new name: Jyoti, Jasmine, Kali, Jazzy, Jase and Jane. Jasmine's metamorphoses are closely associated with the hybridity of her identity. In metamorphoses, Jasmine asserts herself. Jasmine's self-assertion is two-sided. On the one side, in self-assertion Jasmine embraces her hybridity. By assuming a forward-looking attitude, Jasmine seeks agency associated with hybridity, cuts her Indian ties and takes initiative to change, act and adapt. In the process, she gets re-rooted in her host country. On the other side, Jasmine tends to Orientalize herself in her self-assertion. Self-orientalization might be used by Jasmine as tools to survive in the strange land, but at the same time, it reveals Jasmine internalized vein of Orientalism.

The self-assertion in metamorphoses deconstructs stable identity and celebrates hybridity. Hybridity emphasizes mutability rather than status quo. Mukherjee's depiction of the immigrants' seeking agency associated with hybridity to get re-rooted in a strange land, although sometimes in a compromised way, works in the contrary to the stereotyped victimization of the immigrants in postcolonial literature. The positive attitude and heroic struggle to transform and adapt certainly is empowering in narrative of migrancy and corresponds to the model minority's aspiration of settling down in their new land.

On the other hand, however, *Jasmine* reflects Mukherjee's strong Orientalist stance in her aesthetics of fusion. Firstly, it is shown in Mukherjee's reinforcement of colonial binarism, namely, her constant privileging of American culture over Indian one. In the novel, the depiction of Indian culture is constantly associated with backwardness and oppression. In Jasmine's retrospect, India is condensed into a rather disturbing picture, the cruel caste system, the overall poverty, the stupidity of its people and the miserable status of women. In contrast, American culture is shown as liberating and full of hope. America is viewed as a promising land which offers freedom and possibility of success to even the marginalized.

Secondly, it is shown in Mukherjee's detextualization tendency in literary writing. Reflected in the novel, Jasmine's metamorphoses to some degree echoes the postmodernist celebration of the performativity of subject construction. Jasmine's seemly easy adaptation and happy hybridity show that Mukherjee to a large degree ignores the social, economic and political factors which are constantly at work. *Jasmine* also reflects Mukherjee's celebration of adventure and territory expansion, which is in strong collusion with American new imperialist discourse.

Thirdly, it is shown in the ruptures in the narrative of the novel. In *Jasmine*, on the one hand, Mukherjee tries to speak for the subaltern woman, Jasmine. On the other hand, Mukherjee constantly subjects the protagonist to superior and Orientalist gaze. The conflicting impulses result in a text full of ruptures which are similar to those detected by Bhabha in the imperialist discourse.

Mukherjee's Orientalist stance in her writings is strong in this period. In interviews, Mukherjee also speaks vocally about severing her own Indian ties and about killing one's old self in order to become a new confident self. Mukherjee's Orientalist stance in this period might rise out of her anxiety of breaking free from the influence of exilic writers and the wish to narrate from a different angle. Or it might rise out of her privileged background and elite Western education, which is further spurred by the urge to secure herself a new cultural identity and get accepted by the mainstream Americans.

The Holder of the World reflects the rebelliousness in transgression. Travelling from the Puritan town of Salem, Massachusetts to London, then to the East India, the protagonist Hannah changes from a Puritan maid to an Old World wife, then to a bibi of an Indian Raja. Hannah demonstrates rebelliousness in transgressing gender and racial boundaries to get re-rooted wherever she chooses to settle down. In the social and racial discourse of the seventeenth century, the superiority of men over women and the white over the black is beyond challenge. As a white woman, Hannah is subjected to the disciplinary power to stay docile to the patriarchal leaders in the family and also she is constantly admonished to keep her chasteness from the lecherous Oriental Other. Bravely ridding herself off the yokes of the patriarchal and racial power structure, Hannah transgresses gender and racial boundaries to get re-rooted. Besides, Hannah's liberation of female sexuality and celebration of other forms of female sensuality further subverts the binary opposition of the Men/Women and the White/Black.

The rebelliousness in transgression narrated in the novel has a universal relevance for by depicting a white woman's cultural translation from the West to the East, Mukherjee shows that re-rooting applies not only to those migrating from the East to the West, but also to those migrating from the West to the East. Transgression is a boundary negotiation in hybridity. By advocating transgression across gender and racial boundaries to get re-rooted, Mukherjee unsettles the Men/Women, the White/Black and the West/East binary constructions in Western metaphysics. Compared with *Jasmine*, which advocates assimilation, *The Holder of the World* may be deemed more counter-hegemonic in its bold deconstruction tendency. The novel may be read as a postmodernist and postcolonial response to *The Scarlet Letter*. Through rewriting Hawthorne's canonic works, Mukherjee succeeds in subverting the white, male American national myth of origin. Also in an implicit way, the novel attacks the American imperialist discourse of world expansion.

The novel reflects Mukherjee's moving away from strong Orientalist stance and total identification with Western cultures to tentative re-affirmation of her Indianness. The re-affirmation shows in Mukherjee's appraisal of Indian natural beauty, cultural heritage as well as in her adoption of a total vision in narrative which resembles the technique employed by the ancient Moghul miniature painting. Besides, the depiction of connectedness between cultures and peoples, and the promotion of equal love to all human beings show the budding of Mukherjee's cosmopolitan ideas.

Desirable Daughters and *The Tree Bride* show self-reflection in immigration. In the two novels, Mukherjee depicts a very autobiographical protagonist Tara in her self-reflection after years of immigration. In *Desirable Daughters*, Tara evaluates different cultural affiliations represented by her two sisters and herself. On the one hand, Tara condemns Didi's expatriate sentiments and ghettoized way of living. To Tara, indulging in nostalgia and shunning any adaption to the host country show only cowardice. On the other hand, Tara criticizes Parvati's affiliation to new narrow Indian nationalism. In her perception, the new nationalists' constant resorting to cultural authenticity and originality are quite narrow-minded and hypocritical in nature. However, Tara also has to face her own disillusion in getting fully assimilated into the host country.

In *The Tree Bride*, Tara goes on with her self-reflection as she embarks on roots search back to India to gather materials for the book she is writing. In waving together the story of the legendary Tree Bride in Indian history, Tara reaffirms the strength of Indian culture and its people in fighting for national independence. Revisiting sins and traumas of colonial rulings and at the same time experiencing world terrorist attack rising out of ethnic hatred, Tara gradually gains new insight that breaking down of fixity of identity, getting rid of racial antagonism and embracing of cultural differences are of primary importance in immigration. In self-reflection, Tara fosters her double affiliations both to her homeland and host country, and matures into a rooted cosmopolitan.

The self-reflection in immigration reflects the further maturity of Mukherjee's aesthetics of fusion. Mukherjee changes from the negation of her homeland culture to the reaffirmation. Besides showing strong affiliations to both her homeland and her host country, Mukherjee promotes the fusion of universality and respect for cultural differences. Both her affiliation to locality and promotion of universal fusion echoes the rooted cosmopolitanism advocated by Appiah. Also in the two novels, the depiction of economic drives of colonial expansion and exploitation shows Mukherjee's concern about political and material circumstances. Mukherjee's interest in the social context reflected in the two novels is in sharp contrast with her privileging of the performativity of self-fashioning in *Jasmine*. Moving away from detextualization to retextualization, the stance of Mukherjee's aesthetics of fusion changes from an Orientalist one to a rooted cosmopolitan one, by replacing an either/or with a both/and ideology.

The depiction of immigrants' identity constructions from self-assertion in metamorphoses, rebelliousness in transgression to self-reflection also reflect the change in Mukherjee's aesthetics of fusion. Mukherjee's writings of immigration may be located in a sense at the crossroads of critical reflection. In the postcolonial era, after a rather long period of rigorous exploration of rootedness and rootlessness, many critical thinkers and writers begin to drop previously held essentialist or binary stance to resort to more open and dynamic interpretation and depiction of migrancy. Such a shift in focus is also a response to social, economic and political changes in the contemporary world. Mukherjee, situated in relation to a broader community of postcolonial writers, may be classified as one of the best representative in this trend of change.

This book studies the writings of immigration in Mukherjee's major novels, and the development and maturity of Mukherjee's aesthetics of fusion. The author of this book hopes that this study may contribute to the re-evaluation of Mukherjee's novels and her writing aesthetics.

Works Cited

Primary Sources

Mukherjee, Bharati. Beyond Multiculturalism: Surviving the Nineties[J]. *Journal of Modern Literature*, 1996, 20(1): 29-34.

Mukherjee, Bharati. *Desirable Daughters* [M]. New York: Hyperion Books, 2002.

Mukherjee, Bharati. *Jasmine*[M]. New York: Ballantine Books, 1989.

Mukherjee, Bharati. *The Holder of the World*[M]. New York: Alfred A., 1993.

Mukherjee, Bharati. *The Tree Bride*[M]. New York: Hyperion Books, 2004.

Mukherjee, Bharati & Suzanne Ruta. Decoding the Language: Bharati Mukherjee Tells Suzanne Ruta Some of the Stories behind "Desirable Daughters"[J]. *The Women's Review of Books*, 2002(19): 13.

Secondary Sources

Abraham, Markose. *American Immigration Aesthetics: Bernard Malamud & Bharati Mukherjee as Immigrants* [M]. London: Author House Publishing, 2011.

Abrams, M. H. & Geoffrey Galt Harpham. *A Glossary of Literary Terms* [M]. Beijing: Foreign Language Teaching and Research Press, 2010.

Alexander, Meena. *The Shock of Arrival: Reflections on Postcolonial Experience*[M]. Boston: South End Press, 1996.

Ameena, Meera. Bharati Mukherjee[J]. *Bomb*, 1989(29): 26.

Anderson, George & Manilal Bhagwandes Subedar. *The Development of an Indian Policy (1818-1858)*[M]. London: G. Bell, 1921.

Appiah, Kwame Anthony. *Cosmopolitanism: Ethics in a World of Strangers*[M]. New York: W. W. Norton & Company, 2006.

Aristotle. *The Politics*[M]. Cambridge: Cambridge UP, 1988.

Barker, Chris. *Cultural Studies: Theory and Practice*[M]. London: Sage Publications Ltd., 2008.

Baskaran, G. Nature as Healer: An Eco-Critical Reading of Bharati Mukherjee's *The Holder of the World*[J]. *Language in India*, 2012(12): 390-396.

Berreman, Gerald D. Race, Caste, and Other Invidious Distinctions in Social Stratification[J]. *Race Class*, 1972,13(4): 385-414.

Bery, Ashok. *Cultural Translation and Postcolonial Poetry*[M]. New York: Palgrave Macmillian, 2007.

Bhabha, Homi K. *The Location of Culture*[M]. London: Routledge, 1994.

Bhabha, Homi K. The Third Space[G]//*Identity: Community, Culture, Difference*. Ed. Jonathan Rutherford. London: Lawrence & Wishart, 1990.

Blaise, Clark & Bharati Mukherjee. *Days and Nights in Calcutta*[M]. Saint Paul: Hungry Mind Press, 1995.

Braziel, Jana Evans & Anita Mannur. *Theorizing Diaspora*[M]. Malden: Blackwell Publishing, 2003.

Breckenridge, Carol A., et al. *Cosmopolitanism*[M]. Durham: Duke UP, 2002.

Bressler, Charles E. *Literary Criticism: An Introduction to Theory and Practice*[M]. Upper Saddle River: Pearson Education, Inc.; Beijing: High Education Press, 2004.

Buell, Lawrence. Hawthorne and the Problem of "American" Fiction: The Example of *The Scarlet Letter*[G]//*Hawthorne and the Real*. Ed. Millicent Bell. Columbus: Ohio State UP, 2005.

Butalia, Urvashi. *The Other Side of Silence: Voices from the Partition of India*[M]. Durham: Duke UP, 2000.

Butler, Judith. *Bodies That Matter*[M]. London: Routledge, 1993.

Butler, Judith. *Gender Trouble: Feminism and the Subversion of Identity*[M]. London: Routledge, 1990.

Burton, Rob. *Artists of the Floating World: Contemporary Writers between Cultures*[M]. New York: America UP, 2007.

Carter-Sanborn, Kristin. "We Murder Who We Were": Jasmine and the Violence of Identity[J]. *American Literature*, 1994, 66(3): 573-593.

Castles, Stephen & Mark J. Miller. *The Age of Migration: International Population Movements in the Modern World*[M]. New York: The Guilford Press, 1993.

Cheah, Pheng & Bruce Robbins. *Cosmopolitics: Thing and Feeling beyond the Nation*[M]. Minneapolis: Minnesota UP, 1998.

Chang, Yoonmee. Beyond the Culture Ghetto: Asian American Class Critique and the Ethnographic Bildungsroman [D]. The University of Pennsylvania, 2003.

Clifford, James. *Routes: Travel and Translation in the Late Twentieth Century*[M]. Cambridge: Harvard UP, 1997.

Dascalu, Critina Emanuela. *Imaginary Homelands of Writers in Exile: Salman Rushdie, Bharati Mukherjee, and V. S. Naipaul*[M]. New York: Cambria Press, 2007.

Day, Frank. *Bharati Mukherjee*[M]. New York: Twayne Publishers, 1996.

Davis, Mike. *Late Victorian Holocausts: El Nino Famine and the Making of the Third World*[M]. London: Verso Books, 2001.

Dhawan, R. K. *The Fiction of Bharati Mukherjee: A Critical Symposium*[M]. New Delhi: Prestige Books, 1996.

Dirlik, Arif. Chinese History and the Question of Orientalism[J]. *History & Theory*, 1996, 35(4): 96-118.

Dlaska, Andrea. *Ways of Belonging: The Making of New Americans in the Fiction of Bharati Mukherjee*[M]. Vienna: Braumuller, 1999.

Drake, Jennifer. Looting American Culture: Bharati Mukherjee's Immigrant Narratives[J]. *Contemporary Literature*, 1999, 40(1): 60-84.

Edwards, Bradley C. *Conversations with Bharati Mukherjee*[M]. Oxford: Mississippi UP, 2009.

Edwards, Justin D. *Postcolonial Literature* [M]. Hampshire: Palgrave Macmillan, 2008.

Esterbauer, Verena. *The Immigrants' Search for Identity*[M]. Saarbrucken: VDM Verlag Dr. Mullter, 2008.

Foucault, Michel. *Discipline & Punish: The Birth of the Prison* [M]. Trans. Alan Sheridan. New York: Vintage Books, 1977.

Gabriel, Sbarmani Patricia. "Immigrant" or "Post-colonial"? Towards a Poetics for Reading the Nation in Bharati Mukherjee's *The Tiger's Daughter* [J]. *Journal of Commonwealth Literature*, 2004, (39): 85-104.

Gauthier, Marni. *Amnesia and Redress in Contemporary American Fiction* [M]. New York: Marni Gauthier, 2011.

Genette, Gerard. *Paratexts: Thresholds of Interpretation* [M]. New York: Cambridge UP, 1997.

George, Rosemary Marangoly. *The Politics of Home: Postcolonial Relocations and Twentieth-Century Fiction* [M]. Cambridge: Cambridge UP, 1996.

Grewal, Inderpal, Caren Kaplan & Robyn Wiegman. *Transnational America* [M]. London: Duke UP, 2005.

Hall, Stuart. *Colonial Desire: Hybridity in Theory, Culture and Race* [M]. London: Routledge, 1995.

Hall, Stuart. Cultural Identity and Diaspora [G]// *Identity: Community, Culture, Difference*. Ed. Jonathan Rutherford. London: Lawrence and Wishart, 1990.

Hall, Stuart, Sean Nixon & Jessica Evans: *Representation: Cultural Representations and Signifying Practices* [M]. London: Sage Publications Ltd., 1997.

Hawthorne, Nathaniel. *The Scarlet Letter* [M]. New York: New American Library, 1980.

Huggan, Graham. *Interdisciplinary Measures* [M]. Liverpool: Liverpool UP, 2008.

Hutcheon, Linda. *The Politics of Postmodernism* [M]. London: Routledge, 1989.

Kandiyoti, Deniz. Identity and its Discontents [G]// *Colonial Discourse, Postcolonial Theory*. Eds. Patrick Williams & Laura Chrisman. New York: Columbia UP, 1994.

Kaplan, Caren. *Questions of Travel: Postmodern Discourses of Displacement* [M]. Durham: Duke UP, 1996.

Koshy, Susan. Bharati Mukherjee[G]//*Resource Guide to Asian American Literature*. Eds. Stephen Sumida & Sau-Ling Wong. New York: MLA, 2001.

Leong, Liew-Geok. Bharati Mukherjee [G]//*International Literature in English: Essays on the Major Writers*. Ed. Robert L. Ross. New York: Garland, 1991.

Loomba, Ania. *Colonialism/Postcolonialism*[M]. New York: Routledge, 1998.

Lowe, Lisa. *Immigrant Acts*[M]. London: Duke UP, 1996.

Madsen, Deborah L. *Feminist Theory and Literary Practice*[M]. London: Pluto Press, 2000.

Mandal, Somdatta. *Bharati Mukherjee: Critical Perspective* [M]. New Delhi: Pencraft Books, 2010.

Mariani, Philomena. *Critical Fictions: The Politics of Imaginative Writing* [M]. Seattle: Bay, 1991.

McHale, Brian. *Postmodernist Fiction*[M]. New York: Methuen, 1987.

Mills, Sara. *Discourses of Difference: An Analysis of Women's Travel Writing and Colonialism*[M]. London: Routledge, 1991.

Mills, Sara. Knowledge, Gender, and Empire[G]//*Writing Women and Space: Colonial and Postcolonial Geographies*. Eds. Alison Blunt & Gillian Rose. New York: The Guilford Press, 1994.

Milner, Andrew & Jeff Browitt. *Contemporary Cultural Theory: An Introduction*[M]. London: Routledge, 2002.

Morison, Samuel Eliot. *The Oxford History of the American People*[M]. New York: Mentor, 1972.

Morton, Stephen. *Gayatri Spivak: Ethics, Subalternity and the Critique of Postcolonial Reason*[M]. Cambridge: Polity Press, 2007.

Mura, David. A Shift in Power, a Sea Change in the Arts: Asian American Constructions[G]//*The State of Asian America Activism and Resistance in the 1990s*. Ed. Karin Aguilar-San Juan. Boston: South End, 1994.

Nayar, Pramod K. *Postcolonialism: A Guide for the Perplexed*[M]. New York: Continuum, 2010.

Newman, Judie. *Fiction of America: Narrative of Global Empires*[M]. New York: Routledge, 2007.

Newman, Judie. Spaces In-Between: Hester Prynne as the Salem Bibi in Bhararti Mukherjee's *The Holder of the World*[G]//*Borderlands: Negotiating Boundaries in Post-Colonial Writing*. Ed. Monika Reif-Hülser. Amsterdam: Rodopi, 1999.

Nelson, Emmanuel S. *Bharati Mukherjee: Critical Perspectives*[M]. New York: Garland Publishing, Inc., 1993.

Nyman, Jopi. *Home, Identity, and Mobility in Contemporary Diasporic Fiction*[M]. New York: Rodopi B. V., 2009.

Obourn, Megan. *Reconstituting Americans: Liberal Multiculturalism and Identity Difference in Post-1960s Literature* [M]. New York: Palgrave Macmillan, 2011.

O'Hearn, Claudine Chiawei. *Half and Half: Writers on Growing Up Biracial and Bicultural*[M]. New York: Pantheon Books, 1998.

Owen, Cory. *Perpetuating Self: Postcolonial and Immigrant Hybridity in Bharati Mukherjee's Jasmine*[M]. Ann Arbor: UMI Dissertation Publishing, 2010.

Papastergiadis, Nikos. *Cosmopolitanism and Culture*[M]. Malden: Polity Press, 2012.

Parry, Benita. *Delusions and Discoveries: Studies on India in the British Imagination 1880-1930*[M]. Los Angeles: California UP, 1972.

Peters, John Durham. Exile, Nomadism, and Diaspora: The Stakes of Mobility in the Western Canon[G]//*Home, Exile, Homeland: Film, Media and the Politics of Place*. Ed. Hamid Naficy. New York: Routledge, 1999.

Pratt, Mary Louise. *Imperial Eyes: Travel Writing and Transculturation* [M]. New York: Routledge, 1992.

Ravichandran, M. & T. Deivasigamani. Immigration and identity in Bharati Mukherjee's *Jasmine* and *Desirable Daughters*[J]. *Language in India*, 2013, (15): 552-555.

Said, Edward W. *Orientalism*[M]. New York: Vintage Books, 1979.

Said, Edward W. *Culture and Imperialism* [M]. New York: Vintage Books, 1993.

Sanga, Jania C. *Salman Rushdie's Postcolonial Metaphors: Migration, Translation, Hybridity, Blasphemy, and Globalization* [M]. Westport:

Greenwood Press, 2001.

Saraithong, Wilailak. Citizen of the World: Post-colonial Identity in the Works of V. S. Naipaul[D]. Washington State University, 2001.

Sen, Asha. From National to Transnational: Three Generations of South Asian American Women Writers[J]. *Asiatic*, 2009, 3(1): 54-68.

Shaopin, Luo. Rewriting Travel: Ahdaf Soueif's *The Map of Love* and Bharati Mukherjee's *The Holder of the World* [J]. *The Journal of Commonwealth Literature*, 2003(38): 77-104.

Scheffler, Samuel. Conceptions of Cosmopolitanism[J]. *Utilitas*, 1999, 11 (3): 255-276.

Schultheis, Alexandra W. *Regenerative Fictions: Postcolonialism, Psychoanalysis, and the Nation as Family* [M]. New York: Palgrave Macmillan, 2004.

Showalter, Elaine. *A Literature of Their Own*[M]. Princeton: Princeton UP, 1977.

Spivak, Gayatri Chakravorty. *A Critique of Postcolonial Reason: Toward a History of the Vanishing Present*[M]. Cambridge: Harvard UP, 1999.

Spivak, Gayatri Chakravorty. *In Other Worlds: Essays in Cultural Politics* [M]. New York: Methuen, 1987.

Spivak, Gayatri Chakravorty. Can the Subaltern Speak? [G]//*Marxism and the Interpretation of Culture*. Ed. Cary Nelson. Urbana: University of Illinois, 1988.

Steinberg, Sybil. Bharati Mukherjee[J]. *Publishers Weekly*, 1989, 236 (35): 46-47.

Sturken, Marita & Lisa Cartwright. *Practices of Looking: An Introduction to Visual Culture*[M]. Oxford: Oxford UP, 2009.

Tandon, Sushma. *Bharati Mukherjee's Fiction: A Perspective*[M]. New Delhi: Sarup & Sons, 2004.

Viswanathan, Gauri. *Masks of Conquest: Literary Study and British Rule in India*[M]. London: Faber, 1990.

Waugh, Patricia. *Literary Theory and Criticism*[M]. Oxford: Oxford UP, 2006.

Weagel, Deborah. *Women and Contemporary World Literature*[M]. New

York: Peter Lang, 2009.

White, David Gordon. *Tantra in Practice*[M]. Princeton: Princeton UP, 2000.

Young, Robert J. C. *Colonial Desire: Hybridity in Theory, Culture, and Race*[M]. London: Routledge, 1995.

Zhong, Mingguo. Self-orientalization and Its Counteraction against the Cultural Purpose of Gu Hongming in His Discourses and Sayings of Confucius [J]. *Theory and Practice in Language Studies*, 2012, 2(11): 2417-2421.

Zoon, Atia Anwer. *Bharati Mukherjee's Female Protagonists: A Search for Female Identity*[M]. Saarbrucken: Lambert Academic Publishing, 2012.

Walkowitz, Rebecca. *Cosmopolitan Style: Modernism beyond the Nation* [M]. New York: Columbia UP, 2007.

黄芝. 变幻莫测的"卡莉女神": 解读芭拉蒂·穆克尔吉的《詹丝敏》[J]. 解放军外国语学院学报, 2007(3): 93-97.

石海峻. 地域文化与想像的家园: 兼谈印度现当代文学与印度侨民文学 [J]. 外国文学评论, 2001(3): 24-33.

徐珍岩, 张丽. 离散中的女性主体性身份建构: 解读芭拉蒂·穆克尔吉的《茉莉花》[J]. 大学英语(学术版), 2010(2): 114-116.

杨晓霞. 流散往世书: 印度移民的过去与现在: 兼论印度流散小说创作 [J]. 深圳大学学报(人文社会科学版), 2012(6): 10-16.

尹锡南. 芭拉蒂·穆克尔吉的跨文化书写及其对奈保尔的模仿超越[J]. 国外文学, 2010(1): 148-153.

王宁. 叙述、文化定位和身份认同: 霍米·巴巴的后殖民批评理论[J]. 外国文学, 2002(6): 48-55.